# McLeary's Mulligan

## Bridget Bell Webber

Dark-N-Stormies
An Imprint of Grace Abraham Publishing
Bristol, Virginia

GRACE ABRAHAM PUBLISHING
13335 Holbrook Street
Bristol, VA 24202

Copyright © 2004 by Bridget Bell Webber
All rights reserved,
including the right of reproduction
in whole or in part in any form.

Manufactured in the United States of America

ISBN: 0-9741090-3-7

# McLeary's Mulligan

To Sheridan,
With thanks
for your patience, guidance
and grace under pressure. You are
a consummate professional!
Warm wishes,
Bridget
August 13, 2006

# Acknowledgments

- To the members of my writing group, Cynthia Polansky Gallagher, Wendy Sand Eckel, and Jon Coile, I give heartfelt thanks. Your enthusiastic support and thoughtful advice were indispensable.

- I am also grateful to all those who read parts of this book and offered encouragement, comments, and inspiration. I'd like to thank Bob Thomas, Larry Olmsted, Vernon Nily, John Daniel, Barry Butler, Marilyn Marx, Allan Arlow, Mike Behan, Elaine Mailliard, Debbie Dorsey, Dana Granieri, my father, H. Clark Bell, my brother, Kieran Bell, and my sister, Kathleen Roberts.

- A good number of golfers spent time with me, sharing the rewards and challenges of the sport they love. I offer special thanks to Barbara Aldersley, my golf partner and friend.

- To my editor, Mary Bargteil, for your extraordinary talent and boundless patience, thank you. And to Judy Webber and Shannon Benil, I present my sincere gratitude for your input.

- To Reed and Chase, my children, I am truly grateful for your tolerance and understanding. To Jennifer Riffle, nanny-extraordinaire, I appreciate your Herculean efforts to keep my office door shut.

- Finally, I'd like to thank my husband, Don, for his stalwart faith. This book is possible because you love me.

*For Mother, the late Joy Kieran Bell,
a golfer of uncommon character.*

# Prologue

### Charleston, South Carolina

"I'm *fired?*" Chase McLeary whispered to his agent.

They were seated in the window table at Magnolia's. A busboy delivered glasses of water with floating lemon circles to the linen-topped table and glided away.

A trickle of acid clawed its way up from Chase's stomach into his mouth. Shoulders rounded, he swallowed hard and forced it back down, feeling the weight of how far he'd come in pursuit of his dream.

Countless hours hitting balls, backbreaking drives cross-country, cheap motels with splurges at Shoney's; he'd earned every inch of his ascension to the ranks of golf's elite. And now he was giving it all back.

"Call it whatever you like. It's over." Jake Nathan adjusted the gold bar atop his Hermes tie before reaching into his briefcase. He handed Chase *Golf Digest Magazine*. "Hot off the press. Page fifty-six."

Hands shaking, Chase fumbled to the article situated beneath two prominent photos. In the left one he sported a blue blazer and accepted the National Collegiate Athletic Association's Golfer of the Year Award. On the right he wore an orange jumpsuit and held a numbered placard. He read the lead and pushed it aside. "I know I screwed up. Right now I'm the scandal of the day, but this story will fade. I promise. Give me a second chance."

Jake leaned back. "Sorry. No Mulligans."

"Come on," Chase said, his voice cracking. "My wife died less than a year ago. I've got a toddler to raise. Between the medical bills and the funeral costs, I'm totally broke. You can't expect me to just snap back. Give me some time."

Jake appraised the lunch specials. "The sympathy card's already been played." He pushed back the menu. Two young women seated nearby smiled. Jake cocked his head in acknowledgment.

"You arrogant, son-of-a—"

"You want to blame someone? Look in the mirror." Jake snapped his fingers. "The minute you were arrested is exactly the moment that your career as a professional golfer ended."

Chase bumped his water glass but saved it from spilling. "It was a terrible mistake."

"I'd say. You almost killed your son."

The sound of ice cubes tinkling against glass turned into ambulance sirens. The disappearing sight of River, bruised and broken in Roper Hospital Emergency room as the police dragged Chase off in handcuffs, flashed before his eyes.

"I was in so much pain." He rubbed the tops of his khaki pants and removed a long piece of string. It reminded him of that time, after the radiation, he awoke to find clumps of Terry's hair on her pillow. It was only one of the escalating humiliations she had suffered as the cancer overtook her body.

Chase snapped back his head. "Try to understand. All I could think about was numbing it and . . . that's not important anymore. As soon as I get through rehab and community service, I'll start making my way back up the money list." Remorse assailed him. He remembered the look of love and respect on his late wife's face when he broke fiftieth on the money list. *I'm so proud of you.* What would she say if she were alive today? *What have you done to our son? What have you done to yourself?* Chase's breathing labored. He stared into Jake's eyes. "I'm a rising star. You said so yourself."

"More like an imploding star." Sunshine sliced through the blinds. "Anyway, time is up." Jake donned his wraparound sunglasses. "Your endorsement contracts have been canceled."

"What?" Chase tugged at the collar of his light blue polo shirt. He ached to be outside, swinging a club, flexing his arms in a soothing rhythm.

Jake's chin dipped and rose twice in affirmation.

Chase rubbed the front of his shirt. The glistening skin beneath was a good three shades lighter than his cheeks and muscle-roped forearms. "You can't do this to me. I've got fines to pay, massive attorney fees, a mortgage, childcare . . ."

"Spare me." Jake signaled for the waiter and instructed him to increase the air conditioning. "You've embarrassed me and wasted my time. Do you have any idea how much your failed personal life has cost me in terms of money and reputation?" He lowered his jaw. "I hand-picked you out of Clemson, I introduced you to golf's elite on a silver platter and you've made a fool out of me." He took a deep breath. "You're my first mistake."

Outside the window a beer truck was stopped at the light. There were three liquor stores within a two-block radius, begging Chase to succumb.

He jerked his chair back from the table. "I was good enough for you before your company went public. Where's your loyalty? What about the little guys like me who helped put you on the map?"

Jake sipped his water. "I fail to see how your pitiful playing record and felony arrest speak favorably of my business acumen."

"Fine. I don't need you. As soon as I get back on my feet, I'll find a new agent. Sponsors will be lining up to sign me. I'm a great golfer and you can't stop my return to the PGA Tour."

Jake leaned forward, his smoky eyes narrowed. "This isn't just about you and me anymore. I can't afford to be embarrassed. Neither can my partners. Neither can our investors. OneSport Corporation is the new worldwide leader in athlete representation and sports marketing. Nothing gets in our way."

Chase scowled. "Are you threatening me?"

Jake crossed his legs. "All I'm saying is that we are golf's most formidable business presence. *Anyone* who wants to be *anyone* in this business needs OneSport on his side. We, on the other hand, don't need you. You're a loser, Chase McLeary, and I'm betting that you will *never* play pro golf again."

# Chapter 1

*Twin Palms Country Club*
*Mount Pleasant, South Carolina*

"I can do it this time," Chase McLeary said, dodging an army of colorfully clad weekend warriors. "Give me a chance." Strong coffee and musk aftershave overpowered the bustling lobby as he struggled to keep up with the man's brisk pace.

"Sorry, kid. Not interested." Tank Mazzola, a retired Wall Street stockbroker with chiseled cheekbones, maneuvered deftly through the crowd like an aging quarterback.

"At least take a minute to hear me out." Chase used the sleeve of his frayed yellow polo shirt to mop his brow, careful to avoid scraping his freshly shaved skin on the Wando High Golf Coach patch emblazoned on the arm. A whiff of pine scented deodorant pricked his nose.

Tank stopped. "You're wasting your time." He dug a pinkie into the crevice of his cleft chin. "Even if I wanted to, I don't have the money to sponsor your comeback bid." He slid into an overstuffed lounge chair and exchanged sandals for soft spikes.

Chase sat across from him and removed his sports cap. He ran a hand through short blonde hair marred by a slender gray stripe above the right ear. "But Marty thought . . ."

Tank grunted. "He doesn't know what he's talking about. Marty's a caddie who spends too much time thinking about ways to spend other people's money." He yanked the laces tight, leaned forward and put both hands on his knees. "Every dollar I've got and then some is invested in my new business. But even if I had the money, why would I give it to you? What makes you think you're still good enough to get back on the PGA Tour after, what, a decade?"

Chase frowned. "Six years. Seven if you count the season I cut short to be with my wife during the chemo."

"Sorry." Tank panned the lobby. "Maybe when my business gets off the ground we can do something . . ."

"Hold on. I want to answer your question." He waited for Tank's eyes to meet his before holding up his pointer finger. "There's only one reason I'm not playing on Tour, and that reason is Jake Nathan."

"The OneSport guy? Why?"

"He was my agent. After I got into all that trouble he fired me. Then he blacklisted me."

"Maybe he did and maybe he didn't, but either way, I don't see how that kept you from getting through Qualification School and earning your way back on Tour." Tank scratched his upper lip with the back of his thumbnail. "OneSport rules the golf industry, I'll give you that, but no amount of blacklisting can keep a guy from sinking birdie putts if he's got the talent."

"That's just it, I couldn't win on my own merit. He totally abused me." Chase took a deep breath. "It took me two seasons to get out from under my legal troubles. After that, Jake made sure I couldn't get into any tournaments on sponsor exemptions so I had to go to Q-School. My first attempt, he had somebody slip an extra club in my bag and got me disqualified. The second year he sent child welfare activists to heckle me. I couldn't hear myself think much less putt. Then he . . ."

Tank held up a hand. "Hold on." After checking the number display, he flipped open his cell phone. "Where are you?"

"We're not coming," Trip Boswyck, one of Tank's business partners, said. "They canceled."

Tank groaned. "Let me guess." He pressed the telephone tight to his ear.

Chase jiggled the heel of his golf shoe as he waited.

"OneSport," Trip said. "They've got every pro golfer locked down tight. These kids are petrified of getting on OneSport's bad side and won't even give us an hour of their time."

Tank sighed. "I'll call you later and we can talk it through."

"You on your way back?"

"Nah. It's not like I've got anybody to go home to. The course is packed but as long as I'm here, I might as well see if I can get in on a game." He snapped the phone closed and looked at Chase. "Okay, you got a raw deal. Welcome to America. Those OneSport guys are jerks, believe me, I know, but they can't keep you out of the game forever." He pointed a finger. "If you're half the player you say you are, then golf is in your blood and you won't quit until you're back on top."

"That's what I've been trying to do, but I need help and nobody believes in me anymore." Chase leaned back in the chair, head tipped up.

"You want my advice? Lose the pity-party. You screwed up and you're still paying the price, but talent and perseverance always come out on top. Stay confident, keep at it and one day things will turn around."

Chase opened his mouth to speak but then closed it. "Sounds like your playing partner bailed," he said, gesturing toward the cell phone. "I've got a threesome going off in half an hour. You're welcome to join us so long as you don't mind a couple of beginners."

Noisy throngs of golfers hustled through the doors, anxious to get out on the course. Tank hesitated. "Okay, but just so we're clear, my joining your group doesn't mean anything. I told you about my financial situation. You can't get blood from a stone."

\* \* \* \* \*

## *Midtown Manhattan, New York City*

OneSport Corporation, a moniker created from the last names of its three marquee partners, Joe O'Hara, Jake Nathan and Mort Epstein, occupied the 41st–49th floors of the Burlington House Building on Sixth Avenue. Together with its sister company, OneSong, it employed hundreds of men and women to represent the brightest stars in sports, television, film and music.

The owners met in the corner conference room for their weekly briefing.

Joe took his usual seat by the door and eyed Jake's latest fashion statement. "Jeez, what did you pay for that suit? Couldn't you afford a matching tie?"

Jake ripped away teeth-whitening strips and tossed them in the wastebasket. "Not everyone likes wearing a brown polyester uniform every day, bean-counter."

"Bite me," Joe replied.

Mort scratched his dark but thinning hair and swiveled around his black leather chair. "What happened with Alvarez?" Scalp snowflakes dotted the front and sleeves of his dress shirt.

"We got him," Jake said.

"How much?" Joe asked.

"He gets thirteen percent to use our racket and clothes." Jake checked his reflection in the glass trophy cabinet.

"What about Hilliard?" Joe asked. "You didn't give up the non-compete, did you?"

OneSport's Lord of Leverage, Joe could work miracles with cash. Borrowing, investing, selling, manufacturing, Joe knew the serial number on every dollar in and out of the company.

"No. Same deal. From now on, everyone we represent in the tennis industry uses and wears our stuff."

"Stop patting your own back." Mort adjusted his thick glasses. "We haven't penetrated the sports market the way we've gotten entertainers signed. If we don't step up, OneSong will be funding OneSport in three to six months."

Mort pursed his lips, awaiting an appropriate response. He cranked the chair lever a few times in an attempt to raise himself to Jake's height.

"OneSong clients are easier," Jake said. "With musicians, it's all about image. They want the latest sound and the newest clothes. My cocker spaniel has more talent than some of these kids. Athletes are different. They're married to their equipment and some of them can't play without their lucky shirts. Fear not. I'll get them sooner or later. I always do."

Joe sniggered at Jake. "You gotta' love this guy. Employees love him, the media loves him, clients love him and he really loves himself."

"Why not? I've got the kind of star quality that makes women cheat on their husbands and men open their checkbooks."

"And an ego to match," Joe added.

Jake held up his middle finger.

"Enough," Mort said. "There's a problem with golf."

"No way," Jake said. "Things are moving great. We've been signing talent on the PGA, Nationwide, European and Austral-Asian tours like mad. It's baseball I'm worried about."

"Shut up for a minute. We're about to kiss our golf market goodbye," Mort said.

"Don't tell me you're worried about another agency?" Jake said. "We're the pace car, laps ahead of everyone else."

Mort poked at the sleek chrome intercom in front of him.

"Tonya," he said to their shared executive secretary. "Scrounge me up one of those double chocolate doughnuts."

Cute, but not too cute, and smart, but not too smart, Tonya had the right combination of street smarts and survival instincts to flourish under their results-oriented, yet laissez-faire management style.

"Okay. Coffee's on the way," she said. "Joe? Jake? Anything for you guys?"

"Bagel with butter," Joe said.

"Only bottled water for me," Jake said. "I ate my bran muffin and yogurt at 7:30 after racquetball." He flexed his arm muscles.

"Don't you ever sleep in?" Tonya asked.

Jake grinned. "Is that an invitation?"

Mort shut off the intercom and shook his head. "Cut the crap. Are you trying to get us sued?"

Joe poked at his PDA to check the latest line on tonight's Yankees game. "If you're thinking about changing our business plan, I'll need time to rework the budget numbers. Expanding our golf operations wasn't supposed to hit the sheets until next fiscal year."

Mort passed out a sheaf of papers. "Then you'd better get busy. This is a feasibility report for a new golf club manufactured under the name Trubird Group."

Jake's eyes flashed down the page. "I'm not buying it," he said, arms folded. "These stats say we're about to get shut out of the golf market by a company I've never even heard of."

Joe lined up the pages in a neat row, underlined sections and jotted notes in the margins as he read.

"Believe it. These clubs are cheaper than any others out there," Mort said. "And well-engineered to boot."

Joe whistled. "The profit margins are off the charts. They'll have the whole market. Where did you get this?"

"The more important question," Mort said, puffing out his chest, "is what can we do to protect ourselves and eliminate this threat? Golf is a money sport. It's white-hot right now and will only get richer unless Trubird enters the mix."

"A full set of their sticks sells for less than five hundred bucks," Joe said. "These guys are sticking it to everybody else in the business. How can they do this?"

"Who cares? Why are you worried about cheap knock-off clubs?" Jake asked.

"Because," Joe said, "the profit margin in name brand equipment is the best kept secret in golf. Manufacturing expenses total around a quarter of the retail price, and soft costs like research and development and advertising make up maybe another twenty-five percent. We sell premium drivers for four hundred and twenty nine bucks a pop. They cost us less than two hundred to make."

"Consider our target market," Mort said to Jake. "The high-end golfer willingly spends twenty-five hundred bucks for one of our sets. A weekend hacker might pay five hundred for the same bag. What's the difference between the two? Confidence brought on by sheer advertising dollars."

"No way," Jake said. "Technology has made clubs hit the ball longer and straighter. Look at how much money Augusta spent to lengthen their holes."

"You're missing the point," Mort said. "Most of today's knockoff clubs have the same technology as the name brands. But you don't see Tiger Woods carrying a no-name putter on the eighteenth green at the PGA Championship, do you? Endorsements sell golf clubs, not technology. Trubird is dangerous because their clubs are priced at rack rates and they boast better technology like longer-lasting shafts. They should be charging more than we do for a set." He smacked the table. "Not less."

Jake flicked a dog hair from his lapel. "Why is this Trubird Group different from every other company we've had to muscle aside? We've got solid contracts with all the important players and nobody wants OneSport as an enemy."

Joe frowned. "Because these numbers are scary. There's too much potential. If they can get a decent Tour professional to hawk their cheap clubs, our profits will vaporize. Trubird will take over and OneSport products will be outdated and overpriced-like beta videocassettes. Our inventory will jam the warehouses and we'll take a huge hit on our balance sheet. You know how tight cash flow is. This would ruin us."

"Why don't we buy it; make it our own?" Jake asked.

"Impossible." Mort turned to Jake. "Your old friend Trip Boswyck is one of the equity partners. He'd rather go bankrupt than do business with us. His reputation was everything, and you made him a laughingstock. I told you he'd come back to haunt us."

Joe rolled his eyes. "He still claims you promised him a piece of OneSport in return for all his golf contacts back when we started the company."

Jake shrugged. "I never promised him anything; that's why the lawsuit was dropped. He just assumed a lot. Anyway, why can't we come up with a copycat club? We could start a marketing blitz to steal their edge. Who else is in on this?"

"Aside from the designer, there are two other backers plus Boswyck," Mort said. "And no, we can't come close to duplicating these sticks. They're using new technology with an integrated process to produce their clubs, from driver to wedge."

"What new technology?" Jake asked. "Trans-beta forging? Alpha mirage? Individually matched shaft systems? Thermoplastic grips? We do all of that stuff."

"No," Mort said. "They've created a new material to work with, found a way to ensure consistency in flexibility and that's only part of the innovations. We're talking a whole new mousetrap."

"I still think we can come up with something similar," Jake said.

"At what cost?" Joe asked, clicking his mechanical pencil on and off. "Considering how much capital we've sunk into developing our own line of equipment, starting from scratch would kill our third quarter numbers, maybe fourth quarter too. Plus, if we do any more off-balance sheet financing, the auditors will go nuts."

Jake waived a hand. "Screw them."

"I'm serious," Joe said. "The post-Enron, WorldCom, Tyco accounting world is terrified. They're not willing to bend over for us anymore since investors are successfully suing them. This isn't the time to sink big money into research and development. Trust me."

The partners sat in silence. Mort put a thumb in his belt and rocked back into the quilted leather. "We don't want to look bad by taking someone else's lead. Plus, matching Trubird's price would put us in the red for years. The last thing we want to do is decrease our profit margins."

"Yeah," Joe said. "And after that last bump to our expense accounts, I'm running out of magic to disguise our personal spending."

Jake's eyes narrowed. "Then where are we?"

"Out of time," Mort said. "The patent is nearly approved and word has it they want to introduce the full set mid-season." He placed both hands flat on the table. "We're the leader and everyone is gunning for us. If Trubird succeeds, it will open the floodgates for challenges to every aspect of our business. Trubird clubs can never hit the market. We have to sabotage their introduction in a way that will ensure total failure."

Joe twirled his pencil, baton style. With the other hand, he pulled a fruit flavored antacid from his shirt pocket and popped in into his cheek. "How?"

"I say we use the full extent of our relationships, sponsors, endorsements, or anything else we have, to ruin anyone in bed with Trubird." Jake folded his slender fingers.

Mort nodded and turned to Joe. "Find a way to hold up every aspect of their business plan and bleed the partners dry. We need to know where Trubird's principals are most vulnerable and whom they've approached for funding. Bury them in paperwork, sue, threaten breach of copyright, hurt their other investments - whatever you can think of to draw down their bank accounts and put them out of business."

"Done," Joe said.

"We're OneSong." Jake stood. "We've got nothing to worry about."

# Chapter 2

Trip Boswyck and Satch Wyzinski, two of Trubird Group's four partners, met at their makeshift offices to discuss project developments. Housed inside an eighteen hundred square foot air-conditioned warehouse, the unofficial headquarters was jammed full of equipment, materials and machines.

"Where's Tank?" Satch asked, tossing his ponytail while tinkering with a prototype five wood.

An engineer from Cal Tech University, Satch was Trubird's creative genius. Brilliant and outspoken, he was dismissed from the corporate-sponsored research team that developed Liquid-Metal™ after voicing his unpopular belief that LiquidMetal,™ while a goldmine for golf manufacturers, was imprecise and grossly overpriced.

"He'll be back this afternoon." Trip, as Chief Operating Officer, coordinated all of the company's financial, legal and public relations duties.

After hanging his navy blue blazer on the door, he looked for a clean place to sit amidst the noisy golf graveyard. Broken shafts, balls and club heads lay everywhere. A wall-mounted television blasted a history channel documentary on German U-boats and the bass-thumping beat of salsa music blared from a portable stereo. Trip snapped off the music and searched for the remote control.

"How can you work in this environment? Don't you ever clean up?" He picked up an empty fast food container that littered the desk and brought it to an overflowing trashcan. After lifting the lid, the aroma of stale hamburgers and pickles knifed the air.

"Cut me some slack. Unlike you, *I* spend twenty hours a day here. I've slept on that old sofa more nights than I can remember," Satch answered. He put down the club and scratched a few notes on a clipboard filled with measurements.

Trip tossed two empty soda cans and sighed. "I can't believe we haven't signed a golfer up yet. This is insane. I'm the former PGA Commissioner, for crying out loud."

"Don't beat yourself up. Without you we wouldn't have had the clout to get our foot in the door with some of those athletes and venture capital guys."

"A lot of good it's done us," Trip said, perching cross-legged on a metal stool. "Jake Nathan's influence has made my past connections virtually useless. I know that somewhere there's a golfer who is willing to take a chance and cross OneSport. We've just got to find him before we go bankrupt."

Satch pulled a four iron from a stack of clubs and headed for the loft-and-lie machine against the wall. His greasy fingers were black from knuckles to fingertips. "This'll cheer you up. Watch." He bent the club until it broke.

"I hope that wasn't one of ours."

"Nope. That was the competition's cast iron club. Bend the club-head five degrees and it snaps like a twig. Here's one of ours." He slipped one of Trubird's irons on the machine, wiped his hands on his jeans and jerked the levers.

"Take it easy, will you? Those loft and lie machines are two grand a pop and you've gone through three in the last six months," Trip said. His irritation subsided as he watched the club respond.

"How much did you adjust that?"

"Seven degrees." Satch held up the club.

"Excellent." Trip pumped his fist. "Flexibility is our hallmark and that's exactly how Trubird is going to corner the market.

Our clubs will turn high-handicappers into decent players because they are consistently forgiving, even with a bad swing. They bend without breaking. The guy with a bad slice will hit straighter than ever before because the club flex will help straighten his shot."

"And the good player will enjoy more length and accuracy." Satch flipped off a sandal to scratch the bottom of his foot.

"Between our new grip system, our ultra-forged irons, the shaft flexibility, and our weighted accu-driver, the golf world won't know what hit it." Trip inspected the ceiling. "If we can get one golfer to try using our clubs, that's all we need to break through OneSport's monopoly. After his first hole he'll buy into the whole Trubird concept. I can feel it. I can taste it. We're so close."

"Yeah. Once I perfect the wedge, my job is done and we're ready to roll." Satch yanked one of the demo clubs.

"I thought you had that wrapped up already."

"I did, until I reworked the cost figures into your marketing model. Titanium costs around ten bucks a pound but nickel costs more, around seventeen. I reconfigured the composition to change the proportions of the other metal materials to keep our price down without sacrificing accuracy. But don't worry, I've almost got it."

"Almost won't cut it." Trip buttoned the cuff of his pin-striped dress shirt. "Do it."

Satch cracked his knuckles. "Leave the technical side to me. You concentrate on signing up our guinea pig." He typed rapid fire into his computer.

"Did those papers arrive?"

"Over there." Satch gestured. "They came by courier from the attorneys."

Trip opened the envelope and pulled a pair of glasses and a pen from his breast pocket. He read the documents slowly and carefully.

"Everything okay?" Brushing loose hair from his forehead, Satch re-taped a grip.

"Looks fine so far."

"I almost didn't sign for it. Thought it was misdelivered. How come it's addressed to Boswyck Partners?"

"Just a formality." Trip looked up over his glasses.

Satisfied with the grip, Satch took several practice swings. "Trip, I need a favor." He held the club for moral support.

"Let me guess. You can't come up with the next installment." Trip circled something on the back page.

Satch swung the club hard. "We're tapped out and Ally won't let me put a second on the house. The bank won't lend me a nickel because I don't have any collateral. Can you loan me the money for this installment?" He braced for the answer.

Trip put down the papers. "This won't be the last installment. You don't have any other resources?"

Satch shook his head.

Trip hesitated before answering. "Okay, I'll loan you the money. But only if you're willing to put up your Trubird shares against the note."

"How does that work? I'm a scientist with two PhD's, but I can't even balance my own checkbook. Financial terms are a foreign language.

"We'll do a promissory note at the market rate of interest. So long as you pay me back on time, you keep your shares."

"Sounds good to me." Satch swung the club.

"I'll have the attorney draw it up today. Sign it tomorrow and you're all set."

"Thanks. I really appreciate it." Satch moved his attention to the Trubird driver.

Trip nodded. "My pleasure."

* * * * *

"Dad? Earth to Dad."

"Sorry." Chase turned to his eleven-year-old son. "What did you say?"

"When do we tee off?" River repeated amid the whoosh of balls being struck all around them in the linear practice area. His shorts hung low on his underdeveloped hips and one sock refused to stay above his ankle.

"Ten minutes." Chase filled his lungs and smiled. Never was he so secure as when he stepped outdoors, club in hand, ready to play the game he loved. A well-struck ball brought with it the feeling of purity, like a resonating guitar string or a nothing-but-net foul shot.

Playing a casual round on a beautiful day was almost reward enough for the talent he possessed. Almost. A peanut-sized knot formed in the base of his throat. Having tasted the thrill of life on the PGA Tour, he ached to be back there, testing his skills against the best players in the world.

After placing another ball on the mat, he glanced up at his favorite moving target, the caged tractor-like ball sweeper traversing the range. After a gentle swing of his five iron, he didn't need to follow the ball's path with his eyes to know he hit his target. The metal plinking sound the golf ball made as it bounced off of the roof confirmed what he already knew. The man inside yelled a familiar greeting.

Chase waved before pausing to watch a windsock inflate, deflate and then invert with the change in breeze.

He sipped a bottle of water and pointed at yet another of his son's shots sailing down the left side of the fence.

"See that hook?" Chase said. "You're swinging too hard. Let the club do the work. If you want to get any better," he said, handing his son a five iron, "put that driver away."

"No way." River grunted and tugged at his cowhide necklace before tightening his grip on the club.

"What good is playing if you can't get the ball in the fairway? You know what they say. Drive . . ."

"Yeah, yeah." River recited his father's mantra. "Drive for show, putt for dough." Propelled by another monstrous swing,

River barely made contact, sending the ball off the toe of his driver backward toward an approaching figure.

"Ugh!" Tank grabbed his crotch and dropped his bag.

Chase covered his eyes with his hands.

"Sorry, sir." River scrambled over to apologize. "That had to hurt. I'm really sorry." Waiting for the man to recover, River fiddled with the waistband of his purple boxers and looked to his father for help.

"Some swing," Tank said through clenched teeth. "Two inches higher and I'd be a freaking soprano."

"Next time you want to pound a driver," Chase said, "make sure nobody's around."

"And make sure nobody's jewels are in the way," Tank added.

"River, meet Mr. Tank Mazzola. He was going to be our fourth before you scared him off," Chase said.

"What kind of name is Tank?" River asked.

"Nickname. Got it in the Navy." His grimace began to fade as the throb subsided.

"Cool," River said. "You still want to play?"

Tank took a deep breath and exhaled the last vestiges of pain. "Depends. You gonna do that again?"

"I promise you he won't," Chase answered, staring down his son.

Tank nodded. "All right. We set to tee off? I've got some business to take care of right after our round and . . . hey, looky there." Tank flipped up his sunglasses to get a better view. "I'd like to get a piece of . . ."

"Mom, we're over here," Chase quickly called out.

"*Mama mia*," Tank whispered. He used his hand as a spatula to tuck his shirt into the front of his linen pants and winked at River.

Maddie McLeary, Chase's fifty-two-year-old mother, was dressed in pink and beige golf attire, resembling Ann Taylor's older sister more than a serious golfer. She tugged her high tech pull-cart, complete with water bottle, Evian atomizer and matching towel, next to Chase.

"Mom, this is Tank Mazzola. He's going to be joining us."

She extended a manicured hand and then brought it up to adjust her ash blonde hair.

Tank took a step forward. "The pleasure's all mine. Mmm. Smells like Shalimar."

Maddie backed up a step. "Good guess. Uh, you're welcome to join us, but we'd hate to slow you down. River's a beginner and I'm not very—"

"Not a problem." Tank picked up his clubs. "So, were you a child bride or what? I never would have figured you for Chase's mother." He led the way toward the first tee.

Maddie turned around and looked at her son.

*Be nice to him*, Chase mouthed.

She shrugged and they assembled around the tee box. "Come here, River," she said. "You can hit from the reds with me."

"No way. I want to hit from the gold tees with Dad. The reds are for girls. Besides, I can make it to the fairway."

"Go with Momma, River," Chase said. "If you come in under fifty strokes on the front nine, you can play the golds on the back nine. Tank, what's your handicap?"

"My backswing. Mind if I take the honors?" Tank addressed the ball with a brief waggle. He took an easy practice swing and then repeated it in front of a ball.

Chase nodded. "Right up the middle. Nice shot. Looks like you've played this game before."

Chase teed up his ball. After one practice swing, with a loud crack of his three wood, Chase's ball sailed nearly one hundred yards in front of Tank's and landed dead center of the fairway.

Next, Maddie drew her supple arms back and forth with a graceful swing. Her effortless drive sailed one hundred and thirty yards up the right side of the fairway.

"Allow me." Tank stepped forward to remove her pink tee from the ground.

"Give me a break," Maddie said under her breath.

River stuffed his tee into the ground. "Watch this."

Chase shook his head. "Put it back."

"But dad, I . . ."

"Put that driver away. You've done enough damage with that thing this morning."

"Why can't I just . . ."

"Watch your stance. Here, look where you're aimed." Chase gave River an unwanted lesson.

Tank inched closer to Maddie.

"Your son's a born teacher. Lots of patience, but *that* one." He nodded at River. "Piss and vinegar, pardon my French. You're gonna have your hands full with that kid."

"Don't I know it. River's got his mother's temperament." Maddie pulled at the fingers of her golf glove, adjusting the fit. "She passed away when he was only a baby," she added.

"What about you? Married?"

"Widowed."

"Sorry. Recent?"

River swung hard and missed the ball completely.

"No, Jim died more than fifteen years ago," she answered. "And you?"

"My Lucille, she's been gone twenty-five years, God bless her. Wish I could say the same for my second wife, that conniving witch." He picked grass from his cleats with a broken tee.

She laughed. "Bad divorce?"

"Satan himself wouldn't want that wench. Thank God for the prenup. Both my daughters warned me about Trish, but I was only listening to one thing at the time, if you know what I mean." He winked.

A pink cloud crossed Maddie's face.

"That one's gonna be good," Chase said, watching River's shot sail one hundred twenty five yards down the left side of the fairway.

"Come on, Dad. We can take these guys. How about it, Tank? Me and Dad against you and Momma. Give us a stroke a hole, match play format."

"You're on. Doll, this looks like easy money." Tank hitched up his tan slacks.

Maddie switched hands to pull her cart. "You shouldn't have given up any strokes."

"I know what I'm doing."

Maddie's eyes shone. "We'll see."

Tank finished out the first hole with a par and Maddie made double-bogey, for a team total of plus two. Chase made birdie and it took River nine strokes to get in the hole which, adjusted for their one stroke handicap, put the younger pairing at plus three.

At the second hole, a par four with pot bunkers along the left side, all four players had decent drives. Chase's drive landed ninety yards from the green in the light rough.

River, still in the fairway, hit his fourth shot. A lofty pitch, his ball touched down eight feet from the flag.

"Great one," Chase said. With a decent lie in the rough, he selected his sixty-degree loft wedge. "After I hole this, Tank and Momma might as well head for the clubhouse because they're not going to see the lead again."

Tank belly-laughed.

Squaring up the face, Chase took a long lazy swing. Together the foursome watched the ball soar over the greenside bunker, land six feet from the stick and roll slowly until it died in the cup. River erupted in victory whoops.

Maddie turned to Tank. "Glad you know what you're doing."

From the corner of his eye, Chase watched Tank slowly stroke his chin, a thoughtful look on his face.

Chase's heart skipped a beat. Just maybe . . .

Tank, eyes riveted on Maddie's shapely bottom, abruptly turned and scurried after her.

Chase's shoulders sagged. It figures.

\* \* \* \* \*

The engagement luncheon for Mort's daughter at the Pierre Hotel on Manhattan's Upper East Side ran late into the afternoon. The intoxicating fragrance of sweet Stargazer lilies and earthy Belgian chocolates lingered throughout the candlelit room.

Jake and Joe cornered the father-of-the-bride-to-be at the bar.

"Sorry we missed your toast," Joe said.

Jake nodded. "She looks great."

"Off limits for you." Joe lightly punched his partner on the arm.

In a mild but rare state of scotch-induced melancholy, Mort's eyes stayed trained on his daughter. "Hope she holds off on kids for a few years. Not sure I'm ready to be a grandpa." He loosened the knot in his tie.

"I'll drink to that." Joe clinked his soda glass against Mort's. "Hate to be a buzz-kill, but we need to meet first thing tomorrow."

Jake swirled his crystal balloon of cabernet. "Why?"

"I reviewed the weekly financials out of our Los Angeles, Miami, London, Tokyo and Sydney offices," Joe said. "We've got some problems with our licensing and royalty contracts. Also, counterfeit apparel and products are costing us a fortune."

Mort gestured. Young girls in couture and boys in designer suits dotted the room. "This is what it's all about, you know? Giving your family the best, better than you ever dreamed."

Jake shrugged. "Wouldn't know. Lifelong bachelor."

Joe patted Mort's arm. "Great party. Is that carpaccio? Talk about over the top. Can't wait to see you bury that one in our advertising and promotions budget."

"Thanks for coming, guys. See you in the morning." Mort looked across the room toward his wife. Petite and blonde, she wore a short red cocktail dress and important jewelry. She smiled and crooked a finger towards him.

"She hasn't been this happy in years," he said. "I may actually get lucky tonight."

Jake raised his glass. "Mazel tov."

\* \* \* \* \*

By the eighteenth hole, the oldest and youngest players stood together off the right side of the fairway in mild rough. Chase and Maddie, barely off the green, waited for their respective slower partners to hit.

River, whose ball was farther from the hole, pulled out a three wood and surveyed the distance. It was one hundred yards uphill to the pin.

"Kid, you're gonna hit it so far over the green that I can five-putt and *still* win the hole," Tank said.

River didn't flinch, turning his head between practice swings. "This one's going in the cup, Old Man."

Tank chuckled as River made contact with the ball. Both players watched the white streak fly over the green into the neighboring fairway.

River stamped his foot. "You jinxed me."

"Watch and learn." Tank stepped up to his ball with a pitching wedge and frowned when his ball skimmed the ground and stopped halfway up the hill.

"Worm-burner!" River shrieked in triumph.

Tank cursed. "I've got another name for that shot."

Up on the putting green, Maddie shielded her eyes and squinted down the fairway. "I wonder what's so funny. River's practically rolling on the ground down there."

"Whatever it was, I'm sure you don't want to know. Tank may have gotten out of the Navy, but his mouth never did."

Maddie wiped her neck with a handkerchief. "You know, Tank is the only other person besides your dad to call me 'doll,' although that's probably their only similarity." She fingered the locket around her neck. "How do you know him?"

"Let's talk about it later."

Tank and River made their way to the green where Chase casually rolled in a twenty-two footer for another birdie.

Maddie was next.

"Mom, did you read the break carefully?" Chase asked.

"Stop talking. Of course, I did." Maddie lined up her shot for the second time. She drew back her putter.

"You know, with this being for the win, I want to make sure you noticed the heavy spike marks around the cup. No pressure." Chase held up his hands.

"Shush." She lined up her putt.

River produced a burp lasting a full three seconds.

"Cut it out, you two," she said.

Tank ambled over and whispered into Maddie's ear. She nodded, relaxed her shoulders and sank the putt.

Maddie turned to River. "I believe you hit from in front of the tee box, dear, on this last hole."

"So?" River scratched his backside.

"Two stroke penalty, son. We practically had it won before your grandma even touched the ball." Tank shook hands all around. "Come on, kid. I'll buy you lunch."

The packed clubhouse, situated off the eighteenth hole, bustled with noisy golfers bragging about forty-foot putts and that holy grail of topics, the perfect round. The room was so cold you could practically see your breath as sweaty patrons basked in the dark wood, dim lights, cold beer and quick service. The carpeting was dark green and the tables were set with faux-linen napkins on top of laminated scorecards.

"Compared with my club, this is St. Andrews." Tank eyed the crowd.

"Thanks, we like it," Maddie said.

"Hey, Chase. How'd it go today?" the bartender called while wiping up a spill.

"Not too bad, Willy." Chase waved back.

They ordered cheeseburgers and fries all around, Cokes for River and Chase, seltzer water with a splash of pineapple for Maddie and a draft Coors light for Tank.

"Come on, River. Let's wash up. You're carrying around a divot under those finger nails," Chase said.

"Okay," River said. "I've got to take a . . ."

"Ahem." Maddie wagged a finger.

Tank laughed. "We could use more kids like that in my business. Nowadays, they're all grad school snots who never speak their minds."

As a dancer would, she lifted her drink, careful not to let the icy drops dot the front of her blouse. "I thought you said you're in the stock market. What kind of a degree do you need for that, a Masters in poker?" Maddie asked, smoothing the napkin in her lap.

Tank put his arm around the back of her chair. "Back when I started out, you could work your way up the ranks—just like in the Navy. I started out in the shredding room but I learned fast and finally got my own accounts. I stuck with things I could understand—Blue Chips all the way. None of that junk bond-derivative-index option-cockamamie crap that so many kids are pushing now. I hate that stuff."

"Let me guess. You took early retirement?"

"Yeah, but it wasn't exactly voluntary. They gave me a golden parachute, on account of all the big clients who liked me, and they retired me two years ago."

Tank signaled Willie for another draft.

"I see it all the time," Maddie said, uncrossing and crossing her knees. Her bare calf momentarily touched the leg of his pants. "Young brokers anxious for a commission check will sell anything to anyone whether they need it, want it or even like it."

"Have you always lived here?" Tank asked.

"Yes, born and raised." She took another sip. "So, what kind of business brings you down here?"

"What else? Golf."

Chase led River back to his seat as their lunch plates arrived.

"What about golf?" Chase asked.

River, attacking his French fries, remained mute.

"Tank was telling me about his new golf business." Maddie placed all of her fries onto River's plate and inched her chair away from Tank's.

"Are you building a course?" Chase asked.

"Nope. I'm making clubs under the name Trubird Group," Tank said. "A couple years ago, one of my old clients came to me plugging this idea for a totally new concept in golf equipment: technologically advanced clubs for a fraction of the price. I ain't no dummy. Lots of guys have tried to bag me as an investor. I grilled this guy pretty good. Spent big money on a market study and researched the heck out of the golf industry before I decided to jump in. Along with my buddy Dick and another guy, we've invested a boatload of cash. Trubird sticks are going to revolutionize the whole golf industry from performance to pricing. Soon everyone will be able to afford a set."

Chase wiped ketchup from the corner of his mouth. "What are they made of?"

"Can't tell you that. You know how it is. We all signed confidentiality agreements. But one thing's for sure." Tank leaned in and lowered his voice. "The other money guy is the former PGA Commissioner. Trust me, we're on to something big. Really big."

"Boswyck?" Chase said. "That's a surprise."

"Yep. The whole thing has been hush-hush, but now that the patent is in place, I'm supposed to get my own set of clubs before the next capital call."

"What's a capital call?" River asked.

"It's a high class expression for begging. I give money so this guy can build something; but, then when he makes money, I get a piece of the pie," Tank said.

"Oh. Okay," River said. "Are you going to eat your pickle?"

Tank handed it over as a familiar face signaled him from the bar.

"I don't believe it. Be right back," he said.

River sucked the last of his soda through his straw. "Can I have dessert?" he asked, still sucking.

"Cut that out. Don't you ever get full?" Chase asked. "Never mind. Go ask Willie what's on the menu today."

After River's departure, he filled Maddie in on his failed attempt to woo Tank into supporting his comeback bid.

Maddie pushed away her plate. "Well, maybe if you get to know him better, you can get in on this new golf club venture of his. Do you think it's for real?"

Chase nodded. "I do. If Boswyck's on the inside, this must be a major deal. But I've seen pretty much everything on the market, and it's hard to believe these 'miracle clubs' could be so different, especially if they're cheaper."

Maddie shrugged. "Oh, before I forget. Do you remember my friend Sylvia King?"

"Yes, and don't even think about setting me up with her. She's at least fifty, with calves bigger than mine and . . ."

"No, no, no." She laughed. "Sylvia is happily married and definitely not your type. She simply asked if you're taking on new students. Her niece needs a few lessons."

"Sure, have her call me."

"Great." Maddie reached for Chase's hand. "Since you brought it up, I do know someone . . ."

He pulled it away. "No! No more blind dates."

"Honey, the clock is ticking on your life and there is so much more out there for you. Since Terry died, I've watched you flirt with happiness only to hide behind the wall you've built to keep everyone out." She tipped her head. "Think about River. He's too young to remember how his father used to be. You *need* to find a companion. It's the only way you'll ever regain that which I can't explain, but that which is essential."

"I thank God River is too young to remember how I almost killed him." Arms crossed, Chase turned his head away. "Besides, you're a hypocrite. You haven't had a date in twenty years. Why don't you take your own advice?"

Maddie pursed her lips as River returned carrying an extra large piece of key lime pie.

"You know what?" he mumbled.

"Don't talk with your mouth full," Maddie snapped, more loudly than she intended.

"But Momma, Tank said . . ." River tried again.

"It can wait until you're finished chewing," Maddie said.

River rolled his eyes and Tank returned to the table. "I'm sorry, but I've got to head out. Been having such a good time, I didn't realize how late it was."

"Go right ahead. Thanks for lunch, Tank. It was a fun round of golf," she said.

Chase shook hands and River mumbled thanks from an overstuffed mouth.

"Maddie, is it okay if I get your phone number in case I'm down this way again?" Tank asked.

"Sure." She smiled. "As long as I can show you a few rental properties." She retrieved a business card from her purse.

"What an operator. Anytime, doll." Tank stuffed the card into his shirt pocket and left the clubhouse.

"You know what?" River asked Maddie.

"What."

"Tank bet that guy at the bar a hundred bucks that he could get your phone number."

"What?!" Maddie lurched forward, slapping both hands on the table.

"That's what I was trying to tell you. When I was getting my pie, Tank was saying that you were the cutest broad he'd seen in years. Said you looked like Linda Evans, but with bigger . . ."

"Never mind about that," Maddie said in a clipped tone.

Chase doubled over and howled.

"Why are you so mad?" River asked. "He only said nice stuff, right?"

"Stop it, both of you." Maddie folded her arms across her chest. "I never want to see or hear about Tank Mazzola again."

# CHAPTER 3

The first Trubird partner to arrive, Tank ordered a double latte and carried it to a table at the back of the coffee shop. Stirring the foamy liquid, he thought about Chase McLeary's past accomplishments and mistakes. Tank genuinely liked the former star and wondered if he was their best chance to get Trubird off the ground. Of one thing Tank was confident: the former star needed them as much as they needed him.

The door chime sounded and Satch scuffled through the door, followed by Trip and Dick Fischer, their fourth partner.

Crowded around the small table, they listened to Trip's report. "The last two golfers I approached to endorse our product wouldn't even meet me," he said. "And they're rookies."

"What kind of excuse did you get this time?" Tank asked.

"The truth," he answered. "OneSport warned them to stay away from the competition, and that's what they're going to do. These kids are scared. They don't want any trouble."

"This bites." Satch twisted his silver thumb ring.

Trip sipped his coffee. "OneSport's contracts are strict, I'll grant you, but this is embarrassing. We're not asking anybody to stick his neck out. Simply talking to us won't violate their deals, but I can't even get an audience to make our case. I'm running out of options."

Tank dumped a second packet of sugar into his coffee. "I think OneSport is scared to death of us," he said, licking the cinnamon from his swizzle stick. "Once Trubird gets off the ground, we'll put a huge hole in their market share. They'll be de-throned as the king of all-things-golf. Don't think for a minute they'll let that happen without a fight."

Dick leaned back, grazing a thick hand across the top of his crew cut. "I'm not saying our motives are purely altruistic. Of course I want to make a buck with our clubs, but I'm surprised that none of the professionals you've approached are interested in helping us bring golf to the general public as an affordable sport."

"They're not hungry enough for the money to take a chance," Trip said. "Even the guy who is one-hundred-fiftieth on the money list has still got club and ball sponsors. Probably most of the guys on the minor tours too. And for ninety-nine percent of them, it's OneSport writing the checks."

Satch leaned forward. "They can't monopolize the sports industry. Besides, most professional golfers cherry pick anyway. If they're using Mizuno woods they might have Titleist irons."

"Not anymore, not since OneSport," Trip said. "A few years ago, the company long considered golf's gold standard had annual sales around $480 million dollars and most of the market. Now they're barely afloat. OneSport makes more balls, putters, drivers and irons than any other competitor. They're living the capitalist dream; they want to be number one across the board and they insist on full brand loyalty."

"By eliminating the competition," Satch said.

"Yes," Trip agreed. "What's worse, they're making it impossible for niche companies like shaft-makers and bag manufacturers to stay independent."

Trip drummed his fingertips. "Over the past five years they've bought up the biggest distribution chains and stolen the best talent."

"Then we should pitch our clubs to them," Satch said. "It's not like we're competing with their whole business, just a small piece of it."

"Never." Trip pushed away his cup. "They don't share. They destroy the competition and they're the embodiment of everything that's wrong with the industry. They're a greedy, unprincipled monopoly. If we sold to them, the first thing they'd do is jack up the price and destroy our vision of low-cost golf." He banged his fist on the table. "I hate them. Besides, we'd never retain ownership if we went to them, so forget about joining up with OneSport."

"Then where does that leave us?" Satch asked. "I've put everything I own into Trubird, financially, emotionally, you name it. When are we going to get this thing off the ground?"

"Just hold tight a little longer," Trip answered. "I've pitched the biggest companies in the industry to get more start-up money, but nobody's buying yet. If we can find the right golfer to launch our clubs, our vision will succeed and we'll be set for life. I've invested my reputation and more money than any of you in Trubird. Trust me."

"I don't know." Dick poked the metal bridge of his glasses, pushing them higher up his crooked nose. "Trubird is a tough sell. We haven't been able to tell these pro golfers much before the patent was airtight. Why should they switch to our product? I sure wouldn't want to get sued by OneSport. Those guys have plenty of lawyers and money. And besides, with all the mental wormholes available for a golfer to fall into, why would he want to add another one by using unproven clubs?"

"Because," Satch said, rolling up his sleeves, "our sticks will revolutionize the golf industry. They're better than everything on the market and they're less than half price. These corporate pigs are ripping off the public. Doesn't anybody care?"

Trip looked behind him and put a finger to his lips. "Says us. Believe me, I've called in some favors, but no golfers are willing to bite yet."

"I might know somebody," Tank said. "It's a long-shot, but I've got a feeling about this guy."

"Who?" Trip asked.

"Chase McLeary."

Trip rubbed his forehead. "No way. He crumbled after his wife died and he couldn't buy his way into a tournament on account of how bad he fell into the bottle. That kid hasn't played on Tour in years. He'd probably get drunk before the first hole."

"I talked with the bartender at his club yesterday. In the six years he's been there, he's never seen Chase touch a drop of alcohol. Plus, he still plays like a demon, and everyone loves a comeback."

Trip chewed the end of his mocha-covered straw. "What makes you think he still has it after all these years?"

"For one thing, he hates OneSport. They fired him right after his wife died. Wouldn't even give him time to get his life back together. Now he's got a chance to show them up and to prove he's not a loser. He's got plenty of talent, and would kill to get back on Tour."

Dick shook his head. "When we created Trubird, it was all about giving something back to the average golfer by creating a product that is better and cheaper than anything else on the market. But now it's turned into a war against OneSport. I don't think we'll ever see Trubird clubs in stores so long as they're around with their deep pockets. How did you ever convince me to take them on?"

"That brings up another reason to give McLeary a shot," Tank said. "If we bring him back with our clubs, we've got instant publicity because of his tragic past. Plus, he's outside OneSport's reach because he's not a touring pro. He's got no responsibility to any corporate sponsors, and winning tournaments is not a priority because he's got a day job. No pressure at all. Come on, he's worth a look. Satch, what do you think?"

"Designing these clubs has been my life's work." Satch slid his arm around the packing tube next to him, cradling his newest creation. "Everything, and I mean *everything*, is riding on this guy. If he blows it, OneSport will crucify us with the press, the pros and anyone else who will listen. Aside from making the most of his potential comeback, what makes you think he can score a few decent rounds?"

Tank leaned in. "I've been watching this kid. He's a fighter, a natural athlete and he needs this break; this will put his whole life back on track."

Trip handed his partners a hefty document. "Maybe, but first you better review these ugly cost projections."

Dick's sharp intake of breath was audible. "Sweet lord." Plagued with a history of heart disease, his reaction brought stares from the partners. "I took a second mortgage on my house, and it's already spent. My retirement fund is next. We've got to sign somebody up soon."

"Take it easy," Trip said. "Okay, I'll give McLeary a look, but I'm not hopeful."

Tank tossed his empty cup into the can behind him. "Trust me. You're going to love him. Chase and his mother have a 2:08 tee time tomorrow afternoon. I already called ahead to the pro shop and arranged to have my twosome, you and me, join them."

"We'll see," Trip said. "Now let's talk money."

Tank groaned. "Trubird is sucking me dry. I'm leveraged beyond my worst nightmares. How much do you need this time?"

"The accountant prepared this summary."

Dick stared at the page, his chest heaving. "I don't have this kind of money. Even if I raid the kids' college funds, I'm still short. What happened to all the start-up cash?"

"Don't you read the financial reports?" Trip said. "It's all there: accountant fees, materials costs for titanium, zirconium, copper, nickel, beryllium, chromium, graphite, rubber, loft and lie machines, lab fees, frequency matching processing, flexibility tests. Everything costs money. And now we have serious legal fees."

"More attorney fees? Why?" Tank asked.

"Attorneys' fees. Plural," Trip said. "Some idiot is suing us for patent infringement. Claims we filched his design. I'm sure OneSport is behind it but, as you know, here in America, no matter who sues whom, one person always gets his money, and that person is the lawyer. We've got to defend ourselves. End of story. I need your checks by Friday."

Tank tapped at the pages. "This is it, guys. Either we go forward or we go under. If Chase works, I say we get him ready to play in the Reno-Tahoe Open. This year it's being played the same week as the World Golf Championship-NEC Invitational. The top names will definitely pass on the Reno-Tahoe, which makes it easier for our guy to get noticed. He and Trubird can be the big story of the tournament. It's time for Trubird's debut."

"The Reno-Tahoe is less than one month away," Trip said. "You really think this kid is good enough?"

"Yes."

"After one round?"

"Yes." Tank pounded a fist on the table. "It's time to go for it. We're already way over budget from our initial prospectus. I'm leveraged to the hilt and I know you guys are, too. My gut tells me he's our guy. Gentlemen, let's take the game to OneSport."

# CHAPTER 4

Chase pulled into Twin Palms parking lot as a young woman struggled to load her golf bag onto a cart. He parked two spaces away and observed his new pupil.

Sylvia said her niece was twenty-six, but Jana Witt looked much younger. About five feet tall, she had blonde curly hair that escaped from her ponytail and fell in ringlets around her circular face. Her shapely figure filled out a pair of navy blue shorts and a white top perfectly, and she reminded Chase of a gymnast he once dated.

He approached and was greeted with deep dimples and light blue eyes.

"Chase?" She extended her hand and, in the process, knocked over her golf bag. Balls tumbled out, bouncing in every direction around the parking lot. She scrambled to catch them.

Chase turned to grab one and accidentally stepped on another. He fell to the ground and grazed his chin on the pavement.

Jana laughed and knelt down in front of him. "I'm so sorry."

Her lips were pink and sparkly. He wondered if she had a boyfriend. Using the back of his hand, he blotted the small cut. "I may have to charge you a hazard premium."

"Don't be a baby." She pulled him to his feet. "It's barely a scratch."

He squeezed her hand, noting the lack of a wedding ring. "No wonder your old instructor fired you."

She propped a hand on her hip. "Did Aunt Sylvia tell you that?"

"Come on."

She leaned in. "Don't believe a word she says."

"Let's round up these balls and get started." He led her over to the last spot on the driving range. "By the way, you're not the only person who's had trouble with Mr. Tighlman."

Her dimples turned pink. "He's not a very patient instructor."

"Let me tell you about my own marred history with Thurston Neville Tighlman the Third, also called TNT." He handed Jana her nine iron. "First, show me your grip."

Chase watched Jana squeeze the club as she would a chicken's neck. Her floral scented perfume wafted by his nose. He drank it in before continuing. "When I was in high school," Chase said, rearranging her hands, "I caddied at Charleston Country Club. Have you ever been there?"

"Only once, for brunch. Very classy."

Chase fixed her grip, gently manipulating her manicured fingers. "Thurston was born and raised there. Back then, before he taught golf, he treated us caddies like dirt. Clean the clubs, find the ball, clean the ball, read the putts. He never stopped ordering us around. To top it off, he didn't tip. I mean never." Chase put his club behind her knees. "Bend a little more."

"What a jerk," Jana said, shifting her weight.

"Excuse me?"

"Thurston, I mean." She turned around to grab her water bottle. "Is that your family?" She nodded at the faded photograph pasted to a luggage tag that hung from his golf bag.

"Yes." He bent down, brows knitted. Terry had given him the memento as a good luck charm. The picture was taken in the hospital the day after River's birth. It was a close-up of two beaming parents with a baby in between. "But my wife died."

Jana flinched and put a hand over her heart. "I'm so sorry." She extended her arm toward him but then let it drop to her side. She lowered her eyes.

"Take a practice swing for me."

Jana vigorously complied. Chase glided behind her. "Again but slower. Do it like this." They moved in tandem until her rhythm mirrored his. He stepped around and faced her. "Once more."

She complied.

"Good. Where was I? Oh, yeah, we in the bag room hated TNT. One day, he was showing off his new driver. It had an AJ Tech shaft combined with the Callaway Great Big Bertha head. He spent around 600 bucks on this club. It came with its own tube which was to be inserted into his golf bag to protect it from rubbing up against his other clubs."

She tipped her head. "Shut up."

"I'm serious. Now bring your hands closer to your body and try it again. Good, that's better. Anyway, about TNT, you get the picture. He was asking for it. So one of the caddies, who shall remain nameless, decided to put a small rock in the butt-end of this fancy driver where the grip had a hole." Chase helped Jana bring the club up higher on her back swing, surprised at his own chattiness.

"It had a hole?"

"Yes, it was part of the design. So now there was an incredibly noticeable noise coming from TNT's $600 club. Poor Thurston. That noise was just enough to ruin his day. We got to watch him blow a fuse as he took his precious driver, shaft –protector and all, back to the place where he bought it." Chase put a ball in front of Jana.

"I didn't know you golf types were so vindictive," Jana said, her posture relaxed and her grip softened. She let out a velvet snicker.

Chase touched his watch. "We better get started. Aim for the fifty yard marker."

After spending time on grip he moved to stance, and then covered the final critical area.

"We still need to re-work the proper positioning for your swing. Think hands, hips, then arms," he said. "That's the order I want you to focus on."

"I'll try." She made an awkward attempt.

"Here." Chase moved behind her.

He gently placed his hands on either side of her hips, and helped her through the weight transfer process as her club traveled an arc around her body.

It felt good, touching Jana. Really good. A subtle nagging entered his subconscious, putting him on edge. The way she hopped up and down after a well executed swing or stomped her foot after a poor shot. It was so genuine.

They practiced a few more times with Chase's hands on Jana's hips, reminding him of another time with another partner. Dancing? Teaching?

"Do you understand how the swing is meant to feel?" He forced himself to pull away.

"Yes, but I can't say I'll remember it tomorrow." She rested her club on her foot.

"You'll get it. It only takes practice."

"I guess time's up." Jana put away her club.

Chase felt a stab of disappointment.

"What's the diagnosis, doctor?" Jana asked. "Lessons once a week?"

His heart skipped a beat. "Absolutely. I'll meet you back here next Saturday at eight." He didn't take on new golf students very often; however, he rationalized, with school nearly out he certainly had the time and needed the money.

He loaded her clubs into her trunk. "So tell me. What made you decide to take up golf?" Chase slammed it shut.

Behind the wheel, Jana covered her mouth with her hands. "Oh, no, I can't tell you. It's too embarrassing," she said, pink dimples returning.

"I'm your golf doctor. I need to know everything." He leaned against her car.

"No way." She tucked away a loose curl.

"Cross my heart. I won't tell a soul." He bent forward and put his ear close to her mouth.

Jana started the car and exhaled. "Okay. It was my dad. He told me that I needed some exercise. Plus, he thought that if I learned to play well, I could meet a lot of nice guys." She slowly backed out.

Chase shook his finger in mock disapproval. "Hit the practice range at least twice before I see you next week." Waving goodbye, his eyes shone and stayed locked on her vehicle, pulling away only when it disappeared from sight.

\* \* \* \* \*

Mort opened the Monday morning partners' meeting by flipping through a thick medical report. "Bad news. Let's talk about Bobby Gomez." The first baseball player to sign with OneSport during the company's infancy, Bobby suffered a broken arm in a car accident. The report, prepared by Dr. Vinny Cochera, OneSport's staff doctor, was grim.

"What are we looking at?" Jake asked.

"Multiple breaks." Mort threw his tie over his shoulder and bit into a buttered bagel. "He's out for the season."

Jake frowned. "After all the time we've dumped into him over the years, and he's been playing like crap lately. This will kill the new endorsement deals. What do you think it'll cost us in lost revenues?"

"You don't want to know." Joe licked his finger and mopped up the remaining sesame seeds.

"I say we ditch him," Jake said. "Our time and money is better spent on new talent."

"He has a couple bad seasons, gets hurt and we fire him? Come on," Joe said. "Bobby put us on the map and he's still under contract. We can't simply dump him."

"No, Jake's right," Mort said, his mouth full of food. "We've got a business to run and plenty of other people to think about besides him. Find a way out of the contract."

"How?" Joe asked.

"I don't care how. Find a way," Mort said. "We've got caveats for illegal activities, gambling, drugs and plenty of other stuff that'll invalidate the contract. Everybody's got a weakness."

"I'll take care of it," Jake said, watching late arriving employees scurry past the glass conference room door.

"Good," Mort answered. "Now refresh us on your former client Chase McLeary."

Jake uncrossed his legs. "Why? He's ancient history, a bad mistake long forgotten."

"Apparently not." Mort leaned back in his leather chair and beckoned Jake with a wave of his hand to continue.

Jake exhaled through his mouth and nose. "Let's see. He played for Clemson, won the North South Amateur by five strokes and was named the NCAA player of the year. After graduation he joined the Tour as a rookie and sped through Q-School. Played fourteen consecutive rounds of golf well enough to earn his Tour Card his first year out. Got married, had a son, and all the sports rags tagged him a player to watch."

"When did you sign him?" Mort asked.

"After his sophomore year on the Tour when he was dumb as dirt about the business side."

"I remember that contract," Joe said. "You screwed him pretty bad. He didn't read a word, much less challenge any provisions."

Jake nodded. "The money started rolling in, but then his wife got cancer and died. I swore he'd regroup and regain his former level of play. Instead, he showed up drunk to tournaments. Soon, he couldn't buy his way into a game." He paused to sip his water. "Broke and hustling lessons to make ends meet, he wrecked his car drunk driving and nearly killed his toddler. The kid broke a bunch of bones and was hospitalized for a month. The media went crazy, and McLeary lost all his endorsements. He made me look like an idiot. I had to fire that loser."

Mort pumped coffee from a carafe. "Did he do any jail time?"

"No," Jake said. "His mother bailed him out. Thanks to a couple of $450-an-hour lawyers, he got off with alcohol rehab, therapy, fines and community service. I put the word out for all of our people to stay away from him. He never could make a comeback. Now he teaches school in some one-horse town in the South. Why? What about him?"

"I hear Boswyck is looking at him," Mort said. "I don't have to tell you that would be a lose-lose for us."

Jake laughed. "We've got nothing to worry about. This kid — scratch that, he's not a kid anymore — this guy is a washed up hack. There is no way, absolutely no way, that he will get near a tournament."

"Smart move by Boswyck," Joe admitted. "We've shut Trubird out of the pro market, so he's looking outside our influence."

Jake's nostrils flared. "Smart is the last thing I'd call Trip Boswyck. Anyway, it's a non-issue. Chase McLeary will never succeed in making a comeback. He's not good enough and the pressure alone would eat him alive."

\* \* \* \* \*

"Hi, Momma," River said, as he unlocked his front door.

"Hi, Sweetie." Maddie set down a brown paper bag. "Here are some pralines for you two. A client gave them to me, and I don't want the temptation around."

River dived into the bag. "Look, they're chocolate covered." He stuffed one in his mouth whole.

"Where's your dad?"

"Getting out of the shower. We're going for pizza," River said, mouth full of caramel.

The telephone buzzed.

"Hello. Yeah, he's here. Just a sec." River put down the phone.

"Psst." Maddie motioned to the telephone. *Who is it?* She mouthed.

River shrugged his shoulders. "Dad, some lady's on the phone for you!" He stuck his hand back into the bag of sweets as Maddie strolled to the telephone.

"Got it." Chase grabbed the portable telephone by his bedside while toweling himself dry. "Hello? Hello? Anybody there?"

"Um, hi. This is Jana. Chase?"

Chase brightened. "Hey, there. It's only been two days. Don't tell me you've given up on the lessons already?" He wrapped the towel around his waist and headed for the door.

"No way. I just wanted to see how your, you know, chin was feeling."

Their backs to the door, Maddie and River didn't see Chase coming. He calmly walked to the phone jack and disconnected the cord from the wall. Then he came up behind them, popped it out of the receiver and took the cord with him. The eavesdroppers, left huddling on either side of the mute telephone, did their best to look inconspicuous as they put the disconnected receiver back on the hook.

*Nice try*, Chase mouthed, slamming his bedroom door shut.

"Chase? Are you there?" she said.

He lay back on the bed cradling the phone between his shoulder and ear and continued his conversation. "Sorry, I was getting out of the shower." He pictured her curvaceous smile, the rebel curl peeking out.

"Oh, if this is a bad time, I can call back later."

"Not at all. Now is great. My chin is fine, thanks. How is your back swing? Been to the range yet?" he asked, aware that the gentle fluttering in his stomach was turning into an earthquake.

"No, but I plan to go tomorrow. Gino! Take those two cases of Pinot Noir back to Holson's. They taste like vinegar." Her muffled voice filtered through the receiver.

"Excuse me?"

"Sorry, I'm at work. I manage my parents' restaurant, Wisteria Woods. It's on Prince George's Street."

"I love that place. Do entrees still come with salad and side dishes?"

"They sure do."

In the background, people called Jana's name.

"I'm sorry, I should have known better than to call from here. It's dinner rush hour. Suddenly, I'm very popular." She staved off questions from wait staff and kitchen help.

"I'll bet you are. Anyway, I'm glad you called, but don't worry about my chin. It's fine. Really." He struggled to find something else to say.

"Okay, then . . . guess I'll see you in a few days."

"You bet. Thanks for calling," Chase said, unable to sever the line.

"Chase?"

"Yeah?"

"Oh, I wasn't sure if you hung up yet." She laughed.

He laughed too. "I didn't. But I am now. Take care." He felt like a teenager.

"Bye," she said. Her voice quickly turned into a dial tone.

Grinning, Chase held the phone in his hand, elated and unable to stop smiling. There it was again. He felt like a kid about to sled down a big hill for the first time or maybe dressed up on Halloween night waiting to see if the person behind the door would hand over candy, fruit, or nothing at all.

# Chapter 5

"Good morning, Mother," Chase said. He wore his best linen golf pants, periwinkle blue Nike shirt and a wide grin for their regular Saturday golf date.

"Don't you look nice." Maddie paused to check her watch. "I thought we were going to warm up together. I already hit a few balls. Don't tell me you're running late because you decided to dress up for your mom?"

"Sorry. I had a lesson and it ran over a little." He toweled off his driver.

"Ah, that explains your unusually sunny disposition. Were you teaching Sylvia's niece again? How many lessons has she had? Have you asked her out yet?"

"Come on, Mom, enough with the third degree. She needs a lot of work."

Maddie rolled her eyes but decided, for the moment, to let it pass.

"I guess we're next on the tee."

"Yes, but they're busy today. Arnie put us with another twosome."

"Hey, doll," the familiar voice called out.

Maddie turned and paled.

"Tank. What are you doing back here?" she asked.

"Business. I think my buddy and I are playing with you two," he said, looking back over his shoulder.

"What a coincidence," Chase said with a smirk.

## McLeary's Mulligan

"Hey Trip, come on over."

Chase felt his blood pressure rise as he recognized their fourth. Trip Boswyck, former PGA Commissioner, was a fifteen handicap whose occasionally brilliant rounds earned him a reputation as a sandbagger.

*So Tank really is in business with Trip*, Chase thought.

Trip extended a hand. "Good to see you again. I think we met once before in Orlando. Ma'am, I'm Trip, nice to meet you," he said with a salesman's quick smile and firm shake.

"It looks like they're ready for us," she said, her voice chillier than usual.

Chase eyed Tank. His shirt was already darkened with sweat.

"Chase? Are you coming?" Maddie waved him on.

He tore his eyes from Tank.

"Sorry," Chase said. He put the cart in gear and sped off for the first tee. "Quit pouting. Tank isn't such a bad guy. Don't worry about the other day. That's probably just Navy talk."

"Maybe." Maddie pulled a tube of lipstick from her pocket for a quick touchup.

He parked the cart.

"So tell me more about your, um, lessons, if that's what is really going on."

"Stop baiting me." His deliberate smile and lack of response said it all.

"What's her name? Jane?"

Chase sighed. "You know darn well that her name is Jana. She's a golf student. Don't bug me about her anymore. Deal?"

"Absolutely not. Look at you. You're glowing. I haven't seen you this excited about anyone in . . . well, in a very long time. Why don't you invite her over for dinner? I want to meet her."

"Please, Mom, let's talk about it later," Chase whispered. "Right now, the only thing I need to be thinking about is my next shot."

He had the exciting feeling prickling at the back of his neck that he was auditioning for something important.

*Have some fun. Relax. Play the game.* He shook off the premonition.

"Son, you're on fire today." Maddie watched Chase sink yet another putt in the fifteen to twenty-five foot range for birdie.

"I'll say," Tank agreed. "I only dream about six birdies and three pars on the front nine."

Trip stroked his five-foot putt. It bled left but caught the edge of the cup and rolled in. "What's your handicap these days, Chase?"

"Scratch," he said watching Maddie make bogey.

Tank set up in front of his ball. "Must be nice." He watched his ball slowly trickle four feet towards the hole and circle the cup before dropping in. "Maddie, did you know that an amateur must have a handicap of two point four or *less* to enter a Monday qualifier for a PGA event?"

Maddie turned. "No, I didn't, but it makes perfect sense. With only two or three spots open, the poor tournament people don't want some high-handicapper clogging up their qualifying rounds."

"True. But, boy, I'd love to be good enough to get in just one." He retrieved his ball and replaced the flag.

"Somehow I think Tiger Woods is safe." Maddie turned to Tank. "What are you, about a twenty-five handicap?"

"Twenty two, smarty-pants." Tank pretended to be insulted as the foursome left the green.

Backed up at the tenth tee, Chase's group waited for the foursome ahead to clear the fairway.

Trip sneezed six times in a row.

"It's the lemongrass." Maddie pointed to several bushes next to where he stood. "They planted too many on this hole. Come stand over here by me."

Trip happily complied and the two became engrossed in a conversation about all things horticultural.

Chase made a few baseball-style practice swings and took a sidelong glance. "Tank," he said, only loud enough for the two of them to hear, "what's going on? I don't believe for a second that you and Trip Boswyck became our playing partners by accident."

Tank juggled three golf balls in one hand. "Maybe you're paranoid."

"I get the feeling you want something from me." Chase leaned against his driver.

The group in front of them finally reached the tenth green, making room for Chase's foursome to tee off.

"It's not what I want from you." Tank removed his sunglasses. "It's what I can *give* you. Keep playing this well and we'll talk at lunch."

Like a superhero with rocket-fuel for blood, Chase's body pulsed with adrenaline. "You got it."

\* \* \* \* \*

"Whew, it's hot. Good thing this is our last hole." Maddie fanned herself with the scorecard while Chase drove the cart. "Let's go for a swim with River after lunch."

"I need to stay here a while," Chase answered.

"Why?"

"That guy, Trip, that's Trip Boswyck, the former PGA Commissioner."

Maddie put a hand to her mouth. "Oh, I had no idea. I guess they're meeting about that golf club deal Tank told us about."

"They want to talk to me at lunch. I'm sure that Tank orchestrated this little foursome so that Trip could get a look at my game."

Maddie looked away. "He wants something from you." She frowned, her lips sagging.

"Yeah, but I can't imagine what it is."

Maddie sighed. "I'm such a fool . . . " She looked away again.

"What are you talking about?"

"Nothing. It's nothing." She shook her head. "Chase, don't turn your back on an opportunity, no matter what it is. You're not getting any younger, and you have a son. Promise?" She took off her glove.

"Hey, we've got one more hole. What are you doing?"

"I'm really hot and tired. I think I'll skip the last hole, if you don't mind. Please make apologies for me. I'm not really in the mood for lunch anyway. Oh, and be a dear and take my clubs home with you." She grabbed her purse.

Chase stared at her with one eyebrow cocked. "Are you okay?"

She nodded yes, but her smile was deflated and her shoulders hunched as if she'd been punched in the stomach. "I'm fine. Call me later and fill me in."

"Sure, Mom," he said, puzzled by her sudden mood swing.

Maddie walked slowly towards the clubhouse. She didn't look back.

"Hey, where's Maddie going?" Tank pulled his cart alongside Chase's.

"She's feeling a little tired. Decided to cash out early," he answered.

"We'll meet her inside," Tank said.

"No, she asked me to send her apologies. She's going home for the day." Chase sent his ball two-seventy-five up the right side of the fairway.

Tank's face fell. *Crap: Chase told her about lunch. She thinks I used her.*

Unable to break his thoughts off from Maddie, Tank's tee shot sailed into the left woods. He took an unplayable lie.

"Worst play of the day, partner." Trip teed up his ball.

Tank scowled. "Not quite."

\* \* \* \* \*

The last one out of the locker room, Chase caught up with Trip who was shaking hands with Tank.

"Gotta' run, sport," Trip said, jingling his car keys. "Nice round. Tank, call me on my cell."

Together, Chase and Tank walked through the crowded bar to a table against the back wall. Chase ordered an iced tea and a Rueben. Tank opted for a twenty-two ounce Budweiser and a bacon cheeseburger. "Let's get down to business."

"I'm all ears."

"I already told you about our new type of clubs."

"Not really," Chase interrupted. "You only told me you had one prototype club that hit well, but you didn't tell me anything about what it is made out of."

"Let me finish." Tank sat up straight. "I'm here to make you an offer, but even if you accept it, I can't tell you much more about the clubs until you sign a confidentiality agreement."

"What?"

"You know, a piece of paper that says you can't give away any secrets or we sue you into poverty."

"That wouldn't be much of a stretch." Chase leaned back and patted his front pocket. "I don't even have a savings account."

"Trubird Group wants you to demo our clubs at the Reno-Tahoe Open."

Chase sprung forward in his seat. "Are you serious?"

Tank lowered his voice. "Take it easy, son."

Chase opened his mouth. "I . . . you . . ." He closed it, struggling to respond. "Yes. Definitely, yes. I'm your man."

"Slow down. Before you say yes, let me lay it out for you. We want you to take these babies out for their maiden voyage. Once you swing our club, you'll never want to touch another one. I guarantee it. But the Reno-Tahoe is three weeks away, and One-Sport's going to be none too happy about our debut. We expect you to make the cut, play a few decent rounds, and then you'll be a rich man."

Chase rubbed his chin with forefinger and thumb. "I'm definitely up for it, but do you know how much of a long shot it is to get into a tournament through a Monday qualifier?"

"Yeah," said Tank. "John Daly won the PGA at Crooked Stick in 1991 and he was a Monday qualifier, but you don't have to worry about that. Trip is calling in a favor to get you a sponsor exemption. You're in."

"I can't believe it," Chase said, one hand wrapped around his other fist. "This is a dream come true."

Tank smiled. "Yup. And the Reno-Tahoe is perfect for you. This year it's being played simultaneously with the World Golf Championships-NEC Invitational."

"I get it." Chase nodded. "The biggest names are skipping it, so I'll mostly be up against lesser-known golfers, a definite advantage."

"Plus, Montreux Golf & Country Club is our kind of course," Tank said.

"You're kidding, right? Montreux is a monster. That course is a seventy-five hundred yard par seventy-two."

"I know. It's all about precision drives, irons and tight putts. Trubird clubs, with more consistency and length, are exactly what your game needs to score well at Montreux. You already putt like a demon."

Chase leaned in close, locking eyes. "I'm curious about something. You've seen me play golf exactly twice. What made you decide that I'm up for this? A little while ago you wouldn't give me the time of day."

"Instinct, mostly." Tank broke eye contact to drink his beer. "You're in great shape, you play golf every day and there's no real pressure because you already have a job to go back to in the fall. Plus, you'll get the chance to finally stick it to Jake Nathan and OneSport. My gut tells me this is the opportunity of a lifetime, for you and for us."

Chase felt his pulse beating through his neck veins. "You have no idea how much this means to me. But I've got to level with you. When Jake finds out I'm in with you, there's going to be trouble. OneSport didn't simply fire me, they made me untouchable. I couldn't get a loop at a mini course."

"I know all about that, and then some, from first hand experience. They've got a lock on the business and they've done anything and everything to keep us both out. Do you know what will happen to them when people start buying our low-cost, high-performance clubs? We'll make them and their elitist products obsolete." Tank leaned in. "This is the big league, kid. There's no telling what's going to get thrown our way. I won't lie to you. You've got to come on board ready for anything."

"What would I get out of this deal?" Chase asked.

"Aside from public redemption, you'll make a lot of money, and don't tell me you wouldn't like to return to your former standard of living. For starters, we'll give you $5,000 for signing on. Then you'll get $25,000 if you make the cut to play on Saturday and another $50,000 bonus if you finish in the top twenty-five. Everybody loves a comeback, and if you decide to return to the Tour, we'll give you $150,000 a year to promote our clubs plus one-half percent of the profits. Best of all, you'll finally pay OneSport back for screwing you over when you were down on your luck."

Chase looked at his untouched plate. "But, why me? Why don't you go to one of the rising stars? I'm nobody. It doesn't make sense."

"You're right. You were not our first choice. In fact, I had a heck of a time convincing Trip to even consider you. But at this point, you're our last hope. Virtually all of the golf talent out there is under contract with OneSport. We almost got our legs cut off by their attorneys just for contacting a couple of their guys. Plus, we can't be totally up front with them about our clubs because our patent is only now getting approved," Tank said.

"And I'm cheap." Chase nodded. "I think I'm beginning to get the picture."

"Well, yeah, relatively. But you're also much more of a risk and you've got a . . . a history."

Resting an elbow on the table, Chase held his forehead with his palm. "This is an unbelievable opportunity, but there's a lot to it. I don't want to make a mistake. This could be my one and only chance for a comeback."

"I'm going to be straight with you. Trubird's start-up capital is nearly dry. OneSport has pulled out all the stops to shut us down before we get off the ground. We need a big win and we need it now. The way you play the game, your strengths and weaknesses play perfectly with our profile for Trubird buyers. But we're out of time."

"When can I see the clubs?" Chase asked.

Tank exhaled loudly through his nose. "A complete set will be ready next week."

"That's only a couple weeks before the tournament."

"I know, but that's the fastest the designer can have them ready. He's still tinkering with them."

"Wow." Chase looked down. "Any chance I could get equity? Say five percent?"

"I'll take it to my partners, but there's a provision in our agreement against admitting new partners without unanimous consent."

"Ask them. I'm starting to realize why you chose me. I really am your last chance." Chase pushed back his chair. "How long?"

"We need your answer in forty-eight hours. That's the deadline to lock in your sponsor exemption." Tank grabbed Chase's forearm. "This is right and you know it."

"Forty-eight hours." Chase pulled himself free and walked out the door.

Hunkered over the lobby bar at his hotel, Tank felt his breast pocket vibrate. He extracted his cellular telephone.

"It's Boswyck," the clipped voice said. "What happened?"

"He's ours, but he wants five percent." Tank peeled the label from his beer.

"Can't do it," Boswyck answered. "Double up the bonus if he makes it to Saturday. That should work. Call me later."

Patsy Cline belted out a ballad as Tank ordered another round. His phone was moist with sweat as he dialed information.

"I need the number for a good florist." He pulled Maddie's business card from his shirt pocket and rubbed it back and forth against his lips.

# Chapter 6

"You know, Dad." River zipped up his backpack. "The Chief thinks that Mom still tells me stuff . . . from the spirit world," he quickly added.

"Yeah, your grandfather is one superstitious old Indian." He looked over the evening newspaper. Although he tried to read the words, his mind could grasp nothing besides Tank's offer.

"Sometimes, if I listen really carefully, I think I hear her giving me advice and stuff." River fiddled with the zipper.

"What do you mean?" Chase put down the paper. "What's bothering you?"

"Nothing. I just wondered if you ever . . . talk to her." River retied his shoelace.

Chase answered carefully. "I used to talk to your mom, after she died, all the time. I'd ask her opinion, order her favorite cookies, and watch home videos from when you were a baby, that kind of thing. Sometimes I still pull out old letters she wrote to me, just to see her handwriting. I'll never forget her, if that's what you're asking."

"I'm not worried about that. I think maybe you don't know how great she thought you were." He shrugged.

Chase's heart skipped a beat. "Come again?"

"The Chief. He's always telling me how much Mom believed in you. She told him you were the most talented person she ever knew, and that you were never afraid to 'go for it.'"

Chase looked at River. Terry's smiling eyes and shimmering raven hair stared back at him, loving him, challenging him. He swallowed hard. "Your mother meant everything to me. She was athletic, graceful, artistic; we were like two pieces of a puzzle."

River scratched the back of his neck with sinewy fingers, Terry's fingers. "The Chief said that Mom had visions of me before I was born. She knew I'd look like her, and she knew she wouldn't be around when I grew up."

A smoldering knot formed in Chase's throat. "What else has your grandfather been telling you?"

"Lots of stuff." River looked away. "Like he said that one day everything will be back in balance for us."

"What do you mean? Aren't you happy with the way things are?"

River's eyes fixed on his backpack as he swung it from one hand to the other and back again. "Yeah, I'm happy enough. It's just that . . . I don't know. Maybe there's something else out there for us, that's all."

"Like what?"

The honk of Maddie's horn pierced their talk.

River jumped up. "I don't want to miss the previews. See you tomorrow." He slung his bag over his left shoulder.

"Wait, let's finish talking," Chase said, unnerved by his son's comments.

"No big deal. Forget about it," he answered, halfway to the door.

Chase frowned. "Wait."

"See you tomorrow." The screen door slammed.

He tried to re-focus on reading the paper, but River's puzzling words haunted him until the jingling of the telephone interrupted his thoughts. He snatched up the receiver.

"Hello."

"Uh, hi, Chase?"

His face melted into a half-smile. "Jana?"

"Hi," she said, perky as usual. "I was wondering if we could change my lesson tomorrow until around noon. Would that be okay?"

Chase longed to stand behind her, arms wrapped gently around hers, guiding her through a proper swing. He craved the feeling of warmth from her back and bottom that emanated into his chest as he held the pose a bit too long. "Absolutely. That works out well. My son went to spend the night at my mother's house. Maybe I'll actually get to sleep-in tomorrow morning for a change." He untangled the telephone cord, willing her to stay on the line.

"Great. My hairdresser has a big wedding party to do and he had to change my appointment, because it takes two hours and you know . . . oh, listen to me. Sorry."

Chase pictured her dimples changing size and depth as she laughed.

"I know it's last minute, but are you free for dinner?" he asked.

"Tonight?"

"If you're busy, I understand." He punched the air.

"No, tonight is great, if you don't mind my bad-hair day."

Chase beamed. "How about Poogan's Porch? It's casual, and I think they have live music tonight."

"Perfect. Can you give me an hour?"

"Of course." Chase checked his watch. "I'll pick you up at eight. What's your address?" He reached for a pen and paper.

After hanging up, Chase stood beneath a scalding shower and thought through Tank's offer. It was his best shot at reestablishing his career. Of course he had to take it, no matter what the terms, but was he really ready to return to the Tour?

\* \* \* \* \*

"It's Jana. Marie is going to cover for me tonight." She slipped her fresh pedicure into yet another pair of black sandals. The floor of her closet was littered with rejected skirts, shoes and tops.

"Why? Where are you going?" her father asked.

Jana selected black and white pony print mules and a white sundress. "I have a date with my golf teacher." She checked her underarms for stubble.

"It's about time those lessons paid off. Where's he taking you?"

"Poogan's Porch. Maybe we'll come by Wisteria for dessert so you can meet him. Make sure you save us two pieces of lemon mousse cake."

"No, don't scare him off. Sounds like he's a live one. He won't want to meet your mother and me yet."

"Oh, Daddy." She raced for the bathroom.

"Did you tell him you're divorced?"

"Please. It's our first date." She turned on the shower.

"I knew it. What about him? Any baggage?"

"He's a widower and he has an eleven-year-old son." She switched the telephone to her left hand, stripped off her T-shirt and unfastened her bra.

"Wait a minute, I've heard about this guy. Is he the kid from Mount Pleasant who used to be a golf pro, but then his wife died and he turned into a drunk?"

She braced for a lecture. "We haven't gotten into much personal information, but that's what I hear. Anyway, don't make your mind up about him based on all that stuff. He's a really nice guy."

"That's what you said about Jerry, that dope-fiend-no-good-lying-ex-husband . . ."

"Dad, for the millionth time, I don't ever want to talk about Jerry again. He was the biggest mistake of my life and I've paid for it in blood."

"Yeah, well he was an expensive mistake for all of us. I hope your golf teacher is picking up the check."

Jana flinched at the innuendo. In her former marriage, money flowed one way: toward Jerry and away from Jana. There were loans, ostensibly for down payments on cars, houses, businesses and the like which, without fail, simply disappeared despite fervent promises of repayment. Then there was the embezzlement charge from his former employer, which, although Jerry swore it was all a misunderstanding, was broad enough to taint Jana since the two shared bank accounts.

Finally, there was Tina, the tattooed, blue finger-nailed, big-haired and big-bottomed woman Jana discovered nude in her very own bed, smoking pot with an equally naked Jerry. The divorce was quick, quiet and Jerry was finally out of their lives.

"Is Mom there?"

"She's in the back. I'll have her call you."

"Thanks." Jana tested one foot in the shower.

"Have fun tonight, but be careful." His voice cracked. "Another Jerry we don't need."

\* \* \* \* \*

She was ready for her date except for a pesky section of hair below her left ear. It refused to curl under and she pinned it tight inside the roller to force its compliance.

Zipping around her house, a modest rambler two blocks off the beach, she set an orange vase filled with peonies on the glass coffee table and straightened the watercolor in the foyer. The front door stood ajar and the screen was unlocked in preparation for her visitor.

She peeked out from behind her linen living room curtain. Fifty-two minutes had elapsed since her conversation with Chase. She caught sight of a brown delivery truck lumbering up her street and she recognized Chase's car following it.

"Oh, no. He's early." She turned on her heel for the bathroom. The phone jangled. She grabbed it.

"Hello?"

"Jana, it's Mom. When is your date? Are you excited?"

Jana eyed the door. "Right now, I've got to go. He's pulling into the driveway, and my hair isn't . . . oh, no!"

"What? What is it?"

Jana ran for the paper towels. "Shotzie! Bad dog! Oh, no! He pooped on the kitchen floor and . . ."

The doorbell announced a visitor.

"Gotta' go." She slammed down the telephone.

"Jana?" Chase peeked his head through the door.

"I'll be out in a second," Jana called out behind her. "Make yourself at home."

Chase strolled through the door and continued on toward the sound of Jana's voice.

"Sorry, I'm a minute early," he apologized. "It didn't take as long as I . . ."

Dressed to kill on her hands and knees, Jana held two handfuls of paper towels bearing the obvious byproducts of the naughty Jack Russell terrier cowering behind a chair.

Whipping her head up, the Velcro roller dropped out and spiraled across the floor. It stopped at Chase's feet. As if on cue, a fugitive curl sprang backwards and Jana's face turned scarlet.

Chase cracked up.

"Here, let me help you." He stooped down and tore off a bunch of paper towels.

"Thanks." She laughed. "This is awful. I can't believe he did this. Shotzie never has accidents." She stood and stepped on the trashcan lever.

He turned his head. "Hard to believe such a little dog could make such a big mess."

She moved to the sink, washing both arms up to her elbows with antibacterial soap. "Good thing I wore my best perfume."

"What do you call it?" Chase joined her at the sink. "Eau de doody?"

"Very funny."

He stood close beside her, the heat from his body brushing up against hers.

Jana looked up at him, aware of how much she wanted to reach out and touch him. She tucked the renegade curl behind her ear. "After all that, do you still want to go eat?"

Chase put out his hand, brushed against her cheek and untucked the curl. "Why fight it?"

"Because it, uh, well, it bugs me." She re-tucked the hair.

His eyes locked with hers. "Well, I think it's cute." He folded his arms. "Come on, we can debate it over dinner."

Shotzie barked, animated. He skittered after Jana.

"Stay. You've done enough damage for one night," she said.

Shotzie whimpered.

Jana locked the front door.

"Guess he's not used to visitors," he said.

Jana smiled. *Not yet.*

\* \* \* \* \*

A warm breeze blew through the open windows of Chase's car. Jana leaned back and closed her eyes, inhaling the salty air.

"Don't tell me you're sleepy already?" he said. "It's only ten-thirty."

She wet her lips. "Not sleepy, just content. That seared tuna was delicious and so was the cheesecake. I can't believe I ate that whole huge piece," she said, not a tense muscle in her body.

Chase took his hand from the steering wheel, but then replaced it. "Do you want to go out somewhere? Dancing or something?"

"I'm not really in the mood to go dancing." She searched his dimly lit face for signs of disappointment.

Chase put on his blinker to make the turn for the bridge back to Mt. Pleasant.

"But," she said, eyeing him playfully. "I could go for a swim if you're game. It's such a beautiful night." She stuck her arm out the window. The wind caressed her skin like a dozen fingertips.

"A swim?" He perked up. "Okay. Where?"

"There's a beach access path around the corner from my house."

"Do you always swim at night?"

"Actually, I haven't in a long time," she said, jubilant at the thought of dipping into the warm surf with him.

"Me either. What am I going to use for a bathing suit?"

She snapped her fingers. "I have just the thing."

"Well, how do I look?" He emerged from her bathroom in a pair of her tight gym shorts. They were bright orange with tiny terriers printed all over them and several sizes too small.

Jana howled, sporting a striped blue maillot. "You look mah-velous. Come on, I'll race you to the water." She flew out the front door. The path wound between several houses where the lingering smells of barbecued chicken and citronella candles were strong in the air. Hypnotic strains of reggae music echoed from one of the homes and followed them.

Laughing all the while, they kicked off their shoes at the water's edge and plunged deep into the undulating surf. The warm, salty water lapped against their skin as they bodysurfed along the shoreline.

"Look at this." He motioned her over, cradling something in between his hands. Hair slicked back and rippled chest exposed, he looked like a movie star.

She swam over, pulled toward him like a riptide, and stopped a few feet away. "What is it?" She raised an eyebrow.

"Closer." He cocked his head.

She dug her toes into the soft sand and tiptoed forward.

"Now close your eyes," he said.

"No way."

"Don't you trust me?"

Goosebumps erupted on her neck and tops of her breasts. She sunk down into the water and complied. His powerful hand laid a rope of slimy wet seaweed on her shoulders.

"I knew it!" She shook it off and dove under the water.

He came up behind her and put his arms around her waist. "Come back here."

She wriggled, but he held fast, laughing and tickling her.

"Hey, look up," he said.

"Yeah, right."

Still behind her, his hands ran up her sides until they covered her ears. He tipped her head. "Crescent moon."

She pressed her back into his chest and stared skyward. "It's beautiful." She inhaled as they stargazed. "Smell that?"

"What?"

"That combination of salt, jasmine and wisteria. Blindfolded I could always tell that I'm in the South Carolina low country." She rested the back of her head against his collarbone. "I love it here."

He smoothed the top of her hair, running his fingers across her scalp as they listened to the roaring waves. She shivered. He took her hand, as if dancing, and twirled her around to face him.

She hesitated and then raised her lips. In slow motion he covered them with his own, kissing her deeply and squeezing the tops of her arms.

She hardly recognized the sound coming from her throat. Part purr and part sigh, it blended in with the beating wind and her throbbing heart.

He pulled away. "Maybe we should get back." A wave of discomfort crossed his brow.

"What's wrong? Is it . . . too soon?"

"No, no." He wrinkled his nose. "Not at all." He backed away, the source of his embarrassment evident in the bulging gym shorts he wore.

Jana took his hand. "Come on. I'll put on a pot of coffee. I want to show you my new putter."

They walked back to the house hand in hand. Inside, she stepped behind an oriental screen in her bedroom. "Stay there for a minute while I change."

He complied.

Jana peeled off her bathing suit then flung it. It made a loud suction noise as it hit the floor next to Chase's bare feet, splattering them with cold droplets.

He jumped. "Watch it."

"Sorry." She opened a closet door and rustled around with a package. "Check this out."

Sitting across from each other, feet up on the sofa, empty coffee mugs in their laps, Chase and Jana finally ran out of words.

Shotzie, asleep at Jana's feet, growled.

"What time is it?" She patted the dog on the head.

"Four-thirty." He set down the cold mug. "I better hit the road. I want to get back home before Mom drops River off."

She rubbed the nape of her neck. "Before you go, I think we should talk about my divorce."

He touched her toe and winced. "Any kids?"

"No." She shook her head and gave him the Cliff's Notes on Jerry. "Is River your only child?"

"Yes."

"You said his mother died. Can I ask how?"

"Cancer." He rubbed her foot and looked away. "It was brutal. Fast, ugly, it nearly killed us all."

"I'm so sorry." She took his hand. "You don't have to talk about it if it's too hard."

He kissed her fingers. "No, for once I do feel like talking about it." He let them go. "And now there's not enough time."

"There's something else, isn't there?"

His blue eyes flashed. "I'm . . . a little bit . . . afraid."

She raised an eyebrow. "Of what?"

He hesitated. "Myself, maybe. I'm so close to getting it all back. My career, my self-respect, and . . . other things." He balled up his fists. "I've been waiting a long time for this." Tears welled up in his eyes.

"It's okay." Kneeling forward, she kissed his forehead and put her arms around him.

A minute elapsed before either of them spoke.

"I really have to go." He pulled away and stood.

She reached for his hand. "Hey, what about my noon lesson?"

He smiled. "Don't think I'll go easy on you just because I like you."

She wagged a finger. "Like me? I thought you said I had talent?"

"You do, but not necessarily for golf." He winked.

She threw a pillow at him. "Out, you weasel. See you at noon."

He headed for the door and then retraced his steps, hungry for one more kiss.

\* \* \* \* \*

"Dad?" River called as the screen door slammed behind him.

"In here," Chase called back from the kitchen.

"River, come back here and hold the door for me. Where are your manners?" Maddie's voice chided.

"Sorry, Momma." He rushed back to the door.

"Hey, guys." Chase knelt at the sink.

"What are you doing?" River asked.

"Fixing the garbage disposal."

Maddie raised her eyebrows. "It's about time. Aren't we in a good mood this morning? Do anything interesting last night?"

Chase stuck his head well inside the cabinet. "How was your movie?"

Maddie's eyes swept the room. "Great, if you like disgusting dinosaurs ripping each other's guts out." She searched for telltale evidence that her son had been entertaining.

"It was cool. Two kids starting crying and had to leave," River announced. "Can I go over to Kyle's house and see if he wants to shoot hoops? He was outside mowing the grass a second ago."

"Sure." Chase flipped the switch. The sound of grinding gears greeted him.

"Success." Maddie took a seat at the kitchen table.

The door slammed again as River exited.

Chase washed his hands and sat down next to his mother. "Next time, don't be so subtle about my night life."

She smoothed her hair and crossed her feet at the ankles. "You finally took her out on a date, didn't you?" She clucked her tongue.

"Yes."

"Well?"

"Well, what?"

"Chase, don't be so secretive. Tell me about her."

As he filled her in on his date, his eyes sparkled and there was an excitement about him.

"Smitten. That's what you are," she said.

"Her house is great, small, but it's two blocks off the ocean on Harvey Street. Not exactly the neighborhood I live in. What do you think those go for?"

She answered carefully. "That depends on the condition, but I'd say minimum three-fifty. How long has she lived there?"

"About five years. I think she's got a fair amount of money socked away . . ." he said.

"Don't tell me you're insecure? You have nothing to be ashamed of. You make a good living as a teacher. Besides, it was only a first date. You're not getting married yet, are you?"

He was silent.

"Are you?"

"Of course, not. It's just that . . ." He hesitated. "Oh, I don't know." He leaned back with his arms folded across his chest.

"What's wrong?"

"It's not like I have to impress her, because she's not like that. I only wish . . . "

"You wish what?"

He stood and walked to the kitchen window, his back to her. "I used to be somebody. Chase McLeary the golfer. And now I'm . . . I'm not . . ."

She held her breath. How many times had she prayed for him to utter those exact words so that she could defend him to his worst enemy, himself.

She joined him at the sink and put her arm around him. "You are somebody. You are a wonderful son, a loving father, a terrific teacher and a respected coach."

He turned and gave her a hug. "What's that stuff you take, estrogen? Maybe I need some," he said, squeezing her tightly.

"I doubt that." She pulled away. "Son, you like this girl a lot. I can tell."

"I do, and I haven't felt this way since . . . in a long time. I guess it's freaking me out that she's got money and she's so young. Especially since her ex-husband was such a loser."

"You're about the farthest place you can get from being a loser."

"There's something else," he began, pacing back and forth.

"I thought there might be."

He stopped. "Tank wants to pay me to play in the Reno-Tahoe Open."

Maddie covered her mouth with both hands. "What? Why? You don't even have your Tour Card."

"I don't need one. He can get me in on a sponsor's exemption. Then, I need to play as many rounds as possible."

She sank into a chair. "But why?"

"Remember those new clubs he was talking about the other day? Well, his investor group needs somebody to demo them. You know, show them off to the public, and I'm their last hope." He turned a chair around and straddled it. "Every other player they've asked either is under contract with OneSport or is too scared of crossing them. Those corporate sharks put out the word that anyone going near these clubs will be exiled from the golf industry. Fair play is as important in business as it is on the golf course, and they've eliminated it."

"Wait a minute." She leaned forward. "Isn't that tournament in less than a month? Do you think you're ready?"

"Let's see." He scratched his chin. "I haven't played professionally for a million years, I've never even seen these miracle clubs, and the attention and media pressure will be unbearable."

He leaned back and tugged at his collar. "I'll have to re-live my big failures, both professionally and personally, and—" He stood. "Best of all, if I totally choke, I'll be the laughing stock of the entire PGA Tour."

She inhaled. "And on the plus side?"

He folded his arms. "In my favor, the best players on Tour will be skipping the Reno-Tahoe in favor of the World Golf Championships-NEC Invitational. They're being held the same week, so I won't have Tiger Woods breathing down my neck." He raised one hand. "If I play half-way decent, I'll get a nice cash nest egg as well as commissions from future sales for five years. That could be big money. I could pay back all the retirement money you spent on me, I could jump-start River's college fund and I could maybe even look for a bigger house."

"What else?"

"Personal satisfaction, I guess, to compete again and," he said, pounding the counter, "I could finally get out from under the curse of Jake Nathan. The risks are huge, but I don't have a choice. This is my Mulligan as a golfer, and as a man who stands up for his principles. I'm good enough." He puffed out his chest. "I really am. Plus it would raise my stock as far as River is concerned."

"And Jana too?"

"Yes."

She steepled her fingers. "Let's say you play well because I know you will. After this first one, will you have to enter a certain number of tournaments? What about your teaching job?"

He rubbed his hands together. "If the demo rollout goes well, I'd have to compete in as many events as I can qualify for to heighten market attention on the clubs. Right now, during the summer, it's no big deal. But come September, I'd have to ask for a leave of absence and that's a big risk, I know."

"How long do you have to decide?" Maddie asked, numb with excitement at the possibility.

"Until tomorrow." He stood up again and practiced swinging an invisible club. "This is crazy, isn't it? I've been dying to get back to the Tour for so long. I can't believe I'm actually going to do it. I mean, I won't finish in the top ten or anything; but I think I could make a decent showing. Play a few good rounds, bring home a nice check, what do I have to lose? Right?"

She frowned. "Are you guaranteed a fee no matter how far you go in the tournament?"

"A small one. These guys are smart. The closer I get to the finals on Sunday, the more money I get. What do you think?"

"Are you crazy?" She threw up her hands. "This is the chance of a lifetime. Go for it. What are you waiting for?"

He scratched his palm. "Give me the phone." He punched the buttons. "Tank? It's Chase. Let's tee it up."

Tank whooped. "Kid, welcome back to the PGA Tour!"

# Chapter 7

"Hi, doll, did you hear? We're practically family now," Tank said, his rich voice blasting through her telephone.

Maddie sniffed. "I'm very excited for Chase. I hope you know how lucky you are to have him."

"Absolutely. Hey, I'm staying at the Ashley Inn. You free for dinner?"

"Tonight?"

"Yeah. How about Carolina's at half past eight?"

"All right. Chase and I will . . ."

"Only you. Chase can come another time. I want to pick your brain about that talented son of yours. Grown-ups only, capisce?"

"Is that really necessary? Why can't we-"

"Perfect. Meet you in the bar at eight-thirty."

\* \* \* \* \*

Chase practiced chip shots at the end of the practice tee sporting madras plaid shorts, a white golf shirt and a navy baseball cap.

"Good afternoon. Long time no see." Jana adjusted her crimson golf skirt.

Chase admired her shapely rump. "Too long for me." He pulled her close for a quick kiss.

"Are we disgusting, or what?"

He peeked out from under the brim of his cap, winked and then delivered the ball within inches of the fifty-yard marker.

"You look great." He turned his full attention to his pupil and new girl.

"Thanks." She removed the head covers from her long woods. "I have some big news."

"Don't tell me you're married?"

"Very funny."

"Sorry. You know what they say about things being too good to be true."

"No smoke and mirrors here. What you see is what you get, which brings me to my surprise."

She bit her lip. "You're not gay, are you?"

"Jana!"

"Okay, go ahead," she said, bracing herself against the bag.

"Remember when you asked me why I stopped playing professional golf?"

"Uh-huh. You said your ex-agent had a vendetta against you."

"That was a cop-out," he said, jingling the mixture of loose change, a ball repair tool and several tees in his front pants pocket. "I did get a raw deal early on, but the main reason I haven't been able to get back on Tour is that I lost my confidence."

Chase shared with Jana his deteriorating emotional state during the brutal swiftness of Terry's cancer. He explained how, powerless to stop the disease, he fell into a drunkenness that nearly cost him River's life. He let her inside, to glimpse the pain and embarrassment of losing his career, his lifelong dream, and starting over.

Tears in her eyes, she squeezed his hand. "Chase, I don't know what to say."

He pulled back.

She followed him. "That was a long time ago. You can't blame yourself forever, especially given the circumstances. Your life, so far as I can tell, is just about perfect now. Can I ask why you're telling me all this?"

Chase recounted Tank's offer.

Her eyes narrowed. "So, when you play well with their clubs, everyone will want a set."

"Exactly. Except playing well against the best players in the world is pretty tough." He weighed her lack of enthusiasm. "What's wrong? You look worried."

She twisted an earring. "I think it's a great opportunity, don't get me wrong, and you're obviously excited about it..."

"But?"

"It sounds like they're . . . I don't know." She shrugged.

"What? Say it."

"Sorry if this sounds blunt," she said. "Maybe it's from growing up in the restaurant business; but to me it sounds like they're using you. They plan to market your return as a great comeback and capitalize on your tragedy."

Chase stiffened. "Yeah, but that's how business is done. They invest in me, and I have to perform to reap the rewards."

"Is that really what's important to you?" She touched his chin. "What about your self-esteem? Just because you do well or poorly on any given day shouldn't dictate how you view yourself as a person. What if things don't go your way?"

He looked away. "That's not going to happen."

"But what if it does? The guys you're playing against are awesome."

"So am I!" He jerked his thumb into his chest. "Since I left the Tour, my driving is farther and more consistent, my chipping and putting are great, and I've added new shots, like the knockdown, to my resume. So far as technically playing the game, I am absolutely better than I was before. But that's only part of the equation. The biggest hurdle for most players is coping with the mental pressures of playing golf. Lack of talent is not what prevents guys like me from shooting rounds in the sixties at a tournament; it's brain-lock. There's no substitute for the pressure of competition, and that's something I'm ready for."

Her mouth twisted into a half smile. "You're not afraid you'll choke?"

"No. My only concern is that I'll be playing with a completely new set of clubs."

She nodded. "How long do you have to get ready?"

"Only a couple of weeks. I have to practice like crazy between now and then, so I won't have much time for lessons or much else."

"Uh-oh." She shifted her weight and stared up at the cloudless blue sky. "Is this some kind of elaborate brush off? You don't have to concoct a wild story to get rid of me."

"How can you say that?" he demanded, an angry flash crossing his ice blue eyes. He put both hands on the tops of her shoulders and squeezed. "Finding you has been the best thing . . . well, the best thing in a very, very long time." He waited until she nodded her acceptance to continue. "It's just that I have to practice day and night. I've been struggling to figure out how we can still be together, and I think I found a way-if you're willing to do it."

"Do what?"

"Be my caddie."

"Your what?"

The rumble of passing lawnmowers forced him to repeat himself. "My caddie."

Her mouth twisted as if she'd discovered a hair in her food. She backed up a step. "Your caddie?"

"Yes." He smiled and angled her away from the noise. "What better way to learn the game? You even get paid. Help me practice every day and then come with me to the tournament, walk the course, meet other players and keep me sane; that's all you have to do. I need you there with me, I really do. How about it?"

She turned and scanned the all-male crowd. "Do professional golfers usually have women caddies?"

"It's unusual, but not unheard of. Nick Faldo's caddie is a woman. Come on, Jana. You're perfect, except you might need to start lifting weights because my bag weighs forty pounds."

"Wow." A deep dimple resurfaced. "I've never been to Reno. How would that work? You know, do I have to be with you all the time? I'd have to talk to my dad because I'm usually at the restaurant every night, but you probably play in the daytime. Maybe I could . . ."

"Easy, take it easy. We can work all of the schedule issues out. The main thing is whether or not you want to do it." He held his breath.

"You can't get rid of me that easily." She stood up straight and stuck out her hand. "Count me in. Congratulations. I'm your new caddie."

\* \* \* \* \*

"How about another?" the bartender at Carolina's asked Tank. Light and airy, the restaurant was filled with flowers and middle-aged clientele. Perfect for a first date.

He shook his head and waved a hand over top of the martini glass. "Nah, I'm nursing this one until my date gets here. Don't want to impair my performance," he said as he winked and took another glance backwards.

Tank slicked down his sideburns with his sweaty palm. Dressed to the nines in a lavender Bruno Magli dress shirt, oatmeal linen slacks and a black Prada alligator belt, he positioned his barstool under the air conditioning vent. The timed infusion of frosty air kept him cool and dry.

Maddie slid onto the stool next to Tank. Looks of admiration from men her age, and decades younger, followed her entry.

"You're a vision." Tank took her hand and planted a delicate kiss on her wrist.

She pulled it back. "Cut it out." She placed her clutch on the bar.

"How about a cocktail, doll? Our reservations aren't for another fifteen minutes."

"I'll have a glass of Pinot Grigio, please." She arranged her legs primly beneath her knee-skimming skirt. It was the palest shade of green silk as was the matching tank top peeking out from beneath her sheer white bolero demi-jacket. The pink pearl choker and matching earrings complemented her coral colored lipstick. "Make that two." Tank drained the last of his gin without taking his eyes from her.

"Tank, I want to thank you for what you've done. Chase is perfect for—"

"Hold on." He held up a hand. "No shop talk until we get one thing straight. I didn't invite you out for dinner to talk about Chase."

She frowned.

Tank leaned in. "I asked you out because I like you, plain and simple. In fact, I liked you the first time we met. Before I ever thought of doing business with Chase, I knew I had to get to know you. That's the truth. I want to make sure you understand that I didn't use you to get to him. Him and us, that's two separate things. Got it?"

"Why didn't you tell me that on the telephone?" She fiddled with the napkin beneath her over-sized wineglass.

He eased his barstool closer. "Didn't want to give you a chance to say no to dinner."

She laughed. "You want me to believe that you're genuinely pursuing a relationship with me and not simply hedging your bets with Chase?"

"I sure do."

"Hmm. Using a mother's loyalty to con her into dinner. Pretty presumptuous." She raised her glass. "Cheers."

He touched his glass to hers. "To the beginning of a beautiful friendship."

\* \* \* \* \*

"Hey, did you beat her today, kid?" Tank called out.

River flexed his arm into an exaggerated muscle. "I made a birdie, and check out all of these balls I found!" He dumped out the side pocket of his golf bag to count his treasure.

Maddie parked her pull-cart next to Tank, who stood watching Chase practice putting. Jana squatted directly behind each shot, learning to read the greens. After each ball found the cup, Jana placed another at varying intervals and difficulties on the green.

"Since Chase accepted your offer, they've been at it day and night, those two," Maddie said.

"Yeah," Tank said. "I knew Chase was a pro, but that little lady has me eating crow."

"How so?"

"I'll admit I was dead set against her being caddie. There are too many chances for mistakes out there that could cost us. But the way she encourages him to follow his own gut is magic. And as a career waitress, she memorizes the course layout, stats and management tips like nobody's business. She can recite them back to him like a daily special. I'll bet she doesn't even know what half the stuff means, but he does and that's all that matters."

"I haven't seen him like this with anyone in a long time," she said.

"Yeah, they're in a rhythm and they've got to keep it going. This time tomorrow we'll be in Reno."

"Why are we going out there on Sunday anyway? The tournament doesn't start until Thursday. Before, when Chase was on Tour, he never arrived at a tournament before Wednesday. Too much time for him to get nervous."

"Not to worry. He needs to log at least four practice rounds, memorize the course and study the competition. Most guys will be playing in the Wednesday Pro-Am, so Chase can check out the course up close."

"I checked out Montreux Country Club's website. It looks fabulous."

Tank cleaned his sunglasses using the bottom of his polo shirt. "Yeah, well the real thing can be very different, especially depending on the weather. You remember the 2002 Masters? All that heavy rain and mud killed half the field."

## McLeary's Mulligan

"I'm not worried about rain."

"Well, I'm worried about everything. I've got a lot riding on that kid of yours," he answered, his eyes fixed on Chase.

"So do I," she said evenly.

He gave her a sidelong glance. "Touché."

"Momma, can I get a Coke?" River asked.

"Sure. Ask Willie to put it on my tab. I'll take a club soda. Tank, would you like something?"

"Diet Coke would be great," he answered.

River trotted off to the clubhouse.

"Chase loves your clubs. It took him some time to adjust to the flexibility, but he's driving the ball farther and more accurately than ever," she said.

"He sure is, and so will everyone who uses Trubird clubs. That's why we're all going to be rich." Tank made notes on a card. "Looks like you've been helping River stay out of trouble these last couple of weeks."

"Yes. Business has been a little slow, so I've been able to keep him out of Chase's hair," she said.

He turned his head. "Slow? I thought with interest rates so low it'd be booming."

She shrugged. "I haven't gotten a new listing in nearly two weeks, which is odd, but I'm sure things will pick up soon."

He moved his chin toward Chase. "Do you think he's ready, emotionally? I know there are loads of bad memories out there waiting for him. As soon as he pops up at the press conference, it's gonna hit the fan."

Maddie watched her son gently touch Jana's back and point to the circuitous route the ball would make prior to reaching the hole. "If he is, it has everything to do with her." Maddie motioned to Jana.

"Yeah, looks that way. She's a keeper."

Maddie's eyes smiled their reply.

"Is River excited about flying out to Reno tomorrow?" Tank asked as the boy approached.

"He's been packed for a week."

"Here you go." River handed the adults their drinks.

"Thanks, kiddo. Hey, on the plane tomorrow, did you know they make kids under twelve sit in the cargo bin with the luggage?"

"No way, you're full of it. I've got a window seat and everything."

Tank took a healthy swig of his soda. "Nope, I've got the window seat. I'm serious. It's a new FAA regulation."

"Momma, he's lying."

"You two are worse than brothers."

Tank put his arm around River's neck. "Go ask your dad. He'll tell you I'm right."

River raced to the green as Tank followed.

"Dad! Hey, Dad! You know what Tank said? Hey, Dad!"

She sipped her plastic cup.

I better not have the middle seat between those two.

\* \* \* \* \*

River craned his neck. "This place isn't bad, but I'd rather be at the hotel."

Chase laughed and parked the rental car at the Montreux Golf and Country Club Welcome Center, just off the Mount Rose Highway between Reno and Lake Tahoe, Nevada. Sponsor and press tents were everywhere.

The clubhouse was modeled after a twenty-five thousand square foot French Country Manor house. The cost of membership was about one hundred thousand dollars and included access to Montreux's three dining rooms, wine cellar, full service pro shop and locker rooms, replete with marble counters and hardwood floors.

"Does this place have a pool?" River asked.

Tank's hand gestured like a gun. "Over there, along with tennis courts and a fitness center, but it's members only in Jack's Den. That's Jack as in Nicklaus. He designed this course. It's a combination pine forest and high desert layout."

Chase slipped his arm around Jana's waist. It felt so good, being here, back in the hunt with her at his side. His arms felt powerful, his muscles tingled, anxious to prove that he belonged.

"Mom, why don't you and River take a tour around the place. Jana, Tank and I should go check in. Trip should be waiting for us," Chase said.

She gave her son a hug. "Deep breaths. You'll do fine."

Chase hugged her back. "Don't worry about me. I intend to eat this place alive." He looked up. The crystalline sky welcomed him and a soft breeze kissed his forehead.

"That's my boy."

Jana stepped forward. "Last night I couldn't sleep so I checked this place out again on the Internet." She lowered her voice. "Did you know that the practice area has a huge — like, maybe eighteen thousand square feet — putting and chipping green and, like, six target greens?"

Chase laughed. "Like, really?"

"Like, totally."

"Like, I think I'm going to puke." Tank pretended to stick his finger down his throat.

A passing figure caught Jana's eye. "Isn't that—"

"Don't point." Chase grabbed Jana's hand and squeezed it. "And yes, that's Notah Begay. He set the course record here, shot a sixty-three, in 1999. Don't look now, but see that guy standing at your seven o'clock? That's . . ."

Tank turned away to use his cell phone and, in doing so, he spied Trip not twenty feet ahead, in a heated argument with two men, one of whom was the current PGA Commissioner. Trip pointed to Chase and waved Tank off.

Tank turned back around, pivoting sideways to block Chase's view. "Why don't you and Jana go look over that swanky practice area? I'll get all the paperwork squared away and we can meet back here in half an hour. Okay?"

Chase rubbed his hands together. "Don't you think I should wait with you for Trip? I'm ready to get this party started."

Tank put a thick hand behind Chase's back and nudged him forward. "Nah. He's so long winded you won't get a word in for half an hour anyway. Take a minute together with your girlfriend now while you can. Go on, beat it," he said, with an easy brush off before making his way to Trip's side.

Red faced and hissing, Trip addressed the men before him. "You can't humiliate me like this. After all I've done for you."

"Sorry, Trip," said the current Commissioner, palms raised. "But legal council says we have no choice." He gestured to the stone-faced attorney next to him.

"This is slander," Trip said, sounding part-python. "Don't think I won't sue the Association to clear my name."

The attorney shrugged. "We're done here." They disappeared into the crowd amid handshakes and laughter, not a smidgen of emotion carried over from their unpleasant conversation.

Tank frowned at Trip. "I'm afraid to ask, but I've got the sickening feeling that I'm on the verge of bankruptcy."

Trip lowered his voice. "We lost our exemption."

# CHAPTER 8

Chase, Tank, Trip and Jana stood in a circle off the fringe of the practice green.

"How could they pull the exemption?" Chase asked, chest tight and laboring to catch a breath.

"Calm down." Tank pivoted his head back and forth between Chase and Trip. "Both of you."

"Do you have any idea how I feel?" Trip slapped his heart. "I've sunk every last penny into this deal, and my own people, guys I've known for twenty-five years, stabbed me in the back."

Jana reached for Chase's arm. "What happened? Why are they doing this?"

Trip leaned forward. "All they'll tell me is that somebody filed a complaint against me." His voice dropped to a whisper. "They're saying I gambled on Tour events during my last year as Commissioner. It's total fabrication, but the Association wants to distance itself from any hint of scandal while the investigation is pending, so they took away my exemption."

Tank turned to Chase. "OneSport is behind this, I know it. They've been spreading the word that Trubird will put everyone else out of business. No one wants our clubs to see daylight."

Jana wrinkled her nose. "Sounds a little paranoid, don't you think?"

"No, Tank is right," Trip said. "We're finding out the hard way just how far their influence reaches."

"What can we do? Is it over?" Jana asked.

Chase folded the brim of his cap. Pent up hunger to prove himself worthy of the Tour, to best Jake Nathan, and to earn Jana and River's respect, burned his stomach. He wanted, no, he deserved his life back. "You bet it's not. I'm not quitting now."

Jana opened her mouth and then snapped it shut.

Like a boxer anxious to throw the first punch, Chase smacked his fist into his opposite hand. "Tomorrow I'm going to enter the Monday qualifier and earn myself a spot in the tournament."

"Wait a minute." Jana pulled his shirtsleeve toward her, worry in her eyes. "That wasn't part of the deal. You can't expect to—"

"Expect?" Tank snapped. "Sweetheart, we don't have a choice. Besides, what's he got to lose? He's come this far, so why not?"

Trip shook his index finger at Jana. "If Chase backs out now, Trubird is dead and so is he. We're nearly bankrupt and he'll never see another tournament."

River's voice reached the foursome. "Dad! There's my Dad," River said, galloping over to Chase. His eyes shone with excitement and pride. "Hey Dad. The driving range has balls that automatically come up out of the ground. I can't believe you get to play here. It's the coolest place ever!"

"Hold on a minute," Jana said.

Maddie joined the group and stood close to Tank, her smile fading. "What's up?" She spoke to Chase. "Is something wrong?"

Chase slipped his arm around River's neck, pulling him close. He looked at Maddie and then Jana. "No, there's nothing wrong. In fact, everything's great. I got a raise."

Trip's head snapped up. "What are you—"

"After I make it in the qualifier," Chase said, puffing out his chest, "I'm going to get a piece of the pie, right, guys?"

Trip nodded slowly, eyebrows raised. "One percent of Trubird's receipts for five years?"

Chase cocked his head. "Does that mean I get ownership?"

"No," Trip said, frowning. "But you do get money without any of the debt or liabilities that come with ownership. Deal?"

Chase advanced a step closer, grasping the similarity between a tough round of golf and a business negotiation. "And I still get twenty-five thousand for making the cut and another fifty for a top twenty-five finish, right?"

"Correct."

Chase squeezed his eyes shut, ready to play the game. "Put it in writing and you've got a deal."

Tank slapped Chase on the back. "Atta boy."

"Okay," Trip's face softened. "It's time for full court press. Tank, thanks to OneSport I'm a bit unpopular, so you'll have to take the lead. You know what to do."

Tank nodded. "Come on, guys."

"Where are we going?" Maddie asked.

"Press tent," Tank said. "We're raising the stakes. It's time to introduce the return of Chase McLeary using Trubird clubs. Here comes OneSport's worst nightmare."

\* \* \* \* \*

"Do I have to do everything myself?" Mort spat into the telephone from his office in New York. He scratched wildly behind his ear. Behind him, the television blared a sports drink jingle at maximum volume.

Two thousand miles away, Jake poured a bottle of sparkling water into a glass and stood naked at the window overlooking the northern Nevada mountains. "Relax, I've got it covered," he replied from his room at the Atlantis Casino Resort in Reno. He drank down the cool liquid and then reached for his magenta swimsuit, OneSport's latest design.

"Covered? You said Trip Boswyck wouldn't get his guy anywhere near the Reno-Tahoe. I just watched the special press conference feature on Chase McLeary, your former client, and his comeback attempt using spanking new Trubird clubs in tomorrow's Monday qualifier. These guys are milking the comeback story for all its worth. His mother, his kid, his girlfriend the caddie, everyone is spewing sympathy for this guy. Oh, and the announcer specifically named you as Chase's previous representation. Did you hear that Trubird rep, Mazzola? He called us heartless giants who gave up on Chase too early, that idiot. What the hell have you been doing out there?"

"Mort, I know this guy. Tomorrow, if he even makes it to the first tee, he'll die within the first three holes, dragging Trubird to the grave with him. Chase McLeary was expecting a cakewalk. Glide in on a sponsor's exemption, play a few good rounds and cash Trubird's check. Now that I pulled Trip's exemption, Chase will never make it through the qualifier. His performance will prove that he doesn't have what it takes to play on the Tour, thereby validating my decision to dump him as a client."

Mort inhaled audibly.

"Trust me," Jake said. "Trubird is about to crash and burn, and Chase McLeary will wish he was never born." He pulled on a plush white terrycloth robe.

"You better be sure about that. What if he does make it into the tournament? What then?" Mort asked, a distinct nose-whistle sounding with each breath.

Jake laughed. "Maintain plausible deniability, my friend. All you need to know is that I've got multiple backup plans in the unlikely, no, make that impossible, event that Chase squeaks into the game," Jake said. "You've got to believe me. I know all his pressure points."

"This is our future, Jake." Mort's voice dropped an octave. "Don't screw this up."

Jake pulled the robe tight, caught by a sudden chill. "What about Joe? Where is he with putting the screws to Trubird's partners?"

"Close," Mort said. "He's filed five lawsuits, tapped into their lenders, bought up their loans and mortgages, and started an injunction to halt all production and use of Trubird clubs.

If we can fast-track that one, Chase won't be able to use the clubs in the tournament, and the litigation will definitely bankrupt these guys."

"Good."

"We've got more at stake in golf than I thought."

"What do you mean?"

Mort grunted. "Industry trends are forecasting a surge in two golf markets: women and youth. Within the next two to four years, participation in each is going to quadruple. OneSport needs to own them, uncontested. I want the whole pie."

"Then let me get back to work."

\* \* \* \* \*

Jake strolled across the glistening pool deck, his eyes scanning the crowd from behind metallic sunglasses. He chose a lounge chair at the water's edge next to a middle-aged woman and a young boy.

"This is great!" River yelled. "With that glass cover over the pool, we can even swim if it rains. Come on, Momma, I'll race you again."

"No way." She climbed out of the water. "I'm exhausted. I want to go upstairs and lie down before dinner."

"Not yet. I'm not tired and I want to swim some more. Come on, Momma. I'm not a baby anymore."

"I know that, but I don't think . . ."

"Come on. I'm almost twelve. You said yourself that I'm ready for more responsibility. I swear I'll stay by the lifeguards. Please, can I just stay a little longer? Pretty please?"

Maddie looked around at the well-dressed crowd, and over to the lifeguard behind whom a large clock hung on the wall. She glanced at the other vacationing families and the crisply uniformed hotel personnel. "Okay. But, see that clock? If you're not upstairs in half an hour, you will lose all of your television and swimming privileges for the rest of the trip. Understand?"

"Thanks." He plunged headfirst back under water.

Jake waited until Maddie left and then waded into the water. "Hey, kid." He smiled. "Race you to the other side?"

River backed away, looking up toward the lifeguard stand.

"Relax," Jake said, holding up his hands. "I'm an old friend of your dad's. You're River, right?"

River raised an eyebrow and nodded slowly.

Jake flashed his movie star grin and eased closer. "Your dad never backed away from a race. What are you, chicken?"

\* \* \* \* \*

"I've been calling you for an hour," Mort said.

Joe held one hand over his ear, straining to listen over the crowd surrounding him. Thundering hooves grew to a crescendo amidst cheers, jeers and the announcer's thick Brooklyn accent.

"Hold on." He bolted up the aisle at Saratoga Springs Racetrack in upstate New York. "I'll call you right back." Locked inside the last bathroom stall, he called his partner. "I thought Sunday was my day of rest," he said, sorting through a stack of betting slips.

"You saw the press conference?"

"No. What happened?" Joe tossed the tickets, all losers, in the toilet. He flushed them down.

"Where are you?"

"In the can."

"What?"

"Talk fast," Joe said. His back to the stall door, he rested one foot on the cracked toilet seat. "I'm late for an appointment."

"Chase McLeary is playing in tomorrow's qualifier."

Joe massaged his right temple with his newspaper print stained index finger. "That's great. Let me guess, he's getting a hero's welcome."

"That, and his mere presence make us look bad. You know our competition is eating that up." Mort picked dead skin from inside his lip.

The tinny warning bell announced the start of the next race. Joe was down big money and needed a long shot to score. He snapped the lock. "The injunction to halt all use of Trubird clubs is on-line, but not in time to keep him out of the qualifier. We're talking Tuesday at the earliest." Joe ran a finger down his folded newspaper.

"What else have you got on Trubird?"

The closing bell clanged. Great. Another missed opportunity. "Trip is neutralized and two of the backers are about to get frozen out," Joe said, walking to the sink. "I've got one iron in the fire for Chase's mother, and his girlfriend is easy money. Jake said Chase belongs to him which leaves the inventor for you to handle."

"That hippie Satch is mine," Mort said. "You close the loop on everyone else. If word gets out that Trubird clubs are every bit as good as ours but a quarter of the price, it's only a matter of time before all of OneSport is challenged by similar start-up companies. We'll lose talent and huge market share. Our profits will evaporate."

"Grim Reaper, that's what you are today," Joe said. Two rapid beeps indicated another call. He recognized the flashing telephone number. It was his bookie.

"I didn't get us where we are today by underestimating the markets or the competition," Mort said. "We've got to take these guys down before they get us."

"Done. I'm on it." Joe mentally tallied up his losses for the day.

"Joe, go for the knock-out. No smoking guns."

Joe glanced at his watch. He still had time for one more race. "Bet on it."

\* \* \* \* \*

"Come on, Chase, we've been at this for hours. You're as ready as you're ever going to be. Let's get some dinner and call it a night," Jana said. A bleeding sun stretched across the horizon and a mild breeze lifted her curls.

"No, I'm not hungry and I need another couple of hours practicing long putts. My stroke is still a little off. You go on. I'll meet up with you later." He drew back his putter and stopped short of the ball, adjusting for the shadows.

"Don't freak out now. I think a thick steak and a long soak in the hot tub are just what the doctor ordered." Jana ran her fingers through her tangled hair and pulled her cap tight over her forehead.

"Jana, I can't. Not now. Do you have any idea what I'm in for tomorrow?" He glanced at the handful of golfers still practicing.

"Yes, I do, and you're well prepared for it. Besides, tomorrow you get to play against easier guys than you'll face on Thursday. Consider it a warm-up round." She arched her back and rubbed her lower spine.

Chase rested his putter on the ground. "A warm-up round?"

"I'm kidding. I wanted to lighten the mood a little. Take a few deep breaths, will you?"

Chase watched Jana's renegade curl flip around her ear. It lacerated his concentration. He inhaled deeply and exhaled three times.

"You might not be the most experienced caddie, but you're definitely the cutest."

"Let's go check out the hot tub. Are you coming or not?"

Chase looked down at the club in his hand and then back up at his girlfriend. She was right, of course. A good dinner, a bath and an early bedtime were the best things he could do for himself at this point.

"You win . . . but only if you wear your black bikini." He handed over the putter.

She twirled it baton-style before returning it to his golf bag. Chase laughed.

"In a few minutes," Jana said, "your tensions will be long gone. I guarantee it."

\* \* \* \* \*

"He'll have a heart attack. You can't tell him," Tank begged.

"Are you insane?" Maddie answered. "His son is missing! I've got to tell Chase." She moved from the crisply made twin bed to the desk.

"Keep your voice down and stop pacing," Tank said. "You're gonna wear a hole in the carpet. I'm sure River met some kid and lost track of time. He's only a couple hours late. He'll turn up soon."

"Turn up? What if he was kidnapped? This is all my fault. I never should have left him alone at the pool. I can't believe I—"

"Don't cry. Maddie, Maddie." Tank drew her into his thick arms. She collapsed into sobs. "It's not your fault," he said. "River's practically a teenager, not a toddler."

"It is absolutely my fault." She grabbed a tissue from a painted box atop the built-in dresser and blew hard.

"You checked the pool and the arcade, right?"

"Yes," she answered, sniffling. "And I called hotel security. They're combing the place right now. I don't want to leave my room in case they call."

"Look at me." Tank cradled Maddie's chin. Her soft flesh sent heat spasms through his hand. "River is off having a blast somewhere. He'll turn up any minute. But, if you throw this at Chase right now, we can forget about tomorrow's qualifier. It'll take him days to decompress from that kind of a scare. You've got to trust me."

A knock sounded at her door.

"Mom? Are you in there? It's Chase and Jana. Mom?"

"Oh, no," Maddie whispered. Her eyes brimmed with tears.

Tank felt the panic beneath her skin about to erupt. He held up a finger to his lips.

"Mom? River?" Chase knocked again. "Maybe they already went down for dinner." His voice trailed off as he strode down the hall.

Tank massaged her shoulders. "Promise you'll give me two hours." He waited for her nod before releasing and then turned and opened the door a crack.

She lunged forward to grab his powerful forearm. "Where are you going?"

"To find that grandkid of yours. And when I do, I'm gonna chain him to my freakin' leg."

"Tank, what if—"

"Stop it." He covered her trembling hand with his. "He's fine, and I'm bringing him right back to you. Just promise you won't tell Chase."

"I'll give you two hours, not a minute more." She pulled away. "After that, I've got to tell him."

"Stay by the phone."

Maddie raised her hand to wipe a tear. Tank beat her to it, delicately gliding his callused thumb under her eye. "Don't worry, doll. Piece of cake."

\* \* \* \* \*

"Your room is ten times as big as ours." River pounced back onto the sitting room sofa. "But that bathroom is kind of weird. I've never seen two toilets right next to each other."

Jake laughed. "Only one of those is a toilet. The other is called a bidet."

"A what?"

Jake disappeared into his suite's walk-in closet. "Never mind."

River sucked the last of a soda through a straw. "I really need to get back now." A dull ache pulsed in his stomach.

Jake leaned out. "What's the matter? Not having fun anymore?"

"Are you kidding? I had a great time. No one's ever let me spend that much money in an arcade. And the hat and sweatshirt you bought me are awesome. It's just that my grandmother is going to be mad because I'm so late." River shuddered, picturing Maddie, one hand on her hip and disapproval written all across her face.

"Why? You're too old for a babysitter." Jake perched on the back of the sofa. "Besides, like I told you, I'm an old friend of your dad's. I'm sure your grandmother won't mind, especially since all the grownups are tied up at a special dinner most of the night."

"No offense," River said, flipping his baseball hat around backwards, "but you don't know her very well. She's pretty strict."

"How about some dessert before you hit the road? Don't tell me that burger and fries filled you up."

"What do they have?"

Jake grabbed a leather room service folder from the mahogany desk. "This place makes the best brownie fudge pie in the world. It'll be here in a minute, and then I'll take you back to your room and make things right with your gram." He motioned to the television. "That's a good one."

River's eyes lit up. "Awesome." He lunged for the remote and increased the volume. Months earlier he had unsuccessfully begged Chase to let him see the R rated movie. He settled into the flowered cushion and put his bare feet up on the coffee table. Wait until he told his friends that he'd finally gotten to see it.

Jake dialed room service and then reached for his ringing cell phone. Mort's number flashed on the display.

"Hey, partner."

"What's going on?"

"I have a little visitor. River McLeary has been entertaining me for the past few hours."

"Are you out of your mind? You've got his kid in your room? Security will be breaking down your door any minute."

Jake continued his conversation inside the bathroom. "Relax, I'm not kidnapping him. I only want to borrow him long enough to jerk Chase's chain. Get him good and rattled before tomorrow's qualifier. Trust me. I know what I'm doing."

\* \* \* \* \*

"I've been waiting over an hour to see you, and now you're telling me a ritzy place like this doesn't have enough security cameras?" Tank asked, checking his watch again.

"Mr. Mazzola, please try to calm yourself," the head of the Atlantis Casino Resort security responded. He waived a hand around the television-monitor-ringed-room. "We have excellent security. But it simply wouldn't be feasible to cover every inch of the Atlantis with cameras. Be reasonable and let us do our job. Look at monitor four." He pointed. "I cued up the tape of the swimming pool area from earlier this evening."

Tank jumped forward to touch the front of the screen with two fingers. "There. That's River right there, and that's his grandma."

"Okay. I'll scan his image and distribute it to our people. There's no audio on this. There goes the grandmother," the security chief said.

Tank stared at the images, eyes widening. "Wait." He traded pangs of fear gripping his neck for stabs of anger deep in his gut.

The security chief paused the tape on the image of a man sitting at the pool's edge, next to River.

He circled the image with his finger. "You know that man?"

"Son of a . . . yes. That's Jake Nathan. What's his room number? He's got River."

"Mr. Mazzola." He smoothed his tie. "I'll handle this. I can't give out . . ."

"This is an emergency." He wiped a dot of spittle from his upper lip and scowled at the slight man. "Take me to Nathan's room or I'll tear this place apart looking for him."

"That's against policy. Stay here and I'll—"

Tank made a fist. "Now!"

They hurried to the elevator banks.

"Stay behind me," the security chief said over his shoulder. "This could still be a simple misunderstanding."

Tank grunted, pointing to the tray outside Jake's room. On it sat the remains from three desserts and a pack of bubble gum.

"Mr. Nathan?" The security chief knocked. "Mr. Nathan? Can I have a word with you?"

"Open it," Tank said. He felt the seconds tick away as the man reached for his card key.

"I'm letting myself in, Mr. Nathan," said the chief.

"This isn't a good time," Jake called from behind the door.

"Open up, Nathan!" Tank pounded on the door.

The chain slid off and the door flew open to reveal Jake, naked except for a towel wrapped around his muscular waist.

"Where is he?" Tank demanded, pushing his way into the room.

"Sorry for the interruption, sir," the security chief began. "We're looking for a young boy. You might have seen him at the pool today."

"Who, River McLeary?" Jake asked.

"Yes, do you know where he is?" the security man asked.

"River? River?" Tank tore around the suite, squatted down under the bed and checked inside the closets.

"Sure, I do," Jake answered, gazing at the security man as would a parent struggling with a petulant child. "He's back with his grandmother. I'm an old friend of his father's. We had a little fun earlier, and now he's probably in bed."

The security chief picked up Jake's telephone and dialed Maddie's room. "Hello, Mrs. McLeary? It's security. Has River . . . oh, good. I'm so glad. And he's feeling okay? Great, yes, you're very welcome. Don't hesitate to call if we can be of further assistance."

Jake deserved to be throttled, both for his dirty tricks and for what he put poor Maddie through. Tank stomped forward and stuck a finger in his chest. "I know what you're trying to do, you piece of crap, and it's not going to work."

"Would you do that a little to the left?" Jake said, smiling. "I could use a massage."

The security chief tapped Tank on the shoulder. "Obviously, this was all a misunderstanding." He turned to Jake. "Sorry to have bothered you, sir."

Chest puffed out, Tank stared up into Jake Nathan's mocking eyes. "If you touch that kid or go near him again, so help me . . . I'll kill you."

The security chief opened the door. "Mr. Mazzola, please."

Tank's sweaty fists burned to pulverize Jake's picture perfect grin. He raised them just enough. Jake flinched. Temporarily satisfied, Tank turned and marched away.

"Ciao." Jake slammed the door shut.

At the elevator banks, Tank turned to the chief. "That guy's dangerous."

"I'm going back to my office, Mr. Mazzola. If you have any further problems, I insist that you call me before taking them into your own hands." The security chief stepped into the descending elevator and disappeared.

Tank punched the elevator button three times. "Come on already," he said.

The bell chimed and the doors opened. Tank flinched.

"What are you doing on this floor?" Chase asked, arm in arm with Jana. "Did you switch rooms?"

"No, I, uh, I, I was checking out the hotel." Tank stepped forward and stood alongside Jana.

"I thought you and Mom and River were meeting us for dinner? Where did you guys go?" Chase asked.

"Oh, sorry about that. River, uh, he wanted to explore, and we kind of lost track of time."

"Are you okay? You look funny," Jana said.

Tank took a deep breath. "Fine, I'm fine. Hey, you should be turning in for the night. Where were you two?"

"After dinner we took a long walk. Jana's a great sports shrink." Chase squeezed her shoulders.

"I'm more interested in her caddie abilities." Tank hurried off the elevator. "Well, you two get some sleep. Big day tomorrow."

Jana's room was first off the elevator followed by Tank's room. Chase's sat across the hall next to the one Maddie and River shared.

Jana kissed Chase and then put her card-key in the lock. "Good night."

Chase continued down the hall.

"Where are you going?" Tank blocked the aisle.

Chase walked around Tank and tapped lightly on Maddie's door. "To say goodnight to my mother and my son. Do you mind? What's up with you?"

"I'll bet they're already asleep. You should turn in for the—" Tank said.

Maddie eased open the door. Her eyes scanned from Tank to Chase and back again. "Hi, honey."

"Mom, your eyes are—"

"A little red, I know. Must be from all that chlorine in the pool. River's fast asleep. He had a big adventure—"

"Okay, then." Tank stepped in. "Guess we should all turn in. Come on, Chase. Goodnight, Maddie."

"Goodnight." She kissed Chase's cheek and quickly closed the door.

Chase retired to his room.

A minute later there was a soft knocking at Maddie's door.

"What happened?" Tank asked. "What did River say?"

Maddie pulled her bathrobe tight around her and whispered in the dimly lit hallway.

"He said that some old friend of Chase's took him out for video games, hamburgers and even bought him some sports clothes. He said the man told him that Chase wouldn't mind. River knows better than that; I can't understand how he could do this. I told him that he's not to leave my side for the rest of the trip. As soon as this tournament is over I'm going to tell Chase everything," she said.

"Did you see the guy?"

"No. Your two hours were almost up and I had the phone in my hand when someone knocked on the door. I opened it and there was River. He called the guy 'J' and said he'd just left."

"'J' is none other than Jake Nathan," Tank said.

"Chase's old agent?"

"Yes. Better known as the face of OneSport. Trubird golf clubs must have them scared stiff to pull a stunt like this. They're doing everything in their power to rattle Chase so that he'll choke tomorrow."

Maddie rubbed the front of her neck. "Chase was absolutely devastated when Jake dumped him. He scorched Chase's reputation in the media and pronounced him 'washed-up' as a golfer. I can't wait to see him eat crow when Chase makes it into this tournament."

"Trust me, OneSport won't go down without a fight. The stakes just got higher. From here on out, we've got to watch our backs; and above all else, we can't let Chase know what's going on."

The sound of a chain sliding across the lock startled them.

"It's Chase's door," Maddie said, eyes wide.

Tank slipped his arm around Maddie and pulled her in for a long kiss.

Chase's door opened briefly, and then quickly closed and locked.

Maddie pulled away. "I can't believe you did that."

"What choice did I have? At least now he won't wonder why you're out here whispering to me in your bathrobe."

Maddie pulled her robe even tighter. "How convenient."

"If you want, we could—"

"Goodnight." She shut her door.

Tank touched his lips, the lines in his forehead melting away. Goodnight, doll.

# CHAPTER 9

"Momma, I'm going to the bathroom. Don't wait outside the door like I'm five years old," River said, shifting his weight.

"I'm waiting right here." She pointed to the floor. "If you don't want to be treated like a five-year-old then you shouldn't act like one."

"I'll only be a second. Where do you think I'll go? It's not like I want to miss Dad tee off on the back nine."

She tapped her watch. "Hurry up, then. I'm not going to budge. I don't want you disappearing again."

"This is totally embarrassing." River slipped into the men's room of Montreux's clubhouse.

Maddie stood against the wall in the hallway and waited as two men in pricey sunglasses, crisp slacks and pastel polo shirts emerged from the bathroom. Both had press passes dangling from their necks.

"I'm telling you right now, he's the biggest story today," a tall man said to a shorter one. "Looking for a comeback after a tragedy wrecked his game, cute girlfriend caddie and hot new sticks that he claims are the cheapest on the market. Today is all about Chase McLeary."

Maddie turned away from the men.

"I don't know," the shorter one answered. "He may be leading the qualifier now, but he's got plenty of time to vomit all over himself on the back nine. It wouldn't be his first time."

They paused outside the clubhouse door.

"Let me run with this. I've got a feeling about it. Have you noticed that all of the big guys, players and sponsors, are giving this guy and his clubs the cold shoulder? OneSport put the word out that nobody talks to him, or else. What does that tell you?" the taller man asked.

The shorter man closed one eye and dug his tongue into the side of his cheek. "All right. Get me everything you can find out about him and his sponsor. What's the name again?"

"Trubird Group."

"Yeah. There's a story there. I'm just not sure it has legs."

"Trust me. Legs like a Rockette. Come on. I want to line Chase up for an exclusive interview."

The two men disappeared around the corner.

River flew out of the men's room. "Momma, you should see all the cool stuff in there. They've even got free mouthwash and mints."

"Come on." Her eyes sparkled. "I've got some cool stuff of my own to share."

\* \* \* \* \*

"Tell me again exactly what they said," Tank whispered in Maddie's ear. The twosome huddled off the tenth tee box where Chase and his playing partners warmed up.

An aquamarine sky welcomed the soaring pine trees that barely swayed with the light wind. Chase caught Maddie's eye and gave her a "thumbs up." She gave him one back.

"I'm thirsty," River said. "Can I get a—"

"Ssh!" Maddie and Tank said in unison.

River folded his arms and leaned against a tree with a huff.

Maddie whispered to Tank, "I told you, that guy standing next to Jana thinks that Chase is the biggest story here. He knows that OneSport doesn't want Chase or Trubird clubs to succeed, and he's ready to run with it."

"That's Scotty Branch," Tank said, "the network's new commentator. He's a typical media tramp, but we can use him. I'll work my way over there and start the spin."

"The spin?"

"Yeah. I've got to sell Scotty on Trubird before OneSport gets wind that he's onto them. They have enough clout with the television people, and the advertisers, to bury the story before it's even written."

"Are you sure you know what you're doing?"

"Sure I do. It's all about momentum. I've got to get the media ball rolling today so that when the tournament starts on Thursday there's a built-in audience to promote Trubird clubs. But it's not me you should be worried about," Tank said.

"What do you mean? I've never seen Chase so relaxed; he's doing great."

"I'm talking about his new caddie. That's not exactly standard Tour behavior going on over there."

Maddie turned to see Jana excitedly pointing to a baby coyote that meandered across the fairway. Chase tipped his head back to laugh and drew her close.

"How sweet. What's the big deal?"

"She ought to be focused on Chase's club selection, not the freakin' wild kingdom," Tank muttered.

"Don't underestimate her. Look at how calm Chase is. She's good for him."

"Maybe."

Tank watched Scotty Branch take in the scene and scribble a few lines in his notebook. He had an ear cocked towards Chase and Jana.

Tank turned. "I'll catch up with you on the next hole."

\* \* \* \* \*

"We've seen quail, hawk and now a coyote." Jana turned back to Chase's golf bag. "I wonder what's next?"

"A bear or a mountain lion," he said.

"Very funny. Just keep it in the fairway, Jungle Boy." Jana handed Chase a three wood. "We're looking at a dogleg right with a nice driving area. Aim for that bunker straight ahead."

"Impressive. Did you memorize that off the score card?"

"Nope." She winked. "The Internet."

\* \* \* \* \*

"You're Scotty Branch, right?" Tank sidled up to the reporter as they walked to Chase's second shot.

"Who wants to know?"

"The name's Mazzola. I'm with Trubird Group, Chase McLeary's sponsor. I heard you might like some background on him and the clubs."

"That's right. Your boy is on fire today. Can you tell me why he decided to try for a comeback now after all these years? Word on the street is that OneSport wants both him and his new clubs to disappear."

"Sure, I can tell you all about that." His chin dipped. "And plenty more."

\* \* \* \* \*

"We're doing pretty well today," Chase said. Everything felt good, his swing, his energy transfer, his muscles, even the temperature felt perfect. He and Jana marched to Chase's second shot on the par five seventeenth hole.

"Pretty well? I'd call today's round pretty awesome. I wish my back were holding up as well. I'm going to need some serious time on the massage table later." Jana wiped the rivulets of sweat from her brow. "Are you sure all these clubs are necessary?"

"If you're too tired, I can carry the bag for awhile."

"Over my dead body. I told you I'd be your caddie and that's what I'm going to do." She trudged on until they reached Chase's ball.

Chase cleaned his sunglasses using his shirtfront.

Jana eased the bag off her back and peered to her left. "You had me worried back there."

"My drive?"

"Yeah. It's a good thing this hole is so long and straight, or your ball would be at the bottom of that lake," she said.

"You're right. These Trubird clubs really make a difference. I didn't hit the ball square, but the sweet spot is so big I still got the distance. It would kill me to make back-to-back bogeys after how well I've played."

"I know. If it weren't for that two-tiered green on the fourteenth, you'd be five under par. That pin placement is ridiculous. Nobody is going to make par on that thing," Jana said.

"We'll see. Hey, feel that?"

"What?"

"The breeze is at our back which gives me a decent shot at making birdie." Chase pulled out a five wood.

"Birdie? After that lucky drive? Just stay left of center, keep out of that bat-cave of a bunker, and you'll make eagle." Jana exchanged the five wood with a three wood.

"Is that your professional advice or are you trying to shorten the round so you can ditch my golf bag?"

"Quit complaining and hit the ball already."

"What kind of a caddie are you? You're supposed to motivate me." He took a practice swing and then struck his best shot of the day. Sitting two on the outer rim of the large undulating green, his ball lay thirty-five feet from the pin.

Jana hummed Hotel California as she cleaned his club and hoisted the bag.

Chase held his head in both hands and groaned. "That was really bad."

"I thought it was clever. You know, sung by the Eagles and all."

"You're fired."

"You can't fire me. I'm practically a volunteer. Hey, cut it out!"

Chase tugged at the heavy bag on her back, and she lost a step, falling backwards into him. He wrapped his arms around her, bag and all, in a bear hug. She smelled of lilac and shampoo and water.

"I love you," he whispered.

She tipped her head and let her lips brush against his earlobe. "I love you more."

\* \* \* \* \*

"What's the big deal? It's only a par four," Jana said.

Chase grabbed his driver, put it back, grabbed his three wood and put it back.

"It looks like the Sahara Desert out there." He scratched his head. "Have you ever seen so many bunkers?" He couldn't decide which club was right for his final tee shot.

"Use the three wood and stay left of the bunker on the hill. That's your best play. Go for the solid par. After your birdie last hole, it's all you need," Jana said.

"You promised me an eagle back there."

"Yeah, well, you've got to save something for the tournament."

"What an optimist." Chase reached for the driver. "I don't know. I think I can carry that bunker on the right."

Jana shrugged. "It's your call."

Chase peered down the fairway before taking Jana's advice. His three wood kept him out of the bunkers, but he left his approach shot short. He chipped onto the green and watched his ball roll within four feet of the cup. He looked at Jana.

"Bring it home," she said, matter-of-factly.

\* \* \* \* \*

"Momma, you're squeezing all the blood out of my arm," River complained.

"I'm sorry. I forgot how nerve-wracking this is." Her stomach churned and her pulse raced.

"It's cake," River said. "I could make that five foot putt for par."

"If you had three strokes to do it," Tank said.

"I wish he'd stop reading the green and get it over with," Maddie said. This was a defining moment in her son's life — one that would stick with him forever.

"I think the cut's gonna be minus three," Tank said. "This is for all the apples."

"Come on, Dad. You can do it," River said.

Chase drew back his putter. Maddie crossed her fingers and held her breath as the ball rolled in slow motion towards the cup. "It's not going to make it," she said, covering her mouth with her hand, stifling a cry of anguish.

"Come on, baby, roll." Tank cupped his hands around his eyes.

On its last revolution, the ball fainted into the cup.

"He did it! He did it!"

Maddie embraced River and Tank. Together, they jumped up and down.

"Look." Maddie pointed.

Jana sprinted across the green, hopped up, wrapped her legs around Chase's middle, and kissed him.

"Gross." River buried his nose in the crook of his elbow.

Tank grinned. "I can't believe he did it."

"No," Maddie said, beaming. "They did it."

\* \* \* \* \*

"This is Scotty Branch live, with former PGA sensation Chase McLeary, who just earned a spot in Thursday's Reno-Tahoe Open . . . thanks to an exceptional Monday qualifying round." The reporter smiled into the camera. "Chase, how does it feel to be back?"

"Great. It's been a long time."

"Tell me about your comeback. You're a schoolteacher now, right? Why return to the Tour after a decade? Do you think you have what it takes to compete with golf's best?"

"If so, it's all thanks to these new Trubird clubs I'm using." Chase held up a five iron.

"You and those clubs are making quite a stir. Your driving distance has been phenomenal, and given the number of greens you hit in regulation, some people are wondering if your clubs conform to USGA guidelines for the width and depth of grooves. What can you tell us about Trubird clubs?"

"Not to worry, they were designed well within industry regulations for groove width, COR, and all those technology rules. Plain and simple, Trubird clubs are better and cheaper than anything else on the market. In fact, they actually compensate for any weaknesses in my game. Made of a brand new material, they..."

\* \* \* \* \*

"Are you watching this?" Joe tapped the television monitor behind his desk with the tip of a pencil. "The stock market just opened, and our shares are down five points."

Mort, applying his signature to the contract on Joe's desk, paused to squint at the screen. "It's the media attention on Chase McLeary and Trubird. Some market analysts think golf products industry-wide are overpriced." He pushed his glasses higher up on his nose and resumed signing. "It's not only us. Everybody's down."

"I thought this guy was some washed-up schoolteacher," Joe said. "How did he get into the tournament?"

"Don't worry about it."

Joe strode to the wall thermostat and decreased the temperature. "Jake promised to get rid of this guy. Said this guy would definitely choke." Returning to his desk, he unbuttoned his shirtsleeves and rolled them to his elbows.

Mort stood erect and tucked his hands underneath his armpits. "Those clubs are out now, we can't ignore them. We've got to humiliate McLeary and Trubird so that no one will ever invoke their names again."

"How are we going to do that?"

"Trust me."

Tonya rapped on Joe's door.

"Sorry, boss." She clung to the doorframe, half in and half out of the room. "Your broker's on the phone and he won't take no for an answer. He says it's urgent. Something about a margin call."

"Crap. Put him on hold," Joe said. He opened a drawer and rooted around for a roll of Tums. "Jake better not screw this up. I can't exercise my stock options until our share price turns around, and I need that money now. If we don't put Barb's dad in a nursing home soon, I'll kill myself."

"You're not the only one with money issues," Mort said. "I'm the one with two girls in college, one in grad school, and one getting married."

Joe unrolled the antacids. "Just keep pushing on your end."

Mort nodded before turning on his heel.

Tonya buzzed.

"Not now," Joe said.

"Sorry, Joe, the auditors want a word. They're here."

Men in blue suits entered Joe's office.

"Two partners visiting me at the same time," Joe said. "What's this costing, a grand an hour?" He closed the file on his desk and folded his hands.

"Hi, Joe. We need a minute."

Joe ran a hand through his hair. "Martin, I'm booked solid today. Why didn't you call for an appointment?"

Martin shifted his laptop bag from one shoulder to the other. "Sorry, we just left the SEC. There's a problem."

# CHAPTER 10

"Yeah?" Joe said, tapping the file as though playing a minuet.

"We're in the hot seat," the accountant explained. "Every public company is being scrutinized for inflated assets and profits. Investors are scared and now the politicians are dogging us. You're our biggest client, but you're also ripe for investigation. We've got to do some quick cleanup on your books."

Joe made a winding motion with his forefinger. "That speech probably cost me three-fifty. Get to the point."

"We've got a problem with your stock option plan," the auditor said.

"What about it?" Joe asked with a shrug. "The last time I checked, granting stock options is still legal according to the Generally Accepted Accounting Principles."

The accountant took a minute to respond. "The Dow Jones has a lot of people spooked."

"So? We follow the law, right?" Joe shifted in his seat. The accountant's expression was even more dour than usual. He looked scared.

"Technically, yes. Your financial statements are legally accurate; but, come on, Joe, we both know the big picture is a whole different story."

Joe narrowed his eyes, gauging their seriousness.

The accountant leaned forward. "We need to restate your financial statements." He stuck a finger between his collar and his neck. "It's going to make your profits look bad for a few quarters, but it will keep the feds off your back."

"No way."

"Stop pretending you don't know what this is all about." The accountant frowned. "The days when we sign off on your personal loans, off-balance sheet financing, and stock option expenses are over."

Joe threw down his pencil. He could practically hear his phone ringing off the hook after announcing consecutive losses. "Our shareholders will go nuts with the change in earnings. You'll put us out of business."

"Right now your shareholders have no way of knowing that the underlying value of OneSport is only a fraction of what they think it is. Your financial reports, although technically correct, are misleading." The accountant folded his arms. "Don't tell me that's a surprise."

Joe stood. "OneSport is still the industry leader. We're worth plenty."

"This is serious. Justice Department-style serious. We'll work with you to minimize the bottom line impact, but if you're not willing to meet us partway, then we have to disclose and resign, and that's not going to make your shareholders any happier. Remember when there were the Big Eight accounting firms? We're an endangered species. Joe, this is a deal-breaker."

\* \* \* \* \*

"You're beaming," Jana said.

"I can't help it. This is so . . . surreal," Chase said.

"This ain't your first time in the spotlight, kid. Don't let it go to your head," Tank said.

"I'm not, but it's a good thing I brought extra shirts. Sweating through back to back interviews is taking a toll on my wardrobe."

"Can I have two desserts?" River asked.

"We'll see. First pick out a sandwich," Maddie said. Tucked into a booth inside the Atlantis Resort's lunch restaurant, the five surveyed the menu.

"We've got to milk these television spots for all they're worth," Tank said. "So far you're doing a great job. Trip broke his back trying to land a corporate investor, but no one would give us any money. Now, with a little publicity, and assuming you don't fall apart at the tournament, OneSport's competitors are going to kick themselves for not partnering with us back when I begged them for money."

"Tank, how could you say such a thing? Chase is playing great," Jana said, cheeks red.

"Simply callin' a spade a spade."

"He's right," Chase said. "I've got to prove Trubird clubs make winners."

"You already qualify. No matter what, you're a success," Maddie said, catching Jana's eye. The young woman was proud of Chase and passionate in her defense of his skills. A lump grew in Maddie's throat.

Chase laughed. "Spoken like a proud mother."

A tall redhead in her early thirties approached the table. She spoke to Chase with a disarming smile. "Excuse me, sir. Are you Chase McLeary?"

"Dad, you're famous," River said. "I bet she wants your autograph."

"Kind of. This is for you." She handed Chase a manila envelope.

"Uh, oh," Tank said.

"What's this?" Chase asked.

"Legal papers. Consider yourself served." The young woman sauntered away.

"This can't be good." Chase ripped open the envelope.

"What is it?" Maddie scooted forward wondering how many more hurdles were in store for her son.

Chase flipped through the typed pages on legal letterhead. He handed the packet to Tank and pushed away his menu. "There goes my appetite."

"I don't fu—I don't believe it," Tank said.

"What? What is it?" Jana asked.

"It's an injunction," Tank said. "It says Chase can't play with Trubird clubs in the tournament."

"Why not? Who filed it?" Maddie grabbed the pages.

"A company that claims we stole their golf club design," Tank said.

"What are we going to do?" Jana asked.

"Fight it," Tank said. "It's only Tuesday. Our lawyers have a day and a half to beat this thing."

"What's going on? Why can't Dad play in the tournament?" River looked to Tank for answers.

"Don't worry about it." Tank stood, patting him on the shoulder.

"Where are you going?" Maddie asked.

"To make a few calls and take care of this."

Chase grabbed his arm. "You can fix this, right?"

He shook it free. "Piece of cake. You practice your golf."

River stared at the table, hair falling in his eyes. "But what if—"

Chase glided a finger under his son's chin and stroked the downy skin. "I earned that spot." His smile was confident. "And I intend to play golf on Thursday."

\* \* \* \* \*

"Did you read the injunction?" Tank asked.

"Yes," Trip said. "Our lawyers are scrutinizing it right now. They're worried."

"Why? We didn't steal anyone's design."

"I know that, but you know how bureaucratic the legal process is. It takes time to rebut this kind of lawsuit. They've got to research and build a counter-case," Trip said.

"News flash — we're out of time."

"You think I don't know that?"

"Give me the bottom line. Can Chase use Trubird clubs or not?"

"You'll know when I know."

\* \* \* \* \*

Jana set up Chase's bag in the center of the driving range.

"Where is everybody? I thought this place would be packed," she said, noting the freshly repaired tee spaces and empty trash baskets.

"It will be, but right now a lot of the guys are out on the course playing in the Pro-Am, the professional and amateur tournament," Chase said.

She toweled off his three wood. "How much do they charge the average hacker to play with a professional in one of these things?"

"About four thousand bucks." Chase stretched backwards and rotated his shoulders and arms.

"For a foursome?"

"For a player." He touched his toes and bounced gently from the waist. "They usually set up four amateurs with one pro."

"I can't imagine spending that kind of money for a round of golf." Jana put a hand on her hip. "Plus, why would any pro want to spend the day before a tournament with four high-handicappers?"

Chase rolled up to a standing position. "If you're one of the pros invited to play, it's not really optional. The top names bring in a lot of money at these things, and they're expected to play."

"Why are you stretching so much? Is your back hurting you?"

Chase rubbed his left shoulder with his right hand. "Not really, but it's a little stiff. I didn't sleep well last night."

Jana frowned, noting the twitch in his left cheek. "Maybe you should just putt. No sense getting over-tired."

"No, I need practice."

An hour later, Chase was covered in sweat.

"I'm totally off. I can't hit one straight shot," he said.

Jana looked behind her. Scotty Branch stood whispering with another man. There was something about them that made the hairs on the back of her neck stand up. "You're tired. This whole injunction thing has you spooked. Let's take a break."

"Not yet. Hand me my putter." He turned back to his bag. "Oh, for crying out loud."

"What?"

He leaned in and lowered his voice. "That guy behind you, talking to the reporter, that's my old agent, Jake Nathan."

"Nathan from OneSport?"

"Yeah. Whatever he's telling Scotty about me, it isn't good."

River and Maddie approached.

"Hi, River," Jake called out, intercepting them.

"What the—?" Chase looked up. His mouth hung open as River ran over and gave Jake a high five.

"How does River know him?" Jana asked.

"I don't know, but I'm about to find out." Chase rammed his club into the bag, shouldered it, and marched over to the small group with Jana at his heels.

"So sorry about that mix up the other night," Jake said to Maddie.

She fixed one arm around River's shoulders and pulled him close.

The reporter's eyes darted back and forth.

"What mix up?" Chase joined the group.

"Chase McLeary." Jake extended a hand. "I didn't expect to see you here."

Chase gave it a half-hearted shake. "Hello, Jake."

"Do you know Scotty?" Jake asked.

"Sure. Hi again."

The reporter nodded. "I hear there's some trouble with Trubird clubs."

"What are you talking about?" Chase asked.

"I've heard that you can't debut those new clubs in tomorrow's tournament because of some legal issue. If that's the case will you withdraw?" Scotty raised his eyebrows.

"Who told you that?" Chase asked.

"Can't say. You know how it is. Gotta' protect my sources."

Chase glared at Jake. "Yeah, well, your source is wrong. I'll be teeing off with the best clubs on the market, guaranteed." He patted his golf bag.

"That's big-time pressure," Jake said, nodding sympathetically. "Tying your fate to those untested new clubs is pretty bold."

"Just look at the time." Maddie grabbed River's elbow. Her voice was shrill as she opted to forego the usual conversational courtesies. "I signed up for water aerobics back at the hotel. Come on, River. We don't want to be late."

"Mrs. McLeary, wait," Jake said. "I wanted to apologize again for—"

"No bother," Maddie said, looking everywhere except at Chase. "I really should be going now."

"You're sorry about what?" Chase asked Jake.

"I assumed you knew. River and I were playing at the pool the other day and time got away from us." Jake laughed. "Your mother here got a little worried. She called hotel security." Jake winked at Scotty Branch.

"What are you talking about? When was this?" Chase frowned at Maddie.

"Sunday," Jake answered. "And—"

"It wasn't a big deal," Maddie said, looking to Jana and then back at Chase. "I didn't want to worry you before—"

"Not a big deal?" Chase ran a hand through his sweaty scalp. "My son was missing, and you didn't even tell me?"

The corners of Scotty Branch's lips turned up slightly as he silently scratched in his notebook.

Jana touched Chase's arm, silently pleading with him not to make a scene. "Maybe we should do this later."

## McLeary's Mulligan

Chase poked his index finger an inch from Jake's nose. "Stay away from my family. Are we clear?"

Jake shrugged. "Pity. You haven't changed a bit. Come on, Scotty." He slapped the reporter on the back. "I want to introduce you to Miles Callabrio. I guarantee he'll be in contention come Sunday afternoon." Jake and Scotty strolled away, sharing whispers and laughs.

"Chase," Maddie said, stepping toward him. "It's not what you think. I—"

Chase backed up. "Mom! How could you not tell me?" He turned. "Jana, did you know about this?"

"Absolutely not."

As Chase stepped closer to Jana and farther from Maddie, the younger woman sensed the mother's pain. "Come on, both of you," Jana said. "This isn't the time or the place. Let's go back to the hotel and sort this out."

"I'm sorry, Dad," River said, fists stuffed deep in his pockets. "Tank told me not to tell you and—"

"Tank knew about this, too?" Chase held up both hands.

"I'll never do it again, I promise," River said. "We were having such a good time playing video games and stuff."

Chase pointed at River. "Come on. I want to hear the whole story from beginning to end, and you better not leave anything out."

\* \* \* \* \*

"I wouldn't do that if I were you," Jana said, slowly shaking her head.

Tank stood outside the hotel room shared by Maddie and River. "Why? What's wrong?"

Jana folded her arms across her chest. "A little while ago the four of us ran into Jake Nathan in the practice area. Apparently, he and River had quite a little adventure the other night."

"Uh-oh." Tank winced. "How mad is he?"

"On a scale of one to ten, about a fifty."

Tank rubbed his chin in search of an excuse. "We were going to tell him — absolutely — but not until after the tournament."

"Oh, really?" Jana's voice was thick with sarcasm. "Well, instead, he got to hear the whole story along with Scotty Branch, who just happened to be standing elbow-to-elbow with Jake."

Tank squeezed his eyes shut and groaned.

"How could you keep such an important thing from him?" Jana asked, every bit as furious as if River were her own child. "He's so mad at you and Maddie that he can't see straight."

"Come on, Jana," he said, arms outstretched. "If we told him, he never would have made it in the Monday qualifier. Don't you want him to take a run at this? He needs complete and total concentration to play against the world's best golfers. You can understand that, can't you?"

"All I know is that River is the most important thing in Chase's life. He thinks that you put business above his child's welfare." She paused and lowered her voice. "I think he's right."

He sighed. "I'm going to straighten this out with him right now. He'll forget about the whole thing once I show him this." Tank held up a packet of faxed pages.

"What's that?"

"From our lawyers. Chase gets to play with Trubird clubs tomorrow."

"That was easy. What happened?" Jana asked.

"I don't know, and I don't care," he said.

"Well, good luck. You'll need it." She turned.

"Where are you going?"

"I'm going to run over to Montreux to check in at the caddie's desk. I want to make sure I'm all set for tomorrow morning. Back in an hour or two."

\* \* \* \* \*

"Do you know what I went through to get that injunction against Trubird filed?" Joe asked, running a red light at Madison and 66th Street on Manhattan's Upper East Side while barking into his speakerphone. "Why did you drop it?"

"I had to."

Joe swerved to avoid a double-parked taxi. "Why?"

"I only wanted to jerk Trubird's chain," Jake said. "Even if we keep them out of the Reno tournament, they'd get into another one sooner or later. Now everyone is clamoring to check out Trubird clubs. Look at what's going on in the stock market. We need to make it clear that those clubs are a pipe dream; that they don't work, they're poorly designed, they're technically inferior—whatever it takes for us to reclaim investor confidence. Trubird must fail, here and now, before it builds any more momentum."

"If you'd taken care of this to begin with, our stock price wouldn't be in the toilet." Joe slapped the center of the steering wheel, and raced around a station wagon with out of state plates.

"You're a gambler. Make the most of it. The stock will rebound after the finals on Sunday. Then you can cash in your options and turn a nice profit."

"I'm counting on it." Joe slammed on his brakes. "But first, let's talk about Maddie McLeary's mortgage . . ."

\* \* \* \* \*

"Excuse me." Jana addressed the man seated next to a large folding table. She was in a small foyer outside the building that housed the golf carts. "Is this where caddies check in?"

"Yeah," said the man while flipping through a listing of PGA Tour players. He reached for a pitcher of water that sat among the stacks of brochures on top of the table. "But you can't get your pinafore or your packet until tomorrow morning."

"Oh." She frowned. "What time do you open?"

He looked up and smiled. "Not me. I'm a caddie. A tournament guy should be right back to help you."

"Oh, sorry. Guess I'll wait." She slid into one of the green and white plastic chairs and checked her watch.

He half shut an eye. "You new on Tour?"

"Yes. This is my first time." She knitted her fingers.

"I can tell." He stuck out his hand. "The name's Buzz."

"I'm Jana. Which player are you with?"

"I'm looping for Johnny Hotung. How about you?"

"Chase McLeary."

His eyebrows arched. "Oh, sure, I know Chase. Great guy." He rose. "See you around, I'm going to check out the course conditions."

She hopped up. "Do you mind if I tag along?"

He shrugged. "No problem."

Jana followed her new mentor down the asphalt path that wound around the course. "I really appreciate this. I need all the help I can get."

They stopped at the first tee.

"What time does Chase go off in the morning?" Buzz asked.

"Seven-ten. He's in one of the first groups."

Buzz whistled. "That's a lucky break."

"Why?"

"We're getting half an inch of rain tonight. Chase will have some nice, slow greens tomorrow before they dry out for the later groups."

"I hadn't thought of that."

"Professional courtesy." Buzz looked around. "But, don't tell anyone I'm helping you out. My boss won't like it."

\* \* \* \* \*

The well-decorated offices of Vinny Cochera, OneSport's staff doctor, contained myriad private alcoves for the comfort and protection of its clientele. Star athletes and entertainers dressed down and took turns waiting for the discreet doctor's services.

An actress-turned-receptionist purred into a telephone headset, "Doctor Cochera's office."

"This is Mort Epstein. Put Vinny on."

"He's in with a patient, but if you'd like to hold a minute I'll be happy to—"

"I don't hold. Vinny is OneSport's staff doctor. I'm his boss. I'm your boss, too. Get him."

"Uh, right away, sir."

Mort watched twenty seconds tick by on his watch.

"Mort? What's the problem? You've got my secretary in tears," Doctor Cochera said.

"Our golfers. Are they all complying with the protocol?" Leaning back in his leather chair, Mort bit a hangnail and spit out the remnants.

Doctor Cochera closed his office door and thumbed through his key ring. "Just a second."

"I don't have all day."

"Take it easy," the doctor said. "I'm unlocking the file cabinet now. We shouldn't be discussing this on the telephone anyway."

"Discretion is one thing, paranoia's another. We're talking about beta-blockers not crack."

"Still."

Mort snorted. "They're not banned on the PGA because they're perfectly safe and legal."

"Only when used for high blood pressure and congestive heart failure," he said. "I'm quite certain the American Medical Association would object to their use for decreasing our players' heart rates and adrenaline flow simply so they can putt better."

"Big deal," Mort said. "All the big entertainers use them to minimize performance anxiety. Now, please tell me that all of my guys are using the beta-blockers. We need a good showing at the Reno-Tahoe Open tomorrow. I want everybody calm and calculating."

Doctor Cochera flipped through his notes. "Everyone but Paul Kilroy and Miles Callabrio is on the protocol."

"Why didn't you put them on the stuff?"

"That's privileged."

"I'm going to fire you if I don't get an answer right now," Mort said.

"All right." The doctor sighed. "Kilroy stopped taking them because of sexual side-effects. He couldn't keep an erection."

"Then shove some Viagra™ down his throat, and get him back on. You get paid plenty to deal with these things. Are we clear? Now what about Callabrio?"

Doctor Cochera exhaled. "No, it's too dangerous. He's a diabetic, and beta-blockers reduce blood sugar. If he takes the beta-blockers, he won't have any symptoms that his blood sugar's low. He could die."

"Look," Mort said. "Callabrio's our hottest new property, but he's got a hair-trigger temper. He needs that stuff more than anybody else. Why can't you double-up on his insulin?"

"It's not that simple. The weather conditions, his nutrition levels, everything effects his sugar level. I'd have to test his blood sugar every hole."

"I don't care." Mort pounded his desktop. "If that kid chokes on a pressure putt, and he's not on the protocol, you're fired."

# CHAPTER 11

The grass underfoot felt like plush wet carpeting. Chase inhaled and let the air of possibility fill his lungs; it was a day of new beginnings. He smiled broadly as early morning spectators jockeyed for position behind guide ropes with their Styrofoam coffee cups, cameras, and portable tripod chairs.

"You look great . . . really," Jana said.

"Very handsome," Maddie agreed.

"Thanks," Chase said. He looked down and patted his stomach. "I feel like a walking billboard."

River yawned and rubbed a lingering grain of sand from the corner of his eye. He gave Chase a thumbs-up.

"You won't get much national coverage this early in the morning, but I want the Trubird logo on every inch of you," Tank said, adjusting Chase's collar. "Just in case."

"I like the hat, but the shirt is awful," Chase said. "I hate yellow."

"Play some good golf, and I'll get you any color you want," Tank said.

The starter, a bald man in his mid-fifties, approached with a clipboard and tapped his watch. "Mr. McLeary, after the group ahead leaves the tee, you're up next. Players and caddies only, please, from this point on. Time to clear out, folks."

"You'll do great," Maddie said, head high. "I know it."

Chase recognized the look in her eyes: unwavering support. He leaned over and planted a delicate kiss on her cheek, silently thanking her for never giving up on him.

"Show 'em what you've got," Tank said, punching him on the arm.

"Good luck, Dad," River said. The twinkle in his eyes was vibrant with specks of green dancing at the edges, so beautiful, so familiar.

\* \* \* \* \*

Trip Boswyck frowned, irritated that he was unable to reach Satch at their office. Although he didn't approve of Satch's personal grooming or organizational habits, Trip never before had trouble locating the brilliant eccentric. He hung up and dialed again.

"Hi, Ally, it's Trip." A baby wailed in the background. "Sorry to call you so early. I've been trying Satch at the warehouse since five o'clock this morning, but there's no answer. Do you have any idea where he is?"

"Not really. He called me around midnight and said he was going to pull another all-nighter and not to wait up. He said he'd grab a few hours sleep on the couch. It's not even eight. Maybe he's on his way home to shower and change. Oh, hold on, I have another call."

While he waited, Trip calculated how long it would take for Satch to overnight mail two full sets of Trubird clubs along with the final version seven wood for Chase. The press conference was set for Friday night after Chase, hopefully, made the cut. They needed two demo sets for the media guys and their golf expert to try out. There was no time to lose.

"Hey." A marshal walked over to Trip. "No cell phones allowed on the course, buddy."

"It's an emergency," Trip said, eyeing the overweight hacker.

"No exceptions during the tournament. Give me the phone or I'll call security." The marshal rested one hand, the size and shape of a ham hock, on the radio clipped to his oversized belt.

Trip snapped his cellular telephone shut. "No need. I'll turn it off."

"No, I'm taking it," the guard said, a smug smile on his lips. "Claim it after six inside the clubhouse."

"Are you kidding me? I need to make some important calls. You can't just—"

"Hello, security?" The marshal spoke into his radio.

Recognizing that the last thing he needed was an official escort to the security tent, Trip tossed the marshal his phone. "Fine, take it." He hurried back to the course.

\* \* \* \* \*

"Nice par," Jana said. Golfer and caddie walked briskly from the green toward the next tee box.

"Thanks," Chase said. "But that was only the first hole. The hard part is stringing together a bunch of them."

"You can do it, boss," Jana said.

"I can, I really think I can. Being here is somehow like coming home. Do you smell that?"

"What?"

"A mixture of cut grass, coffee, cigars, hotdogs and the occasional whiff from a port-a-potty. It's the smell of being on Tour and I can't believe how much I've missed it. Pretty soon the stale aroma of keg beer will be added to the mix. Then you'll hear dead silence around the tee box followed by roars from the crowd as shots are nailed and putts are drained." Chase's words came faster. "By Sunday there'll be a mad dash from hole to hole as the leaders battle it out."

"Let's get back to reality for a minute, okay?"

"Okay."

She nodded. "I want you to focus on this next hole. It's a semi-blind, uphill par three, with a lot of trouble to the left. You've got to hit the green."

Moving left to get a better look at his target, a rich, spice-and-rum scent tantalized his nose and jarred his memory. Coco by Chanel. Terry's favorite. He still kept a tiny bottle, half-empty, hidden in his medicine cabinet. Chase turned his head. His heart skipped a beat.

Behind the gallery ropes, a tall, dark skinned woman paused to read her score sheet. She wore a straw hat, a sleeveless pink polo shirt and white shorts that showed off her shapely legs. He knew that face, knew every inch of it. She pulled one foot from a white-strapped sandal and jiggled it absent-mindedly.

She looked up and smiled, her large brown eyes shimmering. She put two hands around her ponytail and dragged her fingers through the silky mane, releasing a few loose hairs into the wind.

\* \* \* \* \*

Maddie, Tank and River fidgeted behind the ropes where only a handful of early-morning spectators looked on.

"What do you think?" Tank asked.

"He looks calm," Maddie answered. She glanced around as spectators began arriving. "Did you see him eat breakfast? His appetite was normal, and I think he slept until at least five this morning. That's a good sign. I remember before, when he was on tour, he liked to eat—" Maddie covered a gasp. The color drained from her face and her hand trembled. She reached out for River.

"Doll? What's wrong? Chase is gonna to tee off in less than a minute. What's the problem?" Tank scanned the crowd. The veins in his neck and forehead swelled and darkened. "Of all the low-down, dirty tricks."

\* \* \* \* \*

"You owe me big," Joe said to Jake.

"Where did you find her? She's perfect," Jake whispered discreetly into his cellular telephone. He stood outside the Montreux clubhouse.

"I got lucky. I scanned all the talent in OneSong's database until I found a match. She's a backup singer and part-time model. We dyed her hair from brown to black, and showed her some old video for mannerisms and clothes," Joe said.

"How long do I have her?" Jake couldn't wait to see Chase's composure shatter.

"Through Sunday," Joe said. "But I need a favor and it can't wait. I've got serious cash-flow issues. OneSport's stock price has got to rally before the market closes Friday at four. You're going to take care of this Trubird problem once and for all, right?"

"Right. As soon as Chase gets one good look at that girl, it's game-over." Jake hung up and scurried back to the course, like a pervert anxious to peek through his secret hole in the bathroom wall.

\* \* \* \* \*

"Hey, I asked you a question. Are you listening to me?" Jana touched the tip of Chase's cleat with her sneaker.

Chase felt his stomach turn. His heart pounded and his mouth grew dry. He forced himself to breathe.

"Chase? What's wrong with you?" Jana touched his arm.

"Nothing. It's nothing." He jerked free from her grasp as if she were a hornet about to impale his skin. He covered his eyes with one hand.

Like a bad psychedelic dream, the memories, both good and bad, washed over Chase. Terry on their first date; Terry, red-faced during the birth of River; Terry blowing him kisses during a golf tournament; Terry, tubes draining fluid from every orifice; Terry in a morphine-induced sleep; Terry, her head swollen and white against the plastic-lined pillow. Terry.

Chase felt clammy all over. His knees buckled. He stopped to take a sip of water, fumbled the bottle and watched it roll away.

A marshal walked over and handed it back. "Are you feeling okay?"

"I'm fine," Chase lied.

The marshal shrugged.

"Honey, you're doing great." Jana handed him a towel to mop his brow. "Come on, focus on the next hole."

Chase turned to Jana, fighting the urge to run straight back to the parking lot and drive away. "I, uh, I . . . Just give me a second." His eyes locked onto the apparition.

Tank waved Jana over to the ropes. She hustled over to meet him.

"We're in trouble," she said. "He was doing great, but the pressure came down on him like a ton of bricks. I think he's having a panic attack."

"You're right. Look over there." Tank pointed. "See the tall broad in pink?"

"Yes."

"She looks exactly like Terry, his late wife, and I mean exactly. It ain't no coincidence." Tank clenched his jaw and lowered his voice. "OneSport is bound to be behind this. You've got to get Chase's head back in the game, Jana. This kind of stunt could sink us. You're the only one allowed out there and the only one who can do it."

"Where's Maddie? She's better equipped than I am to deal with this," Jana said.

"She was pretty shaken up. Maddie ran inside the clubhouse to get herself together." He put an arm around her shoulders and squeezed hard. "Jana, it's up to you. Nobody else can get close."

"Excuse me," the marshal said to Jana. "They're waiting for your player up at the tee."

"What should I say to him?" Jana asked Tank.

"You'll know. Get going before he gets penalized for slow play." Tank chewed his lower lip. "I got an idea. I'll be right back."

"Where are you going?"

"Never mind." Tank trotted back to the clubhouse. "Just take care of him," he called over his shoulder.

\* \* \* \* \*

Jana hurried over to Chase, who couldn't take his eyes from the woman in pink. She stood between him and the growing number of onlookers. "That woman looks like Terry, doesn't she?" Jana whispered, biting back jealous pangs as she took in the high cheekbones and exotic figure.

Chase nodded, and Jana read a mixture of love, loss and desire emanating from his quivering lips as he stared.

"Do you want to get a closer look?" She asked, shifting her weight. "Go find out her name?"

Chase nodded yes and then shook his head no. "I know it's not her, but she looks so . . . so real." His lips parted as he gazed at the ghost. "Like I could reach over and—"

"And what? Go back in time? Start over?" Jana asked, fighting for her place in Chase's life. "Guess what, that's what you're doing. Right here, right now." She stamped her foot. "This is your Mulligan."

"I . . . I . . ."

"Do me a favor."

"What?"

"Look at me."

As if his neck was operated by hydraulics instead of muscles, Chase turned from the apparition.

Jana nodded as she spoke. "Do you remember why we're here?"

"Of course, I do. You can't possibly understand how hard this is." A lone tear escaped down his cheek.

Jana wiped it clean. "It all comes down to this moment." She pressed a hand against his heart. "Are you going to let these jerks manipulate your emotions? They're trying to break your concentration. Are you willing to accept failure?" She smacked the back of one hand into her other palm. "Come on, Chase. Terry was a wonderful, beautiful wife and mother." Her voice softened. "She's gone. That fraud standing over there insults her." Jana leaned in. "That's not her."

Deep wrinkles formed around his eyes and mouth. "You think I don't know that?"

"I want to help you." She stuck out her chest. "These people, OneSport, are sick to pull a stunt like this." She pushed up her sleeve. "If Terry were really here, she'd demand excellence from you. Now get your head back in the game and show them who you are." She took his face in both her hands. "Please. What's it going to be?"

\* \* \* \* \*

"Momma, let me go." River pulled his arm loose. "Are you okay?"

"I'm sorry. I know you don't remember your mother, except in pictures." Her lip twitched. "But that woman looks just like her."

"I guess." He shrugged. "Man, you really freaked out."

Maddie pressed a tissue to her nose and reached into her purse for a tube of lipstick.

"We better get back now." River fiddled with his belt buckle. "Dad's probably wondering where we are."

"This is terrible," she said. "Some really bad people want your dad to fail. They'll lose a lot of money if he plays well with Trubird clubs, and they'll do anything to stop him."

"So they sent that lady here to bug him?"

"Yes."

"Dad will be okay. I mean, Mom died so long ago."

"Honey, I hope you're right."

"Besides, he really likes Jana now," River said.

Maddie tentatively probed. "And you? How do you like her?"

"She's pretty cool, I guess." River shrugged and looked at his feet. "I mean, she likes the same music I do, and she's kind of funny. And Dad's sure been in a good mood since they've been, you know, together, or whatever."

Paging Maddie McLeary. Paging Maddie McLeary. Please pick up the courtesy phone in the lobby, the intercom announced.

Maddie and River walked to a wall mounted telephone.

"This is Maddie McLeary."

"Stand by. I'll connect your party," the operator said.

"Maddie?"

"Missy? Is that you? This isn't a good time. I've got to—"

"Maddie, listen. I went by your house to feed Chester. There's a moving van loading up all of your furniture, and a 'for sale' sign in your yard."

"What?"

"You've got to come back here right away. The guy in charge said he was from your new mortgage company. He said they bought your loan on foreclosure. Maddie, why didn't you come to me? I would have given you the money."

"I don't have a new mortgage company, and I have never ever missed a payment. There must be a mistake. I mean, I might have mailed a couple of checks barely inside the grace period, but I always paid them. They can't just sell my house. I haven't been notified about any of this."

"I don't know what to say."

"Missy, give me the man's name and phone number so I can straighten this out from here. There's no way I can leave right now."

"The company is called OneSport Financial. They also bought the loan on that T-shirt shop you used to own on the boardwalk. He said it was a two-for-one deal."

The T-shirt Shop.

The bottom dropped out of Maddie's stomach. "Oh, no. I think I know how they did it."

"What do you mean? How could they pull this off? You're one of the savviest realtors around."

"Residential, yes, but not with commercial properties. I bought that T-shirt shop to use as a tax shelter, so I rented it out for a small loss. Remember? It's nestled in between a few shops not too far off the boardwalk. It's cheap and it didn't require much rental income to offset the mortgage."

Missy winced. "I remember that after Chase's accident you needed money for medical and legal bills. I thought you sold it."

"Not exactly. I refinanced it and used my house as collateral. Soon after that, a big developer came into the area and put up a competing strip mall with better access to roads. Retailers followed the foot traffic away from the old boardwalk area, and my shop became worthless. I decided to stop making payments on the mortgage and execute a deed in lieu of foreclosure. It was the easiest way to be rid of it. That way the bank would simply take the T-shirt shop and let me out of the loan. I was due at the bank next week to sign the paperwork."

"Oh, no."

"Oh, yes. I'm guessing OneSport Financial offered the bank an above-market price for my mortgage on the shop," Maddie said. "Then the bank would have readily accepted. Now they're calling my home mortgage, since I tied it to the commercial loan which is undisputedly in default."

"I can't believe this."

"Missy, I need you to do something for me." Maddie slowed her voice. "I have no intention of ever giving up my house."

"Name it." Missy said, strong and clear.

"You have to really, really carefully read through the foreclosure section of every local paper for the last week. See if any ads were run publishing the foreclosure of my house. I need to confirm whether or not OneSport gave adequate notice before foreclosing. If they didn't, I can keep it."

"I'll do it right now, but get back here fast so you can fix this thing," Missy said. "I'll bring Chester to my house."

"Thanks. I'm going to call Burt at the office. I'm sure he can help me."

"Don't shoot the messenger, but your big sale fell through."

Maddie squeezed her eyes shut. "Not the two million dollar house. I need that sale."

"Sorry, but I ran into Burt Monday night. He said the house was chock-full of mold. It failed inspection."

"Not mold again."

"Hon, all I can say is you better get your butt back here before some rich retiree turns your living room into a bingo and bridge parlor."

* * * * *

Standing on the second tee box, Chase gripped and re-gripped his club until Jana handed him a new glove. She took away the soaked one, and stood between Chase and Terry's look-a-like.

The double waited until Chase drew back his club before she moved closer to him.

Chase stopped mid-swing and backed off his ball. A dark stripe ran down the back of his shirt, and widened in the middle where his shirt tucked into his trousers.

Jana glared at the woman in pink and stepped over to Chase. "Focus. You're okay," she whispered. "Stay focused."

Chase again hesitated over the ball, fiddling with his club. He took a deep breath, pulled back his club and made a horrific swing, his right knee collapsing as he turned. The small gallery was silent as the white ball streaked far to the left.

"That'll play, as long as it's in the bunker and not in the ravine." Jana grabbed the club and urged him on. "Come on."

On his way to search for the errant shot, Chase couldn't help himself. He took a sidelong glance at Terry's double. She pushed back her sunglasses, and stared up at the blimp floating in the sky. She was beautiful, healthy and young. Maybe too young. Needing further proof or disproof, Chase stole another look. This woman was in her early twenties, not thirties as Terry would be if alive today. And her hair, there was something about it. It was black but without the hint of blue he knew so well.

"Dad, wait up."

"River? What are you doing?"

He wore a blue vest over his polo shirt, and his hair was neatly combed. River exchanged places with the young boy who carried the name and score sign for Chase's twosome.

"Tank arranged it. I get to follow you and your partner around all day. Isn't this cool? You're supposed to be twelve to carry the sign, but they said it was okay since I'm eleven and a half."

Jana walked back to Chase. "I found your ball. Lucky break. It landed outside the left edge of the bunker. Hey, River, what's going on?"

"I'm Dad's official sign carrier. Don't worry, Dad, I won't let that lady wreck your game. I'm here to watch out for you."

Chase looked at his son, so young and full of life. There was Terry's legacy, standing right in front of him. He pulled River and Jana into an embrace.

Tank and Maddie snuck up behind the look-a-like.

"You make me sick," Tank said.

"Buzz off." The woman turned. "I'm just doing my job."

"What's OneSport paying you to impersonate my dead daughter-in-law?" Maddie said. "It's blood money."

The woman shrugged. "I don't know what you're talking about. Leave me alone."

Tank leaned within inches of her nose and scowled. "What are you, some second rate actress? Honey, you'll never work again after the press finds out what you're trying to do to poor Chase. I'll bet your boss didn't tell you that Chase's wife died of cancer, lost all her hair, and never knew her kid. Do you really think someone's going to hire you after this pathetic performance? You'll be lucky to get a telemarketing gig."

The woman stepped away from Tank. He and Maddie stayed glued to the woman's side. Jake approached, flipped up his sunglasses, and began arguing with Tank. Terry's double escaped Tank and headed for the gallery, but Maddie scampered after her, spouting an Olympic-grade guilt complex.

Unaware of the drama unfolding on the sidelines, Chase swallowed. "Okay, guys. Let's do this thing."

"Ready when you are." Jana handed him a pitching wedge.

"I've got a pocketful of numbers, Dad," River said. "Let's see some low scores."

Chase took one practice swing and then gently pitched the ball within five feet of the hole. He made the short putt to save par.

"Nicely done," Jana said.

River gave his Dad a discreet thumbs-up and checked the sign. Chase was even after two holes.

Jana eyed the brouhaha and winced. "Do you want me to say something to the officials?"

Chase frowned. "Like what? That there's a woman who resembles my dead wife and I want her thrown off the course? That my ex-agent kidnapped my kid, and is trying to decimate my concentration?"

"Yeah." She smiled and thrust a hand on her hip. "Why not?"

"Because golf is a game of nerves, and it's my job to ignore everything except that little white ball in front of me. There are plenty of ways to get inside a player's head, if he lets you. Step on his lie, move slightly during his back-swing, jingle pocket change, sneeze at the wrong moment; people have been doing stuff like that for years, but the best players learn to shake it off. None of that stuff matters, not if you're confident in yourself and your game."

"Your color's back."

"Thanks. I'm not going to let you or River down. No matter what else they throw at me. Plus, I've got an idea."

"I'm listening." Jana tucked a hair behind her ear.

"We're going to beat these guys at their own game," Chase said.

"How?"

"You look good in yellow, right?"

"Huh?"

"I need you to get a message to Tank."

* * * * *

Jake felt his cellular telephone vibrate. He surreptitiously inserted the tiny earpiece, and slipped his hand inside his pants pocket to answer it.

It was Joe.

"You better have good news for me," Joe said.

Jake moved away from a nearby marshal and pretended to tie his shoe. He tucked the tiny headset microphone underneath the arm of his sunglasses. "Patience, have patience," he whispered.

"Screw patience. I need money, and our stock has already slipped another three-quarter point this morning. I close on my Hamptons house next week, and my balance sheet's in the toilet."

"That girl," Jake said. "The one you sent. She didn't rattle him as badly as I'd hoped."

"No kidding. I'm watching the Golf Channel right now and Chase is even par after five holes. He's not rattled at all. Did you see that putt on the third? He almost made birdie. And who arranged for his kid to carry the score sign? The news guys are eating that up."

"You have got to be kidding me."

"Jake? What are you . . . oh, great. That's great." Joe stared at the television screen.

"Are you seeing what I'm seeing?" Jake asked.

"Yeah. The camera just picked up two men and a woman. They're all dressed head to toe in canary yellow outfits, with the Trubird name and logo plastered everywhere. Now the woman is handing Chase's caddie a yellow shirt and visor, and she's putting it on over her jumpsuit. Unbelievable."

Jake rubbed his forehead. "What about Trubird's production capability? Did you stop them from manufacturing any more clubs?"

"You could say that. We don't have to worry about mass production, but there was a complication," Joe said. "Call me from a landline, and I'll fill you in. For now, you need to do something about McLeary. Take it up a notch."

They hung up. Jake pulled out his pairings sheet, and scanned the names and starting times. Johnny Hotung was scheduled to tee off in half an hour. He still had time. Jake hurried back to the practice tee and inspected the crowd. "Hey, Buzz, how's it going?"

"Be right there, Mr. Nathan." Buzz joined Jake at the ropes. The caddie looked over his shoulder to where his boss, Johnny Hotung, stood practicing putts.

With caddie fees ranging from five to fifteen percent of a player's earnings, and purse sizes continuing to increase, competition for bags was fierce; Buzz was hungry for a bigger piece of the pie. Unfortunately, among the hundred and fifty or so regular caddies on the PGA Tour, Buzz ranked in the bottom quarter.

Today's caddies needed encyclopedic knowledge of everything about a golf course, not simply distances between holes. Picking the right club could mean the difference between taking home a check, and taking home a big check. Buzz was ambitious, but he lacked instinct. Knowing when to encourage a player and when to remain silent was something he would never understand. He relied too heavily on yardage books instead of forging a personal relationship with his player, resulting in both parties suffering.

"Hi, Buzz. Sorry you didn't make the final cut to carry Callabrio's bag. Your resume certainly is impressive," Jake lied, noting the dirty sneakers and uneven shave. "I take it you got the check I left you."

Buzz looked back again to ensure Hotung was out of earshot. "Sure did. Consider me your eyes and ears out here this week. I'm guessing your caddies probably already tell you most of the dirt." He licked his lips. "What exactly are you looking for?"

"Stay close to Chase McLeary. Let me know everything you can about him."

"You got it." Buzz scratched his armpit. "Mr. Nathan, I'd do anything to get on board with a top tier player. Everybody knows you have the best talent out there. Plenty of your caddies are pulling in more than half-a-million bucks a year, and I want to be one of them. Give me a chance."

Jake folded his arms. "You're not happy with Hotung?"

"He's a chump, hasn't made many cuts all summer, and only finished top ten once." Buzz rubbed the front pocket of his pants. "I can barely pay the rent, you know what I mean?"

"Come talk to me after your round. I think we can do business together, if you're willing to help me out with something."

"Name it. I'll do anything, anything at all."

"Meet me outside the bag room at seven o'clock tonight," Jake said. "We can talk then."

# CHAPTER 12

"Hey, Chase." Scotty Branch joined Chase, Jana and River on the practice tee. "I see you shot even par for the day. Not bad for your first tournament back on Tour."

Chase smiled. "I guess it's a good thing I didn't withdraw like you suggested yesterday."

"I was just fishing." The reporter shrugged. "Anyway, you were right about those clubs complementing your game. No offense, but your long game has never been your strong suit. I compared your stats from prior years on Tour with today's round. You're hitting every fairway, a big improvement."

"Thanks." He waggled his club. "Wait until tomorrow."

"You've got quite a cheering section. I've never seen so much yellow." Scotty shook his head. Maddie and Tank huddled behind him.

"Get used to it. The color of Trubird is the color of the future," Chase said.

Chase put his arm around River. "Scotty, what's the skinny? Any prediction on the weekend cut line yet?" He raised an eyebrow, determined to be one of the players whose score after Friday's round was below the deadly cut line; only those players would survive to play over the weekend.

"Too early to tell, but the greens definitely dried out this afternoon. I'd say you're in the hunt. The leaders are at four under, but I've seen a few big numbers roll in. I think we're looking at minus one after thirty six holes, but who knows?"

"Tank. There you are," Trip said. His tone was clipped and he barely acknowledged Chase and Jana.

Scotty turned to Tank. "You promised our people a demo set of clubs. Can I see them now? We're running a segment on equipment in tomorrow's broadcast. Maybe even a feature on Trubird."

"Hang on a minute." Trip stepped between the two men. "Tank, can I talk to you?"

"Trip? Are you nuts?" Tank used one hand to make a winding motion at his temple. "Give him the clubs so they can do a feature. Didn't Satch send them yet?"

"Come here." Trip pulled Tank away from the group for a private conversation at the fringe of the horseshoe shaped practice area.

Tank broke from the discussion. "Scotty," he called, his tone more somber than before. "How long are you going to want the clubs?"

"I don't know," Scotty said. "A couple hours. Hey, do you want to promote them or not? I'm going out on a limb for you guys. Nobody," he said, pausing to make a circle with his thumb and index finger. "I mean nobody wants Trubird to get any air time." He collapsed the circle and tapped his notebook. "This is your one chance."

Chase searched Tank's eyes. *Why aren't you jumping all over this?*

"You're right. I'll bring them by the media tent in fifteen minutes," Tank said.

Chase waited until Scotty's attention was on another player. "What's going on with you two?" he asked Tank and Trip.

"Come on, kid," Tank said to River. "I'll buy you a snack from the vending machines."

Maddie held up a finger. "Don't leave him alone for one minute."

"Oh, Momma." River tipped back his head and rolled his eyes.

"No need to worry about that." Tank pulled the boy into a headlock and half-dragged, half-chased him to the snack area.

"Last night," Trip began. He squeezed his hands together and his neck twitched just a hair as he spoke. "The Trubird warehouse burned to the ground. We lost everything, our design details, our testing notes, and every piece of equipment. The fire department suspects arson, but they don't have any leads."

Jana covered her mouth.

Chase's knees grew weak. Could this really be happening?

"There's more." Trip cleared his throat. "Satch was asleep on the couch when the blaze started."

"Is he all right?" Chase asked, aware that he was unable to feel his fingertips from squeezing the club so hard.

"No." Trip's voice cracked. "He's dead."

Maddie gasped.

"Smoke inhalation killed him before the firemen could get him out." Trip lowered his eyes. "Not a burn on his body but the paramedics couldn't resuscitate."

Silence filled the space as Trip's revelation sunk in.

Chase felt blood pulsing through his chest. His voice quivered as he spoke. "It's got to be OneSport." He bent over, hands on his knees. "I think I'm going to be sick."

Jana rubbed his back. "What should we do? Tell the police?"

"They'd never believe us," Trip said. "We've got no proof. Maybe the arson investigator will turn up something."

River raced into their midst, a bright orange mustache above his upper lip. "The candy machine's broken," he said. "All I got was a soda."

"River, go hit a few balls," Tank said, gesturing. "Show us what you got."

The boy jumped at the chance.

"Maddie." Tank licked his lips. "Tell them about your house."

"What about it?" Chase frowned. "You better not be keeping anything else from me."

Maddie filled them in. "I put my heart and soul into that place. I can't lose it, and I could never afford the same thing in today's market." Her eyes welled up.

"Okay." Tank held up a hand. "One crisis at a time. Maddie, let's talk after Missy gets back to you. If we're lucky, OneSport may have left us a loophole."

She nodded.

"What are you going to tell Scotty Branch?" Chase asked. "We don't have any clubs to give him."

"Sure we do," Tank answered. "Yours."

Chase put a hand to his chest. "Mine is the only set left!"

Trip nodded. "Exactly. We'll let Scotty poke around with them for an hour or two, and then you can have them back."

"But I need to practice." He took two steps back.

"Chase, this is the ballgame," Trip said, leaning forward. "You can spare an hour. Go get some dinner. I'll have them back in your hands before dessert." He motioned for Jana to hand over the clubs.

Jana looked to Chase. He nodded.

"One hour; that's it," Chase said. "And don't let them out of your sight."

\* \* \* \* \*

Inside a ground floor meeting room of the Montreux Clubhouse, conference tables were lined with golf products, apparel and promotional literature. Cameramen, reporters and production assistants milled around the room, chatting about the first round scores.

"Well," Scotty Branch asked the network's golf equipment technician, "what do you think?"

The tech swung a Trubird seven iron and made contact with a practice ball tethered to a tee. A solid hit, the ball twirled around a metal base, and a three-inch string prevented it from flying through the conference room window. Numbers and letters flashed on a projector attached to the practice tee. "I'm impressed. Can I take them out for a spin?"

"I'll put in a good word for you, but I doubt it. Now come on. It's almost seven, and I'm on deadline. What's the scoop?"

The technician put down the seven iron and picked up the Trubird putter. "These grips are awesome." He rolled a ball up and down a contoured mat into a practice hole. "If it were a woman, I'd marry this putter."

Scotty sighed and took a seat on the edge of the table. "I'm waiting."

"Keep your shirt on. I'm almost done, but this is heavy conjecture. Without playing eighteen, I'm not gonna stick my neck out too far."

"Look, Trip Boswyck will be back any minute to collect them. Maybe tomorrow he can spare a set for you to monkey around with. I'll see what I can do. But for right now, what have you got?"

"Fair enough. First, I checked all of the obvious things, etchings, weight, etc., against the rulebook and the whole Trubird set meets USGA specifications. Here, look at the Trubird driver." He put the putter down and grabbed the large club. "I compared it with the two industry leaders for touring pros. I'm getting better energy transfer and accuracy, at least theoretically, with the Trubird club."

Scotty scribbled in his notebook. "How can you tell?"

"Experience, plus I plotted my shots with the test machine. It's not perfect; but, since we're not on an actual course, it's the only decent way to estimate the projected trajectory of my shot."

"What else?"

"Here, I made you a few notes." He handed Scotty a piece of paper.

Skimming the one page summary, his finger stopped midway down the sheet. "What's this about materials?"

"Unknown. That's the point. I can't quite pinpoint the mixture of materials they used, but it's a whole new compound, and it's awesome. These clubs feel so good. They're like nothing I've ever swung. You said this new company, Trubird, is selling these sticks cheap, right?"

"Bargain basement. So?"

"Man, if these guys go public they'll be the darlings of Wall Street, and the death of everybody else in the golf industry."

Scotty rubbed his pen against his chin. "Yeah, don't think the big guys aren't gunning for them. I wonder . . ."

"You wonder what?"

"Nothing," Scotty slid off the table. "Clean them up and put them back in the bag."

"Taking off?"

"I'm headed for a pot of coffee and my laptop. I'll check in with you tomorrow morning around six."

"Sure wish I could score a set of these clubs." He reached for the head covers.

"Ask Boswyck when he gets here," Scotty called over his shoulder as he left the media center. "And get me a set, too."

A few minutes later, an old friend interrupted the technician. He looked up. "Great to see you, buddy. What's it been, two years ago in Augusta?" He stuck out a hand. "Where's my favorite camera guy been hiding?"

"Taking pictures on the ladies' tour. I had a thing going, but it didn't work out, if you know what I mean." He winked. "You still dissecting golf clubs for the network?"

"You got it." He folded his arms across his chest. "But now I'm the head tech."

"Good for you. Let's go grab a beer and catch up."

"How about the lobby bar? I'm waiting for somebody to pick up this set of clubs, but he should be here any minute."

"What are you, the head tech or the official babysitter?" The friend said with a laugh. "Come on, man, I'm dying of thirst. Leave the clubs here. Nobody's going to bother them. You need a press pass to get in, for crying out loud."

"Yeah, but—"

"I can taste it now, a nice cold frosty one."

The tech grinned. "So you've been on the girls' tour. I thought they were all gay. Which one were you dating?"

The man shifted his camera bags from one shoulder to the other. "Who said anything about one? Come on and I'll fill you in." He lowered his voice. "Plus, I've got some fresh stuff about your old boss and one of the player's wives. You're going to eat this up."

"I think you're full of it, but if you're buying, I'm in." The technician tucked the clubs under a display table and penned a quick note for Trip. After all, he didn't have all day to wait for the pompous ex-Commissioner.

\* \* \* \* \*

Buzz flashed his identification badge as he exited Montreux's golf bag storage room.

"They're not inside," Buzz whispered. "I checked everywhere. Maybe Chase is still using them."

"No," Jake said. "He and his caddie left the range more than two hours ago without them. Did you check everywhere?"

"Top to bottom, and they're not there, but we might as well check over at the media center. That's where a lot of equipment is being demo'd for tomorrow's equipment special. I'll head over there if you want, but I'm sure Chase wouldn't give his actual playing set to the television techs," Buzz said.

Unless he didn't have another set to spare, Jake thought, considering the possibility that Trubird equipment might be on the brink of success. If the sports techs blessed those clubs in front of millions of viewers, Chase's performance would be irrelevant.

"Buzz, I'll meet you over there in fifteen minutes," Jake said.

"Sure, Mr. Nathan. And then can we talk about, you know, what you promised? I'm sticking my neck way out for OneSport. I think I've proven myself."

"Absolutely, Buzz, but first things first."

# CHAPTER 13

"You look terrible," Maddie said.

"I didn't sleep much," Tank answered. "Kept thinking about Satch. Such a young guy, nice wife, promising career, it's eating me up." He reached for a croissant on the courtesy breakfast table set up for players and VIP's in Montreux's lobby.

"I'm so sorry." Maddie placed a hand on his shoulder. "When is the funeral? I think we should all go."

Tank gripped a coffee cup and filled it to the brim. "Why can't they give you a decent mug? I hate drinking out of these thimbles." He drained it and poured a second. "Services are Monday morning."

River, wearing his score carrier's pinafore, returned from the buffet with a plate full of Danish. "Not bad, but they don't have any sprinkle donuts." He stuffed a cheese filled croissant into his mouth.

"Kid, are you going to the electric chair?" Tank asked. He cracked his first smile of the day as he watched River plow through his second breakfast.

"Don't worry about me," River mumbled.

"After what happened yesterday," Maddie said. "It's a wonder Chase isn't dead last. All things considered, I think he did very well."

"Yeah, but he'll have to go low today to make the cut," Tank answered.

McLeary's Mulligan

"I know. What time did you say they're airing the new golf equipment special?" Maddie asked.

"Right after the cut line is predicted, but even if he makes it to the weekend, there's no guarantee that Trubird will be featured on the television special. Last night when Trip picked up Chase's clubs in the media center, Scotty Branch was already gone, so we don't know if his review is good or bad," Tank said.

"He was gone?"

"Yep, and Trip was pretty hot about it, too. He walked in to find Chase's clubs leaning against the wall where anybody could have taken them. He kept them in his room overnight to be safe," Tank said.

"Stolen clubs, that's all we need." Maddie shook her head.

Jana whisked into the room, frowning as she approached the threesome. "Chase's putter is missing."

\* \* \* \* \*

"Mr. Nathan?" Buzz leaned against a tree and whispered into his cell phone. "Have you got a minute? Can we talk about, you know, my situation?"

"This isn't a good time," Jake answered. He cradled the phone against his shoulder and snapped open the morning paper. "I've got a bunch of calls to make, and I'm already late for my meeting with Kilroy down at the practice tee."

"You're not blowing me off, are you? I'm sorry I couldn't get the whole set of Trubird clubs. It was bad timing. Boswyck picked them up before I got down there, but at least I found the putter lying around," Buzz said. "Maybe tonight I could—"

"No," Jake barked, but then thought better of it. His voice turned silky and conciliatory. "Buzz, baby, you're my guy. Of course, I'm not blowing you off, I'm just really busy. Tell you what, today's pairing sheet says that Hotung tees off at nine thirty-seven, right?"

"That sounds right."

"Okay, then. Your loop should be over by one-thirty at the latest. Call my cell after you're through for the day. First we talk about finishing the job you started, and then we'll discuss finding you a permanent place with OneSport. Sound good?"

Buzz punched a fist into his open palm. "Great, thanks Mr. Nathan."

Jake refolded the paper. "Something else."

"Name it."

"Chase McLeary's caddie."

"Jana? What about her?"

"You talked to her the other day, but does she trust you yet?"

"Like a brother."

\* \* \* \* \*

"This is all your fault." Chase paced back and forth in the clubhouse lobby. "I never should have listened to you. I never should have let those clubs out of my sight."

"Hey, if it weren't for me, you wouldn't be here at all." Trip put a finger to his lips. "So calm down."

"Calm down? How many more things can go wrong? I can't take it anymore!" Rivulets of sweat ran down his back and pooled above his belt.

"If those veins in your neck get any bigger you're gonna look like Frankenstein," Tank said.

Jana winced. "Guys, all of you, try to get a grip. Let's talk this out." She pulled off her visor and rubbed her damp forehead.

"There's nothing to talk about," Trip said, teeth clenched. "The putter is gone. I checked with Scotty Branch, who checked with his technician. The tech thinks he may have left the putter on the table. Someone must have walked off with it."

"Somebody . . . as if we don't know who," Tank muttered.

"And we don't have a spare?" Maddie asked.

"Not with us," Tank said. "Dick is down at the warehouse site now going through the rubble from the fire. If there's anything worth salvaging, he'll overnight it to us."

"It doesn't matter now, it's too late. I tee off in an hour," Chase said, twisting his chin with the palm of his hand until his neck cracked.

"Why can't you use your old putter?" River asked.

"Yeah, why can't you?" Jana echoed.

"Because . . . because I can't," Chase said. "Everyone's expecting me to use Trubird's putter, and Trubird's putter is better than mine."

"Chase, your putting has always been the best part of your game," Maddie argued. "Admit it. You don't need Trubird's club to compete on the greens."

"Yes, I do. I really do." His face was pale and he rubbed his aching stomach with one hand.

Jana put her hand over his. "Your mom's right. I know you can do this with your own putter."

He pushed her hand away. "No, you don't."

"Yes, I do."

"No, you don't! You don't know anything about me!"

Making a sound that resembled a hot air balloon pierced with a machete, Jana turned on her heel and walked slowly and deliberately from the room.

Tank and Trip stared at the floor.

Maddie's eyes blazed. "That was totally unnecessary."

"Yeah, Dad. Why are you being so mean to Jana?" River asked.

Chase covered his ears with both hands. "Give me a minute, will you? Mom, stay here."

Tank shrugged. "I'll go get your old putter. It's your call. Come on, River. It's almost show-time."

"I'll check in with Dick," Trip said. He walked away with Tank and River.

River took a few steps and then ran back.

"Dad?"

Chase pulled his hands from his ears. "Yes?"

"It's like you always say. Drive for show, putt for dough." River winked.

"I guess you do listen to me."

"Sometimes." He ran down the hall to catch up with Tank.

Scotty Branch turned the corner carrying a paper cup and a file folder. Multiple passes hung around his neck from brightly colored cords.

"Morning, Chase. How do you feel today? Ready to give those new clubs a workout?" A strong citrus scent emanated from the sportscaster. His tan was smooth and even.

Maddie and Chase exchanged looks.

"Something wrong?" Scotty asked.

"Not at all. I, ah, I'm looking forward to a solid round. Hey, how'd you like the clubs?" Chase asked.

"My program director is putting the finishing touches on my review right now. I don't want to spoil the surprise, but today just might be the day Trubird makes it onto the map. Of course, you have some work to do if you're going to make the cut," Scotty answered.

"Watch me and see."

"Break a leg." Scotty continued down the hall and exited the clubhouse.

Maddie squeezed Chase's arm. "I can't wait to tell Tank. It sounds like he loved the clubs."

"Don't count your chickens."

Maddie's mouth hung open. "What is wrong with you? You're about to get everything you wanted."

"Mom, I'm scared."

"I know you are, but that's part of it."

"Part of what?"

"Part of the game, and I don't mean golf. I'll admit, everything that's going on is pretty over the top." Maddie rubbed the tender skin at the nape of her neck. "But, there you have it. Life is unpredictable. Nobody knows that better than you do."

Chase wiped his sweaty hands on the back of his pants. "I didn't mean it, what I said to Jana."

"I know you didn't. That was the pressure talking." She pursed her lips. "But you need to make it right with her."

"Yeah. With my luck she's probably on her way to the airport."

"Don't bet on it."

"I love her, and I want to spend every minute with her. I'm terrified of letting her down. I'm in way over my head here, and you know it."

Maddie nodded. "Maybe, but I don't care if you make the cut or not, and neither does Jana." She folded her arms. "Nothing is worth losing her."

"But, what if—"

"Stop it. No 'what ifs'. You're too old for that."

Chase hugged Maddie tightly.

"You're right. Mom, I—"

"Don't say anything else. You know what to do." She shoved him. "Go."

\* \* \* \* \*

Jake found Paul Kilroy preening amid a small group of reporters.

"Paul, do you attribute your course-tying round yesterday to the fact that many of the top players decided to skip this year's tournament in favor of the World Golf Championships?" one of the reporters asked.

"No, not at all." Smallish at five feet nine inches, he paused to run a hand over his bulging biceps. "It's all the strength training. I've been playing great this season. I'm hitting every fairway and my approach shots, well, they speak for themselves. Although, I will say that it's nice not having Tiger Woods playing behind me."

"What about Callabrio and Watts?" another reporter quipped.

"Callabrio? That hothead?" Kilroy threw back his head and laughed. "I heard he almost whacked a heckler yesterday. And I left Watts in the locker room praying to the porcelain gods."

The reporters sniggered. "There's quite a rivalry going between you and Miles Callabrio. Same score, same agents, same nerves of steel around the carpet," one prompted.

"Yeah, and I used to date his wife."

Everyone laughed.

Jake patted Kilroy on the back. "That's it, guys. Paul needs to hit the practice range. You can watch him this afternoon at 2:07." The reporters shuffled off.

"Boy, I've never seen you turn away publicity before," Paul said. "Hey, what's that?"

Jake handed him a putter. The logo was stripped from the end of the grip and thin green tape was wound around the shaft.

"Something special."

"Feels good. Nice weight to it." Paul Kilroy turned the club around in his hands. "What're these grips made of? I've never seen anything like them."

"It's a prototype putter that we've been working on. Top secret," Jake lied. "I want you to practice with it for a few hours and use it this afternoon during your round."

"Jake, I'm in the lead for crying out loud. I'm not going to suddenly switch putters," Kilroy protested.

"Try it out. I'll come back in an hour."

Kilroy shrugged. "Okay, but don't get your hopes up."

"Hey, I made you." Jake leaned in. "You work for me, remember?"

Paul Kilroy flinched. "You . . . you can't talk to me—"

Jake punched Kilroy in the arm. "Gotcha."

"Don't do that," Kilroy frowned. "For a minute, I thought you were serious."

\* \* \* \* \*

"Dick? Are you there?" Trip held his left hand over his left ear and pressed the hotel bedroom phone tightly to the right side of his head.

"Trip?" the muffled voice said.

"Yeah, I can barely hear you."

"Hang on, it's the bulldozer. Just a sec." Dick walked through the rubble at Trubird's former warehouse site and sat inside his sedan. "There," Dick said, slamming shut the car door to insulate from the noise. "That better?"

"Yeah. What's going on?"

Dick's exhale was half groan and half sigh. "Police and fire department are still here along with the insurance investigators. They suspect arson, but they're still collecting evidence." Sweat dripped down his temples. He turned the key and cranked the air conditioning.

"Tell me something good," Trip said.

"Can't." He opened the neck of his sport shirt. "It's bad, really bad. The warehouse is leveled. Everything is gone. I couldn't salvage squat." The acrid smell of fire and rot hung in the air.

Trip groaned.

Dick tilted the air vents towards his head. "I know we've got backup files for the designs and all the patent paperwork, right?"

"Yeah." Trip's voice softened. "But rebuilding will take time and money."

"I don't have any!" Dick pulled his sticky shirt away from his chest. "Trip, I'm too old to be this broke. I don't have two nickels to rub together, and I've got kids in college. I'm about to default on my mortgages, and the bank says I'm too big a risk to refinance. Tank is in the same boat." Dick touched his head to the steering wheel. "We're finished."

"Take it easy." Trip said. "I can loan you enough to get by, but you'll have to sign a note."

Dick picked up his head. "You mean it?"

"Tally up what you need and get back to me."

"You'll have it by noon."

"Wait a minute. I'm sending you some paperwork. Sign it, fax it to me here at Montreux, and then I'll wire you the money."

"I don't know what to say." Dick kissed the phone.

"Tell me about Ally, how's she holding up?"

"Not good. She's a total mess, and she needs money for Satch's funeral. Also, I guess you loaned him some money, too. She found the paperwork and wants to know how much his share is worth."

"I'll call her later and see if we can work something out. Right now we've got another problem. Chase is playing without his Trubird putter. It disappeared yesterday, and I think OneSport grabbed it."

"We're goners." Dick wiped the sweat from his upper lip.

"No, the kid can putt. We're so close right now I can taste it." Trip smacked his lips. "After how well he played in the qualifier, Trubird is nearly afloat. All we need to cinch the deal is for Scotty Branch to feature us on network television. That will make all the difference. I have no intention of walking away from Reno empty handed. I swear on my life that we'll see a big payoff."

Dick looked through the sunroof. "Please make it soon."

# CHAPTER 14

"Joe, the auditors are on the phone again. They've been calling all morning. They sound really ticked," Tonya said into the intercom.

"I don't care," Joe said from behind his locked door. "Take another message."

"If you say so . . ."

Joe pulled the half glasses from his nose and rubbed his weary eyes. His stomach growled. He tried to remember the last time he'd eaten a meal not purchased from the vending machine.

Every inch of Joe's normally immaculate desk was covered with financial documents. Piles of reports lined not only the desk, but also the tops of the file cabinets and the conference table. More stacks of paper sat in linear rows along the carpet, from the side of his desk all the way over to the door.

For the past three days, he'd been crunching numbers in search of an answer to OneSport's current financial reporting problems. Since signing on as comptroller, Joe regularly dispatched any and all problems dealing with money, but this situation was, by far, the biggest test of his skills and ingenuity.

The Dow Jones ticker flashed across Joe's computer screen. OneSport shares were down another half point.

Joe folded his hands, extended them, and cracked his knuckles. The plan he devised for resolving this unpleasant situation was truly ironic. It was also, in short, a gamble.

From his detailed research, he knew that Trubird Group had solicited every major sports company to invest in its product, without success. In the wake of the dot-com bust era, none was willing to fork up the substantial venture capital Trubird needed. They were bleeding cash.

For all his deviousness, Joe had not counted on Trubird's low cost clubs getting any positive media attention. This unexpected twist of fate had thrown a major monkey wrench into Joe's carefully laid plans. If golfers industry-wide began to question whether OneSport's high-priced golf equipment was truly worth the money, every other division would be vulnerable to similar scrutiny. And OneSong products and profits would surely follow. On top of their accounting problems, the potential results would devastate the well-paid partners, and Joe wasn't about to let that happen.

The vision behind Trubird clubs was to create a superior product at a fraction of the going market price. Trubird wanted everyone, rich or poor, to play golf with minimal cash outlay for clubs. A nice thought, but then again, altruism never pays. Joe was certain that somebody should profit from Trubird's design improvements, so long as that somebody was OneSport.

Hidden behind one of their fully owned companies, Joe intended to convince the Trubird shareholders that their company was a lost cause, and dangle some cash in front of them for the design patents. Next, Trubird clubs would be reborn as OneSport's newest and best product line. Joe planned to price them over and above OneSport's other clubs. So much for bargains.

First, however, he had to make sure that public interest in Trubird died at the Reno-Tahoe Open. It was imperative that Chase McLeary perform badly enough that no one would give Trubird a second thought.

Joe reached for the telephone.

"Roger, it's Joe O'Hara. Counselor, I need you to clear your calendar for an urgent matter."

"Good timing. I'm not due in court until two. What's up?"

"Remember Excelsior Investments?"

"Sure, your newest venture capital company. But I don't recall there being any activity since we set it up."

"It's about to go active. I want you to immediately make an inquiry on Excelsior's behalf. We're looking to make a purchase, but it's got to be very, very discreet. If anyone catches a whiff of OneSport's involvement, we won't get to first base. No one can find out anything about Excelsior from public records, or any other way, right?"

"Yes. That's what you wanted, complete anonymity, right?"

"Right. Now, here's what I want you to do."

\* \* \* \* \*

Chase found Jana re-cleaning his clubs.

"Jana. I'm sorry I snapped at you." He took the club from her hand, slipped it into the bag, and put both hands on her shoulders.

She shook them off. "It's okay." Her voice was softer than usual, and she refused to look him in the eye.

"No, it isn't." Chase took both of her hands. "I was a jerk, and I'm sorry. It'll never happen again. You do know me. Somehow you've always known me, and I don't ever want to hurt you again." He rubbed his thumbs on top of hers.

Jana pulled one hand free and twirled a loose curl around her ear. A half-smile crept into her cheek. "I didn't mean to take it so personally. You're under a lot of pressure, I know."

"Wait. Let me finish before I lose my nerve."

"This sounds serious. You're not proposing, are you?"

His heart skipped a beat. "Yes, I am. I love you. Jana, elope with me."

"What?"

"Marry me." Excitement and longing filled his grin. "I know we haven't known each other long, but I've never been surer about anything." He pulled her into a hug. "I love you, and I know you love me." His Adam's apple bobbed as he swallowed several times. "You are my only priority right now, except River, of course. After my round today," he said, pulling back to stare into her eyes, "if I don't make the cut, let's jump in the car, drive to Vegas and get married. I know it sounds crazy and impulsive, but you probably already had the big wedding your first time around, and I thought the church and flowers and all that stuff probably wouldn't matter and—"

Jana sprung into Chase's arms and wrapped her self around his middle. "Yes! Yes! Yes! Stop talking and kiss me. The answer is yes!"

\* \* \* \* \*

"Are you sure?" Trip asked.

"I was standing right there. Of course I'm sure," Maddie said. "Scotty Branch is definitely going to feature Trubird clubs in this afternoon's broadcast."

"We may get out of here alive after all," Tank said.

"Alive and rich!" Trip slapped Tank on the back. "I'm going back to the clubhouse to call Dick. He'll want to watch the broadcast, too."

"Watch it?" Tank laughed. "He'll be drunk before they roll the first commercial."

All three stood energized outside the tenth tee, awaiting the arrival of Chase's group. Today Chase would begin his round on the back nine, due to the number of players and timing issues.

"I can't wait to sue OneSport for trying to take away my house. As soon as this tournament is over, I'm going straight to the Charleston courthouse." Maddie tapped her foot.

"Forget the civil stuff, we need to bring in the district attorney. As soon as Dick gets the fire department report, I'm going after OneSport with everything I've got," Trip said.

"I can't tell you how much this means for Chase and River." Maddie brushed against his shoulder.

"I can't tell you how much extra alimony this deal is going to cost me," Tank said.

All three laughed until something caught Maddie's eye.
"Doll? What is it?"
"Isn't that Scotty Branch?"
Tank and Trip whipped their heads around.
"What the—" Tank began.
Their collective hearts sank. A garment bag and a laptop case draped over the newsman's shoulder, and he handed off his badges to the cameraman.
"I don't understand," Maddie said.
"Here he comes. Let me handle this," Tank said under his breath. "Hey, Scotty, don't tell me you're taking off?"
Scotty bit the corner of his lip before answering. "Yeah, sorry, guys. I've been offered the chance to do the third round coverage of the World Golf Championship NEC Invitational. I'm on my way to the airport. Trubird clubs won't make the equipment feature or any other media forum, I'm afraid."
"How nice for you, being offered a plum gig in the middle of a tournament. Let me guess." Tank scratched his eyebrow. "Management pulled our piece?"
Scotty shrugged. "Yeah. They told me if I wanted a shot at the big time, I had to drop any coverage of Chase and Trubird."
"Who's pulling the strings?"
Scotty turned his head and lowered his voice. "News director called me in. OneSport is our biggest sponsor and they don't like you guys in a big way. Whatever Jake Nathan wants, Jake Nathan gets. Good luck." Scotty hurried off to the parking lot as if they were giving away free cars.
Maddie held her chest. "It feels like someone punched me."
"Someone did," Trip said.
Tank clenched his jaw. "This is war."
"And we're out of ammunition," Trip answered.
"No, we're not." Maddie put a hand on her hip. "We still have Chase. He can make the cut. If he plays well over the next three days, nobody will be able to silence him. Trubird can still come out of this poised to take over the golf industry."

"Atta girl. Never say die," Tank said. "Trip? You okay, partner?"

Trip stared in the direction of the parking lot. After two failed marriages and no children, he was completely alone. He was also ruined. Thanks to the recent claims against him, his reputation was forever tarnished. No matter what he did to clear his name, people would always remember the hint of a scandal.

Along with paying off two expensive divorce settlements, Trip had squandered a hefty chunk of money on a lavish lifestyle during his tenure as the former PGA Commissioner.

Every penny he had saved since then was thoroughly sunk into Trubird, his biggest dream turned nightmare. Trubird was to be his progeny, the child he never had. The thought of this legacy failing was more than Trip could take. Jake Nathan and OneSport had won.

He hung his head. It was time to save his own skin.

# CHAPTER 15

"We're lucky I'm starting out on the back nine today," Chase said, staring up into the crystalline blue sky. The dewy grass smelled earthy. He belonged atop it.

"Jack Nicklaus sure knew what he was doing when he designed holes fifteen, sixteen and seventeen," Jana said, counting his clubs for a third time.

"I'm glad we'll have 'the Bear Trap' behind us this morning instead of later when the greens will be like ice."

"I've got to stop smiling this hard." Jana rubbed her cheeks and whispered, "My face hurts."

Chase discreetly squeezed Jana's hand as his playing partner, Tak Yamomoto, was introduced over the loudspeaker. Together, they watched the young player address his ball. Tak's drive split the fairway, but caught a bad bounce and rolled into the first cut of rough on the left-hand side of the generous driving area.

"And now, on the tenth tee, Chase McLeary," the announcer said.

Bending to insert his tee into the manicured grass, a flash of turquoise caught Chase's attention. Underneath his mirrored sunglasses, Chase allowed his eye to catch sight of the woman.

She wore a striped halter-top, stacked sandals and a straw hat, the same kind Terry used to love. He expected her there in his periphery.

Chase lingered down by the ground, taking an extra minute to adjust the tee. He wondered how much money this woman was earning to impersonate the dead. Did she even know how Terry died?

He stole a look at Jana, so full of love and excitement. Dwarfed by the golf bag she toted, Jana gave him a thumbs-up.

Chase smiled, content in the knowledge that Jana wouldn't care if he carded a hundred for today's eighteen holes. If Trubird flew, so be it. If not, Jana loved him and was marrying him, celebrity status optional. He took a deep breath and looked at River, so happy and proud.

*Goodbye, Terry. You know I'll always love you.*

Chase made an extra brief waggle and hit his best drive of the day. It was straight down the middle, into the future, exactly where he intended to go, with Jana by his side.

"Nice shot, Mister McLeary." Jana grinned and took his driver.

"Thanks, future *Mrs.* McLeary."

Jana's eyes sparkled like Christmas morning. "I can't wait to tell my mom and dad. Remember, you promised that right after the tournament we could tell everyone. My parents are not going to believe it."

"Come on now, caddie. Keep it together until I'm done."

"I'm so sorry, you're right." She tightened the elastic band holding her hair. "I don't know which is more exciting, the thought of you making the cut or missing it. Either way we win."

"My thoughts exactly."

The tenth hole was a four hundred and eleven yard par four. Tak's second shot was a six iron out of the rough. A flawless hit sent his ball to the green, with a touch of backspin that left him a twelve-footer for birdie.

For Chase's second shot, Jana hesitated over his short irons. She tapped the end of a club with her pinkie finger three times. "I think you can make it to the green with an eight iron. But I don't like the looks of that huge bunker protecting it in front." She reached for another. "You better use the seven."

Chase lowered his sunglasses. "What's on the back side if I overshoot the green?"

"The collection area."

Chase took his caddie's suggestion and nailed the shot. His ball landed five feet from the flag. After Tak's birdie putt lipped out of the hole, Chase's dropped dead center into the cup.

Arriving at the eleventh hole, Jana whispered to Chase, "I was wondering, but it's not a big deal, can you wear a wedding ring under your golf glove?" She handed him a five iron for the dangerous par three. Chase's tee shot needed to carry the Jones Creek ravine, but avoid the bunker on the front right of the green.

He took the club. "I never wore one before, but I guess I could get used to it." Still considering Jana's request, he hit a solid drive with a gentle fade. It landed on the left side of the green, twenty feet from the pin.

Tak hit his ball into the creek and then headed for the drop zone.

Jana leaned in toward Chase and whispered, "I don't really care about you wearing a ring. I just wanted to distract you from the water shot. Another caddie taught me that trick."

Chase held his comment until after his playing partner hit. Tak's next shot, counted as his third, was a brilliant recovery. It lofted high and rolled within three feet of the flag.

"And I thought you had confidence in me," he whispered, his chin brushing against her earlobe.

"I do, but there's nothing wrong with hedging my bets, right?" She felt his hot breath on her cheek.

"You want me, don't you?" he said with a leer.

"Yes, but don't make a scene. There's plenty of time for that later." She sprinted toward the green, aching for the match to end.

Tak made his putt for bogey, and Chase two putted for par.

Both the twelfth and thirteenth holes were par fours, but the twelfth was uphill, and one of Montreux's toughest holes. Chase's tee shot found one of the two bunkers on the left side of the fairway, but he got up and down to save par, despite the evil back-left pin placement.

Tak's drive missed the small pot bunker on the right-hand side of the fairway, but his second shot left him ten yards short of the green. His sand wedge brought him within eight feet of the flag, but his putter, again, let him down for another bogey.

It looked as if the thirteenth would prove better for Tak, whose middle irons played well on the short downhill hole. He was on the back of the two-tiered green after only two shots, but his ball trickled backwards until it ran off the green.

Chase nailed a three iron off the tee, followed by a six iron to the green. It looked as if his twenty-four foot putt might drop, but it turned at the last minute and he settled for another par. Tak also made par, but was snappish with his caddie.

"What's his problem?" Jana whispered to Chase on their way to the fourteenth hole.

"Back to back bogeys. He's two over after only four holes."

"And you're one under. I think you're making him nervous."

"Me? I doubt that. Besides, out here you can't be nervous about anything. You can't think about your swing or your last putt, or anything besides getting the ball into the hole."

"Well, speaking of that, I'd say this par five is ripe for a birdie. How about it? Just stay away from that pine tree in the middle of the fairway. Aim dead ahead on the uphill straight-away." She handed him his driver.

"You know, before I had this Trubird club I never felt perfectly confident in my drives. These clubs are really going to help people play better golf."

Jana caught Tak giving Chase's clubs a sidelong glance as he nailed his ball, two hundred and ninety five yards.

"Perfect," she said.

Chase and Tak both made birdies on the fourteenth, although Chase came close to carding an eagle after a lucky bounce brought his third shot dribbling within inches of the cup. Chase gave back a stroke on the fifteenth hole when his bunker shot came out hot, and flew the green. Tak gave back two strokes after an ugly three putt took his total strokes to six.

On the par three sixteenth, both players made it look easy by carrying the water and landing on the green's left corner, the hardest pin placement. Tak's putt finally dropped for birdie, but Chase's didn't, leaving him with par.

The par five seventeenth hole was the longest and straightest at Montreux. The fairway was protected on the left by a lake, and the wind was at Chase's back as he teed up his ball. He swung a hair too fast and he sliced the ball. It landed in the light rough. Tak hit his best drive of the day and nearly holed his approach shot for eagle, but it broke away from the hole, and he only needed a few inches for a birdie. Chase's second and third shots were short, leaving him with a wavering eighteen foot putt to save par.

Jana squatted down behind him and read the lie. She'd seen Chase struggle with similar putts. In her periphery, he was scratching his upper lip—a sign of indecision. She stood up. "I'm thinking you should aim high and strike it hard to take most of the break out of it." She smiled. "Then it should drop right in."

"I don't know." He cupped a hand around the back of his neck. "This green reads like a waffle." He walked to the opposite side of his ball to consider Jana's idea, hesitated and then walked back. "I wish I had my Trubird putter."

Jana stuck out her chin. "You don't need it. I'm telling you, this will work," she said, willing him to believe her.

He set up next to the ball, and glided his putter back and forth so naturally that the club became an extension of his arms.

"That's it. Nice and firm," Jana said, nodding her head. "Now do it in front of the ball." She pulled the flag.

He complied and her heartbeat accelerated and throbbed as the ball did a 360 before dropping into the cup.

"Yeah!" Jana raised the flag skyward and gave thanks.

At the eighteenth tee, Chase and Tak were tied at one under par. Jana glanced at the leader board, and then did a double take. For yesterday's round, about fifty players shot better than par and were ahead of Chase's score. But today, thus far,

Chase and Tak had the best score after eight holes, which, once rolled into their cumulative scores, brought them closer to making the cut.

Jana noted how many recognizable names had posted bogeys and double bogeys so far that morning. She suddenly became aware of the goings-on all around her. People were everywhere and cameras, mounted in tall stands, panned the gallery.

"Caddie? Earth to Jana, may I have a club please?"

"Sorry, Chase. I was . . . uh . . ."

"I saw it too, but try to relax. The scoreboard means nothing. Trust me." Chase took his driver.

Jana leaned in. "Are you sure you want that? I mean, are you sure you can carry that bunker on the right? Maybe you should use your three wood."

"You feel it, don't you?" he asked.

She lifted her shoulders. "Feel what?"

"The pressure of competition. To me, it's like jumping into quicksand wearing a metal suit while trying to breathe through a straw. That about right?"

Jana puffed out her cheeks. "Definitely." She peered at him through newfound eyes, amazed at his composure.

He tapped the tip of her nose with his finger, his eyes playful and yet stalwart. She trusted him implicitly.

"Remember," he said. "No matter what happens, we've already won."

"You're right. You're absolutely right. This is all so new to me, but don't worry, I can handle it."

"Good, I'd hate to have to fire you."

She laughed. "Too late. You're stuck with me forever."

"I like the sound of that."

After nine holes, Chase and Tak were tied at one under.

\* \* \* \* \*

Maddie, Tank and Trip followed Chase's journey along the golf course. After today, the field would be cut in half with only the top portion given a chance to play the weekend.

"He's doing great, and he's not far off the cut line. I know he's going to make it to Saturday," Maddie said.

Trip scowled. "It almost doesn't matter, now. Even if he does make it, it's not like he's going to win the tournament. We lost our publicity, and without it we can't get a forum to explain how great Trubird clubs are. Plus, putting has been the best part of Chase's game, and he's not even using a Trubird putter." He hitched up his khaki slacks. "I can't even begin to spin that one."

"Will ya shut up?" Tank said. "What's wrong with you, anyway?" He pushed up the left sleeve of his polo shirt and scowled back. "Maybe you've given up already, but as far as I know, the fat lady ain't singin' yet. So snap out of it."

Trip shrugged and felt three short bursts of vibration from his cellular telephone signaling receipt of an urgent email. "I'm going to check my messages. I don't want them to snag my phone again. Catch up with you at the next hole."

Trip made his way into the clubhouse and found a telephone kiosk with Internet service. He logged on and scrolled through his messages, stopping on one from a sender named Excelsior Investments. He clicked to open it.

*To: Mr. Trip Boswyck, Trubird Group*
*From: Roger Lemur, Attorney for Excelsior Investments*
　*Dear Mr. Boswyck, please contact me as soon as possible regarding a business proposition. Time is of the essence. If interested, you may reach me at 914-679-9790.*

Trip rubbed his left eyebrow, trying to recall the name Excelsior Investments. It was not one of the companies to which he had pleaded his case when Trubird was actively seeking an infusion of venture capital. He did a quick search for Excelsior on three different Internet search engines; each one came back empty.

A burst of applause came from the lobby bar. Trip glanced up at one of the televisions mounted above his head. Paul Kilroy, the tournament leader, had made another long putt for birdie. A spasm of nausea rippled through Trip's stomach. The cut line was slipping away from Chase, taking financial solvency along with it.

Trip dialed the attorney's number, introduced himself and quickly got down to business.

"Mr. Lemur, you wrote about a business proposition. Are you considering an investment in Trubird?" Trip asked, his heart skipping a beat.

"No."

Trip's heart sank. "Then what—"

"We want to buy your patents. Mr. Boswyck, our analysts don't think you'll ever get your clubs off the ground. There's too much opposition from your competitors," the attorney said.

"That's not true. With the right backing, Trubird can rule the market. Just look at the early media interest in our products," Trip said, silently begging the man to reconsider.

"The key word being early," the attorney said. "Sure, you had a press conference, paraded around a has-been golfer and sent a few tremors through the golf markets, but that interest is short lived, if not long gone by now. The big companies control the advertising dollars, so they govern the media. I don't have to tell you that. As former Commissioner, you know how it works."

"Then why do you want the patents if you don't believe in our product? What good are they to you?"

"Cross-application. We think we can apply some of your research to another investment we're looking into."

"What investment?" Trip asked.

"I can't tell you that specifically, but it's in the building materials sector," the attorney said. His voice was hollow, mocking.

Trip sandwiched his lips and shook his head. "I'm not saying yes, but what kind of buyout numbers are you offering?"

"What are you looking for?"

Momentarily caught off guard, Trip hesitated. "Our business plan projected—"

"Your business plan is useless," the attorney said. "Cut to the chase, Mr. Boswyck. Trubird is dead, and we both know I'm your last hope to recoup any money out of it. I don't have time to fool around. Give me your lowest number, and I'll take it to the board. Play ball, and we can ink this deal by sundown. Otherwise, we walk away and you're left holding a corpse, my friend."

Another burst of applause filled the air. Trip looked up to see a television instant replay of Miles Callabrio's last hole. Despite three terrible shots, nerves of steel allowed him to save par and tie fellow OneSport property, Paul Kilroy, for the tournament lead.

Trip squeezed his eyes shut and weighed the odds. Chase might be capable of making the cut, but even if he did, he would never be in contention come Sunday. The kid wasn't PGA material. Why had he let Tank convince him otherwise? With OneSport's stranglehold on the media, Trubird would remain the best-kept secret in golf.

Trip swallowed and put a hand to the painful throbbing in his stomach; it audibly spread to his intestines. More than anything, he believed in Trubird, but believing wouldn't pay the rent. He saw the writing on the wall. OneSport had won and he had lost. It was time to cut bait.

"Mr. Boswyck? Are you still there?"

"Yes."

"Give me a number," the attorney said.

"Two million dollars, firm. That's less than your basic research and development budget for any major manufacturer, no matter what the product. Bottom line, I'd rather go through bankruptcy court and wait another ten years, if necessary, to introduce Trubird than accept less than that. It's my final offer." Trip held his breath during the brief pause that followed.

"Done," the attorney finally said.

Trip exhaled. A temporary spasm of relief shot through his bowels as he listened to the attorney's instructions.

"I'll draw up a letter of understanding for Trubird's sale of its patents, and attach it to an e-mail within the hour." The attorney's voice quickened a hair. "I need it signed today."

"Fine," Trip said. "I'll send you an electronic confirmation, plus I'll print it out, sign and fax it back to you from my hotel. Put in the contract that I get half at signing, and the balance after you receive the patent documents."

"Okay."

"One more thing." Trip rubbed the left side of his shirt. More than any of his partners, he deserved to salvage something, for he had invested everything he had, and everything he was, in Trubird's success. He was sorry, but there wasn't enough to go around. This was survival of the fittest.

"Trubird doesn't own the patents. They were sold."

"Sold?" The attorney carefully annunciated each word. "To whom?"

"Boswyck Partners. Make the contract and the check payable to Boswyck Partners Limited."

# CHAPTER 16

Miles Callabrio was unusually calm today. Known for his legendary temper tantrums, he displayed none of the cocky behavior that often drove his playing partners crazy. Even after missing a short putt for birdie, he refrained from his typical club slamming and bag kicking. Rather, his steps were tentative and his hands shaky.

By the fifth hole, his caddie was worried. They stood on the fairway waiting for Miles' playing partner to hit his ball.

"Miles, you okay? You don't look so good," the caddie whispered, handing him a bottle of water.

Miles took a sip. He pulled at the neck of his polo shirt and rubbed his collarbone. Pale and sweaty, his face looked like he'd swallowed a lemon.

"What, three pars and one birdie aren't good enough for you?" Miles argued. He stumbled but steadied himself using his three wood as a cane.

The caddie handed him more bottled water. "Boss, you're doing great. Take it easy, okay?"

Miles' breathing was audible as he took a practice swing. He lost his balance and nearly fell over sideways, but caught himself at the last second. Looking up, he shook his head, warning off his caddie who was en route to help.

Reluctantly, the caddie backed off and watched Miles take another practice swing. His arms billowed out too far, as he struggled with the weight of the club.

The caddie swallowed hard. He didn't like what he saw. Sweat poured down Miles' forehead and into his eyes. He backed off of the ball, and wiped his forehead onto his shoulder before again stepping up to the ball.

In slow motion, Miles brought the club back and then snapped it forward with a whooshing sound, as he made contact with the ball. After completing the downswing, he blacked out, lurched sideways and fell to the ground.

\* \* \* \* \*

Over on the par four third hole, two groups behind Callabrio, Chase's bag grew heavy on Jana's shoulders. She straightened her back for a moment to relieve the pressure.

Chase's playing partner, Tak, surveyed his ball. A deep ravine protected the green on the right, and Tak's second shot, although safe, gave him a scare when his ball rolled within inches of the hazard.

Jana continued walking. "I've got a great feeling about these last nine holes. You're in good shape. Let's keep it that way."

"You sure you're okay with my bag? You looked tired," Chase said.

"Stop worrying about me. Focus on making the cut, will you?"

Chase nodded. "These greens are getting faster by the minute. The afternoon players are going to have their work cut out for them. I bet everyone with a cumulative score of two under par makes the weekend rounds. Three under at the most."

"We're at two under right now, so how about a little cushion? Here's the plan. Make this par and then birdie the next hole, it's a par five. Then, all you have to do is make par or better on the last five holes and we're home free."

"One birdie, six pars coming right up," Chase said, pulling his five wood out for his second shot.

His ball came off the club clean and flew down the left side of the fairway. It was still dribbling onto the two-tiered green when a golf ball streaked through the woods, separating the third hole from the adjoining fifth hole.

"What was that?" Jana asked.

Tak and his caddie motioned for Chase and Jana to hurry over.

"Where did that ball come from?" Chase asked.

"The fifth fairway," Tak answered. "Somebody shanked their ball sideways through those trees. Chase, I've seen some weird stuff over the years, but this one takes the cake. You better call an official. You're going to need a ruling on this one."

"What are you talking about?"

"That ball knocked yours into the cup for an eagle."

Jana sprinted over and looked into the hole. "It's true. It's in there. Does it count? Do you get to keep the eagle?"

A marshal hurried over and radioed for assistance. Two officials soon arrived in a special golf cart to speak with both players and caddies. Everyone confirmed that the ball was still rolling when deflected by the other ball.

The officials huddled together reviewing a golf rulebook and the marshal turned to Chase.

"That was Miles Callabrio's ball. They took him away on a stretcher," the marshal said, holding his radio against his ear.

"What happened to him?" Chase asked.

"Maybe a heart attack. Who knows?"

The rules officials joined the group. "Pursuant to rule 19-5, your ball is holed without penalty. You may card your eagle."

"I don't have to put it back? I thought that—" Chase said.

"Had your ball been at rest when hit, you would have had to put it back. But since it was in motion when hit by a ball from another group, it's the 'rub of the green.' Lucky for you." The officials hopped back into their cart and drove away.

Barely able to maintain their composure, Chase and Jana watched Tak finish the hole with a measly par.

"This is awesome," Jana said. "Remember that good feeling I had a minute ago?"

Chase grinned. "Don't even think about it. If you use the word 'climax' they'll have to carry me away in stretcher."

\* \* \* \* \*

"It counts? The eagle definitely counts?" Maddie asked.

"You better believe it," Tank answered, putting his meaty arm around her shoulders and giving her a squeeze. "That fat lady still isn't singing. I wish Trip would get back here so I could rub it in."

"Maybe he's inside watching the television coverage so he can keep track of all the scores," Maddie offered.

"Wherever he is, I'm sure he's celebrating. With that eagle, Chase will definitely make the cut. There's no doubt in my mind. Trubird clubs are in the finals!"

\* \* \* \* \*

Trip wasted no time fleeing Montreux. By the time he reached his hotel's business center, Excelsior's purchase contract was on his email. He printed it, read it twice and then had the hotel shift manager witness his signature before faxing it back to Excelsior.

He raced upstairs, threw his clothes into a suitcase and packed up what remained of Trubird's promotional materials. Anxious to catch a flight home, he sent for the bellhop, and stood waiting with one knee propped on the desk chair.

Images of his partners filled Trip's brain. He betrayed them all, and Trip needed to disappear quickly before they came after him for an explanation of his deception, and for the money they would never see. There wasn't even enough cash left to pay Chase's appearance fee.

He momentarily shook off the guilt. After all, it was just business. Trubird's failure to get to market was not something any of them ever imagined or planned for. And none of their opinions mattered now anyway. Trip controlled more than sixty-six and two-thirds percent of Trubird's issued and outstanding voting stock, and that made him the majority shareholder. He could do anything he wanted with Trubird.

The four Trubird partners originally started out equal partners, with each owning twenty-five shares. But when Satch borrowed money from Trip, he paid little attention to the paperwork. All he cared about was funneling money into his bank account. In fact, Satch had signed a demand note for the loan, which could be called due within forty-eight hours of formal notice.

That's exactly what happened. Satch died on Thursday and Trip wasted no time in formally demanding payment of his loan in a lengthy document sent to poor Satch's widow. He doubted she had even read the letter yet, much less understood its contents; and even if she had, there was no money to repay the note. Thus, the loan was in default, and therefore Satch's twenty-five shares now belonged to Trip.

Dick signed an identical promissory note for his loan from Trip, who called his note at the same time he called Satch's. He was gambling that Dick had also not yet read the notice, but even still, Dick had no other resources for that kind of money. His twenty-five shares would also go to Trip.

Tipping the scales with seventy-five shares, Trip did not need shareholder approval before selling Trubird's patents to Boswyck Partners, his consulting firm. He simply convened a meeting with only him in attendance, made the motion to sell, seconded it, and the deal was done. The timeline was tight, but he had meticulously prepared proper documentation. The transaction involving Trubird's only asset was perfectly legal and safe from attack by minority shareholder lawsuits.

Ironically, in return for the patents, Trubird's compensation did not consist of any cash at all. Instead, Trip simply forgave the hundreds of thousands of dollars of start-up loans and consulting fees that Trubird owed him for his past services.

Trubird was dead. Trip had to get out from under.

"Bellhop. I'm here for the bags."

The young boy rolled a cart inside and grabbed Trip's suitcase and a large file box of Trubird flyers and promotional items.

"You're here for the Reno-Tahoe, right? Did you hear what just happened on the third hole? It was amazing—"

"I don't want to hear anything more about the tournament. My guy is about to get cut. If you want a decent tip, get me a cab."

\* \* \* \* \*

"Okay, Joe. I'm putting them through," Tonya said.

Joe watched the two blinking lights on his telephone become steady. "Jake, you there?"

"Yes."

"Mort?"

"Pick up the handset," Mort said into his cellular telephone. "I'm getting too much static from your speakerphone."

Joe complied. "Gentlemen, I just spent two million bucks out of our R&D budget on OneSport's newest venture."

Jake sucked air through his teeth. "Can this wait? I'm a little busy right now."

"Listen to me," Joe said. "I bought Trubird's patents out from under them. We're going to repackage those clubs under our name, jack up the price and make a bundle."

"How did you pull that off?" Mort asked.

Joe recounted the details of his negotiations hidden behind the Excelsior name, and then voiced his observations about Trip.

"He's screwing over his partners," Jake said.

"Looks that way. It won't be long before they figure out they've been had and follow the trail back to us," Joe said.

Jake peeked at his watch. "I've got to hand it to you, Joe. The market doesn't close for a couple hours. I'll go check in with the media tent and hype OneSport's newest clubs. Kilroy already is using the putter. That should turn around our stock price and fix your personal balance sheet in time to close on that mini-mansion in the Hamptons."

"You've got that right, but hurry up and check your e-mail," Joe said. "I drafted a press release for you to use. Three points minimum, Jake. I need three points."

"Hold on," Mort said. "We still have one loose end to tie up. Chase McLeary."

Jake groaned. "He's the luckiest idiot I've ever seen. That eagle was a total fluke. Too bad about Miles, though. I heard he's in intensive care. How many years are left on his contract, anyway? He's one expensive vegetable."

"I'll deal with Miles. You worry about McLeary," Mort said. "He's still playing in the tournament, and that means Trubird is clinging to life. Jake, take care of this. Drive a stake through his heart. I'm not going to ask you again."

\* \* \* \* \*

After signing off on his card in the scorekeepers' tent, Chase accepted warm congratulations from fellow golfers for making the weekend cut. Besides his eagle, he made four pars, a birdie and a bogey for a two-day combined score of four under par.

As he emerged from the tent, Maddie and River enveloped Chase in hugs and Tank punched him playfully in the arm. By his side, Jana beamed, bursting to announce their engagement but enjoying the secret.

"Come on, guys," Chase said. He pulled away from the celebration. "Let's not make a total scene."

"We're so excited for you," Maddie said.

"Tell me about the equipment special. Was Trubird featured?" Chase asked.

"No," Tank said. "OneSport threw its weight around. Our piece got pulled, but don't worry. The fact that you're playing this weekend will give us good press."

"Not as good as national coverage. Don't snow me," Chase said.

"Okay, you're right," Tank said. "But so long as you finish the tournament playing as well as you've been, I know we can get enough interest going in Trubird to rebuild the warehouse. You know as well as I do that we can make a fortune with these sticks, and I ain't gonna give up, no matter what OneSport throws our way. Remember, you get a fat bonus for finishing in the top twenty-five."

"Where's Trip?" Chase asked.

"Probably out buying the champagne," Tank said. "He can't be far."

"I better hit the range for an hour. Let's meet back at the hotel," Chase said.

"But Dad, you just finished. Why do you have to practice now?" River complained.

Tank put his hands on River's shoulders. "Come with me, kid. Ain't it time to feed that bottomless pit stomach of yours?"

Maddie pulled Chase aside. "You and Jana made up?"

"Yes. Everything's fine."

Maddie smiled as she watched Chase walk away carrying his clubs and holding Jana's hand.

"Maddie? Doll, you coming?" Tank repeated.

Tears pricked her eyes and she looked away. "Sorry."

Tank turned around and touched her chin. "You okay?"

"Sure."

He nodded toward Chase and Jana's retreating forms.

"They make a great team, you know?"

"I do know."

"Then, why do you look like you probably did the day he left home for his first day of kindergarten?"

Maddie frowned. "You certainly are intuitive."

Tank winked. "That's because I'm strong yet sensitive. A real Renaissance man and mighty handsome to boot, don't you think?"

"Buy me a glass of wine, and we'll talk about it." She pointed to a small crowd. "What's going on over there?"

Jake Nathan and Paul Kilroy stood in the middle of half a dozen reporters.

## McLeary's Mulligan

"Who cares? Come on. I'll get you that drink."

"There's your proof, gentlemen," Jake said. He pointed to Paul and the putter he was holding. "It's from OneSport's newest line of golf clubs. Put to the test today, its maiden voyage was a huge success."

"Paul," a reporter asked. "Tell us about it. What's so different about this flat stick?"

"My score," Paul answered.

The crowd sniggered.

Another reporter manipulated his Palm Pilot. "In the last hour, OneSport shares jumped two points on the New York Stock Exchange. Did you expect introduction of this new line of clubs to translate into profits so quickly? And, if so, why did you wait until now to unveil them?"

"Of course, we expected it, and I predict it'll go up at least another point before today's close. We wanted to keep our designs a secret to prevent the competition from throwing together knock-offs for the Tournament. These days you can't be too careful."

"When can we see the rest of the clubs?"

"Soon. Very soon."

\* \* \* \* \*

"Tank?"

"Dick, it ain't even reveille. You couldn't wait a couple hours to call?" Tank asked. He rubbed his eyes and peered at the clock. Three forty-five a.m.

"We got big trouble," Dick said.

"What now?"

"Enemy on deck."

"Who?"

"Trip."

"Where is he? After all the excitement yesterday, I at least expected to hear from him."

"We've been torpedoed."

Naked except for his gold watch, Tank sat up, swung his legs around the side of the bed, and shook off the last vestiges of sleep. "What are you talking about?"

"I got up to go to the bathroom, and I noticed a certified letter on my dresser. Annie forgot to give it to me because she had a migraine and—"

"I'm trying to get some sleep here. Can you hurry it up?"

"Sorry, Tank. Anyway, Trip loaned me some money and made me sign a promissory note. The paperwork looked regular enough, but this certified letter I opened says that he wants the money now."

"He's calling the note? Why? He knows you don't have any money to pay him back right now."

"The heck if I know, but Ally's in the same boat because Trip loaned Satch some money, too. It says we've only got forty-eight hours."

"What's the date on the letter?"

"Friday. I tried all of Trip's telephone numbers, but I can't reach him anywhere."

Tank stroked his scratchy chin. "Have you got a copy of our partnership agreement?"

"Yeah."

"Fax it to me along with a copy of both promissory notes for you and Satch and Trip's letter. I don't know what's going on, but I'm sure as hell going to find out."

"Tank, I'm broke. This was my last chance. I . . . "

"Don't start with me, just get me that stuff and we'll take it one step at a time. Got it?"

"Okay. But I've got one more piece of bad news. I was going to call you about it first thing, but I guess that's now. I was watching the Golf Channel a couple hours ago. They re-broadcast a press conference where Jake Nathan and Paul Kilroy introduced OneSport's latest line of clubs," Dick said.

"So?"

"So, do you think it's a coincidence that the only freaking club they presented was a putter?"

"It's ours."

"No kidding, but how are we gonna get it back?"

"Make no mistake, I'll get it back, and when I do I'm gonna ram it up Jake Nathan's ass."

"He'd probably enjoy that too much. You better beat him over the head with it," Dick suggested.

"Send me that fax."

"Aye, aye. What time is your meeting with that golf ball guy?"

"We're having breakfast at eight-thirty to see if we can do business together," Tank said.

"You think he's serious, right?"

"He's definitely interested in Trubird, and especially Chase on account of his history."

"History? What do you mean?" Dick asked.

"The golf ball guy is a card carrying member of AA. He used to be a really bad drunk and lost everything. But once he got sober, he totally turned his life around. The whole idea of helping a fellow recovering alcoholic is a major motivator. I promised him Chase hadn't touched a drop since the accident. Even better, OneSport is no friend of his either. He told me OneSport put the squeeze on all the national distribution chains not to carry his golf balls."

"So, the enemy of my enemy is my friend."

"You got it, now stand strong. I'll call you in a couple hours."

\* \* \* \* \*

Showered and dressed, Jake bent down to pull on his loafers. Finding an all-night pharmacy in Reno was a lot harder than it would have been in Manhattan, but Jake succeeded. Just after midnight he picked up the prescription and made it back to the hotel, with enough time for a decent night's sleep.

Vinny wasn't thrilled about calling in the prescription, especially since Jake was intentionally vague in describing why he needed the drug. When Jake confirmed its likely side effects, and asked one too many dosage questions, the good doctor started to balk. But as OneSport's staff physician, Vinny Cochera had crossed the medical ethics line years earlier. He was in much too deep to deny Jake anything he wanted.

He reached for the bottle of Valium and shook it. Timing was everything. Although Trip quickly signed the contract and cashed his deposit check, he managed to screw up Jake's delicate timetable when he packaged up the patent documents and sent them to Excelsior. Trip, that idiot, didn't mark the right box on the delivery slip, which meant the package wouldn't arrive at Roger's office until Monday morning.

Because Trip needed the rest of his money, Jake didn't doubt the former Commissioner's word that he'd sent everything as promised. But the stakes were too high to take any chances. The joy of gloating to Chase and that Mazzola guy would have to wait until Monday. Besides, it would take a while to re-register everything with the U.S. Patent Office.

Jake and Joe had gone round and round before deciding the next course of action to be rid of Trubird once and for all. They had two objectives: discredit Chase as a player and expose Trubird clubs as fakes. It was agreed that Jake would handle the first objective and Joe the second.

Jake poured all of the pills into his hand and slipped them into his pocket. Then he reached for the pint of scotch he'd purchased last night. After dumping most of the bottle's contents down the bathroom sink, he returned the nearly empty container to its brown paper bag, and stuck it in his briefcase.

He was due to meet Buzz in ten minutes. If all went according to plan, by the end of today's round, Chase McLeary's comeback attempt would be over, and the media would be frenzied over the latest gossip.

Chase McLeary was back to being a drunk.

# CHAPTER 17

After an early morning breakfast of bagels, fruit and coffee, Chase and Jana headed for the putting area and waited for Chase's tee time. While her secret fiancé lined up long and short putts, Jana failed to push away thoughts of marriage from her mind. Would it be today or tomorrow? What would she wear? Her suitcase contained khaki shorts, black slacks, polo shirts and a lightweight raincoat. Not exactly wedding day attire.

"Jana."

"Yes?"

"I bet I can guess what you're thinking about instead of my lip-out on that last six-footer."

"You caught me. I promise I'll try to focus, but don't blame me if I skip my way around the course today." She smiled. "This is killing me."

"You're all checked in over at the caddie desk?"

"Yes, all set. They even asked me to pay up and join the Professional Tour Caddies Association."

Chase turned to greet another player who wished him well.

"I missed that," Chase said.

"What?"

"Respect. Before, when I tried to make it back on Tour, I was a total mess. Guys would look at me, and all I could see was pity and disgust in their eyes. Now they're truly pulling for me. I can't tell you how long I've waited for that, and how much it means to me."

"This calls for a toast." Jana unzipped the large pocket on the side of Chase's golf bag. She pulled out two small, colored sports drink bottles and handed one to Chase. She unscrewed the top and wound her arm around Chase's in a "lover's toast."

"Pretty fancy. No water today? Where'd you get these?" he asked.

"I have my sources. Anyway, here's to my future husband and what promises to be a great day of golf."

They each took a sip and then leaned forward, pressing their lips together for a good luck kiss.

Thirty feet away, Jake and Buzz studied the couple, admiring the drink bottles spiked with crushed Valium.

"She wasn't suspicious?" Jake asked.

"Nope. I wished her luck, gave her the bottles and told her that's what all the guys drink on Saturdays," Buzz said.

"As long as Chase sucks down at least four ounces, everything should go according to plan. I put enough dope in those drinks to tranquilize an elephant. Everyone will think he's three sheets to the wind."

"I did my part, now a deal's a deal, right?" Buzz propped a fist on his hip.

Jake slid his tongue across his top teeth and smiled at Buzz. "Welcome to OneSport."

\* \* \* \* \*

It was Saturday morning in New York City and Joe was pleased with himself for getting things under control. Last night he spent two hours on the telephone negotiating with the auditors. Finally, they cut a deal.

After heated threats from both sides, Joe agreed to let them retroactively restate OneSport's financials for all of the adjustments they were demanding, except the stock options, so long as they held off doing the restatement until the fourth quarter.

By that time, according to Joe's calculations, the negative financial impact of the restatement would be nearly offset by

OneSport's new golf profits, courtesy of Trubird. It was a win-win situation. The auditors got most of what they wanted and the investors would still receive their usual dividend checks. Of course, all of this would transpire without necessitating any pay cuts for Joe, Mort or Jake.

OneSport's stock price rallied Friday afternoon, following Jake's press conference, in time for Joe to sell off another block of shares for a seven-figure profit. Now Joe could hardly wait for the full line of Trubird clubs to be rolled out. That would mean another spike in OneSport's share price, and Joe had plenty of stock options left in his quiver.

Crossing Sixth Avenue, Joe spotted a five-dollar bill stuck in a subway grate. He snatched it up and tucked it inside his breast pocket. He smiled at the omen.

*Lady luck, here I come.*

\* \* \* \* \*

Tank was beyond nervous. He never figured Trip for the backstabbing type. He had yet to look over the documents Dick faxed to the hotel, and he didn't want to make any premature accusations. But Trip had vanished from Montreux without a word, and that didn't go in his favor.

During the cab ride to the golf course, Tank tried to focus on the positive: his breakfast meeting. Hal Vos was larger than life. A six-foot-two-inch recovering alcoholic with a new lease on life, he poured all of his time and energy into developing a golf ball company. His company, like Trubird, was struggling to get out from under the eight hundred pound gorilla known as OneSport.

Hal was both sympathetic and solicitous of helping Chase succeed, but he was also a businessman. He needed to make money and wanted a business alliance that was economically viable. After minimal back and forth, he and Tank agreed on the basics for structuring a deal that married Trubird clubs with Hal's golf balls.

The fate of their venture, however, rested on one thing and it was a deal-breaker. Chase had to finish the Reno-Tahoe Open in the top ten. Tank begged Hal to reconsider setting such an arbitrary benchmark of success, but Hal was adamant. He was not about to let an unproven company ride his coattails, not for the amount of money Trubird needed to rebuild. He wanted assurance that Trubird's technology was every bit as good as promised, and in Hal's mind, Chase's ability to finish in the top ten was proof enough that both he and the clubs were worthy.

Pulling into Montreux's parking lot, Tank calculated the odds that Chase could earn a top ten finish. After two rounds, which included his spectacular eagle, he sat amid a pack of five players who shared nineteenth place.

A top ten finish was possible, but not without shooting rounds in the sixties both Saturday and Sunday. *Chase has his work cut out for him*, Tank thought as he scampered through the crowd in search of Maddie. He caught up with her mid-way up the fourth fairway.

"Hey, doll," Tank said. A few extra lines crossed her smooth forehead, and her usually full lips were taught. "What's wrong? Are we still at four under?"

Maddie nodded. "Thanks to a great sand save on the second hole. It's only a one hundred and seventy yard par three, but we nearly dropped a stroke back there. How was your meeting?"

"Long. I'll fill you in later on the details. Bottom-line, Chase has to finish near the top of the pack for Vos to play ball with us. I think he's a straight shooter, but he's also our last chance. Of that I'm sure."

Maddie brushed her palm against Tank's cheek. "Don't let the pressure get to you, too."

Her voice was rich with compassion and the deep concern of a loving friend. She dropped her hand and gave his shoulder a tender squeeze.

Tank ached to hug her.

"Doll, when this is over, I want to —"

"Don't." She squeezed her eyes shut. "Let's get through today, okay?"

Tank bit his tongue. "Right."

"Have you seen Trip?" Maddie asked.

Tank filled her in on Trip's mysterious disappearance from the tournament and on his cutthroat financial tactics.

"You don't think that after all of this he'd bail out, do you?" Maddie hugged herself.

"Worse. I think he's got one hand in the cookie jar, and he's using the other hand to stick a knife in my back. I'm going to figure it out after the tournament."

Maddie knit her eyebrows. She and Tank walked down the fairway. "I know you don't want to hear this," she said, "but I think something is wrong with Jana. She doesn't look right. Her perky little march down the course has been dragging more and more with each hole. I think she's sick."

Tank squinted. "How can you tell from here? It's probably just nerves. The course is playing pretty slow today. Maybe she's over-thinking each shot."

They watched Chase take out his three wood and wait for the group ahead to clear the green. Resting his bag on the ground, Jana leaned forward and put her hands on her knees. She turned and Tank caught sight of her face. Pasty and frowning, she kept fanning herself, although the temperature was cool and the sky overcast.

Tank made a fist and punched it into the palm of his other hand. "What else can go wrong? She's gonna puke," he predicted, silently cursing his luck.

"Is she swaying? Oh!"

Jana wilted to the ground. Chase dove next to her and dropped to his knees, attempting to revive her. Seconds later, River, Maddie and Tank crouched down alongside Chase.

As the marshal radioed for help, murmuring circulated throughout the crowd. From the corner of his eye, Tank saw Jake chatting with spectators. He tipped his hand to his mouth as if holding a bottle. Tank cringed, praying that Hal Vos wasn't anywhere in sight.

"What happened?" Maddie asked. She blew on Jana's hairline and felt her pulse.

"Jana, honey, Jana. Say something." Chase put his lips to her forehead and squeezed her hand. He looked up at his mother.

Tank guessed the look on Maddie's face was similar to the one she wore upon learning of Chase's accident years earlier, complete fear. He supported her trembling back with his hand.

Chase patted Jana's cheeks. "She kept saying she was fine, but she didn't look right, all sweaty and thirsty. I knew something was wrong." He cupped his hands behind her head, guarding it from the grass.

"Tank, give me some water to splash on her face," Maddie said.

Tank tore through the pockets of Chase's bag, and pulled out two empty bottles of red sports drink before finding a bottle of water. Tossing it to Maddie, he caught a whiff of something familiar. He followed his nose to another pocket and retrieved a brown bag. He peeked inside and saw the whisky bottle.

"Wait a minute." Tank stuck his nose up next to Jana's and inhaled.

Chase shoved him away. "What are you doing?"

"Take it easy. I'm trying to smell her breath, not kiss her," Tank said.

"Why?" Chase asked.

"'Cause that empty bottle of booze in your golf bag makes me think she's passed out drunk, except her breath is clean," Tank said.

"Bottle of booze? That's not mine, and it's not Jana's either," Chase said.

Tank unscrewed the empty sports bottles, and ran them under his nose. "Nope, definitely no booze in there either. Where did you get these?"

"I don't know. Jana got them," Chase answered.

Tank shook the full bottle of water, noting the seal was broken. A thin layer of sediment turned into snowflakes and whirled around inside the bottle.

"What have you had to drink this morning?" Tank asked Chase.

"Only a sip of that red stuff. It's too sweet for me."

"Any of this water?"

"No. Why? Do you think she's been drugged?"

"I think whatever happened to Jana was meant for you."

Tank backed away to make room for the paramedics. One of them noted Jana's slow pulse, shallow breathing and dilated pupils, while the other asked Chase a few questions about Jana's health history. Tank handed the paramedic the bottled water and voiced his suspicion about possible drugs. He kept the brown bag hidden.

"Which one of you wants to ride in the ambulance?"

"I will," Maddie offered.

"No, I should—" Chase began.

"No. That's the last thing she'd want you to do." Maddie walked alongside the stretcher. An oxygen mask was placed over Jana's mouth and nose. "Chase, finish your round. I'll take care of Jana."

"Is she going to be okay?" River asked, his voice soft and confused as he watched the crowd part for the spectacle.

Tank reached for Chase's golf bag, furious with OneSport for putting all of them through this emotional crisis. "She'll be fine, kid. I'm sure it's nothing serious. Now come on, you can show me the ropes."

Chase looked up. "What are you doing?"

"What do you mean, what am I doing? You're not gonna carry your own bag, are you? Now let's go," Tank said, determined more than ever to see Chase succeed. "You left some meat on the bone back there with that tee shot. Let's nail this one. For Jana."

\* \* \* \* \*

Johnny Hotung failed to make the cut, leaving Buzz fully available to assist Jake with official OneSport business. He and his co-conspirator huddled behind a port-a-potty near the fourth tee.

"How can you blame this on me?" Buzz asked. "It's not my fault the girl chugged it."

"That dumb broad." Jake swatted at flies.

"She's going to be okay, right?" Buzz looked over his shoulder. "She looked pretty bad."

Jake laughed. "Don't tell me you're growing a conscience now?"

"Hey, I didn't know you were going to use so much of that stuff or I wouldn't have—"

"Shut up. You screwed up my plan and now I've got to switch gears."

Buzz shrugged and jingled the change in his pockets.

Jake sidestepped a muddy spot and put a handkerchief over his mouth. Brow furrowed, he weighed his options. "Even without the girlfriend massaging his ego, Chase is still playing pretty well. Nobody expects him to win, but he's definitely in the hunt, and my gut tells me he's not going to fold. Yeah, time to change tactics. Chase McLeary may have nine lives, but I've got ten bullets."

Buzz's adrenaline kicked in. "If you're thinking about doing anything drastic, then I'm out of here." He stepped backwards.

"No, you're not." With a vice-like grip, Jake grabbed his wrist. "I own you now, Buzz. You've already crossed the line, so you'd better hunker down, do your job and enjoy the rewards."

Buzz shook free. "Do I at least get some kind of retainer or something?"

"Better," Jake said. "You're picking up a new bag."

Buzz beamed. "Whose? When do I start?"

"Tomorrow you carry Paul Kilroy's bag."

"Kilroy? The leader?" Buzz's eyes popped. "But he doesn't even know me. The first place cut of the purse is more than half a million, which makes the caddie fee around fifty grand. His regular caddie isn't going to just hand it over."

"I'll take care of him," Jake said, checking his watch. "He's a OneSport asset. Lesson number one, Buzz. What OneSport wants, we get, no matter what the cost. The most important thing right now is for you to be next to Kilroy so you can keep a close eye on Chase McLeary."

\* \* \* \* \*

Chase made par on the fourth hole, but then carded a bogey on the fifth. On the sixth hole, after a poorly hit tee shot, Chase and Tank walked to Chase's ball on the fairway. A rumble of thunder passed overhead.

"Don't say it," Chase said.

Tank looked up at the dark clouds and shrugged.

"I know I should have used the driver, but this is one of the tightest driving areas on the course. I guess I got scared."

Tank stared ahead. "Don't worry about it. You're doing great. We've only given back one stroke."

"Maybe we should call the hospital to check on Jana."

"I'll find out how she's doing when we make the turn, but I'm sure she's fine. The paramedics didn't seem too worried. Somebody slipped her a 'mickey' is all," Tank said.

"I hope you're right." Chase studied the left to right slope. "Okay. I've got to hit the left side of the green or I'll wind up spinning down into that chipping area, don't you think?"

*If you don't wind up in the bunker on the left-hand side*, Tank thought. "Sounds good."

Chase's ball came up short, landing in the bunker. He groaned.

"That ain't bad. You can get up and down for par," Tank said.

"I'm off my game."

"Get your head straight," Tank said, a bit too forcefully. He swallowed hard. "What I mean is, you've grinded your way to a good finish before, so shut up and do what good golfers do. Make your par and move on."

"I need Jana," Chase whispered.

Tank shared a similar thought as he watched Chase hesitate while striking his sand wedge. *Crap*. The ball made it out of the bunker, but left him with a twenty-foot putt for par. He missed it right, and the resulting bogey pushed his cumulative score to two under.

Now in sole position of twenty-third place, Chase was leading Trubird in the wrong direction, and Tank had no idea how to turn him around.

On the eighth hole Chase's drive off the elevated tee was nearly perfect. It flew three hundred yards dead center of the fairway. Tank was certain they would pick up a stroke when his second shot avoided Galena Creek and rolled onto the very narrow green to sixteen inches from the flag.

But his birdie attempt nearly became a bogey after he pushed the short putt right, leaving himself a five-footer coming back for par. The par putt caught the cup's edge and dropped in.

As Tank slipped Chase's putter back in his bag, he caught sight of Jake Nathan standing by the ropes. Smug as usual, Jake was taking furtive glances at Chase's golf clubs. Tank strengthened his grip on the bag and caught up to Chase as dark storm clouds rumbled overhead.

"This next one's a par five," Tank said. "We need a quick birdie on the ninth, and then I'll call your mother to find out about Jana. Come on, kid. You can do this."

Chase's face softened as he removed his three wood, and then exchanged it for a five iron. "Thanks for the vote of confidence, but I can't get my head together until I know she's okay."

His comment turned out to be prophetic. Chase's decision to go for the green in two proved costly when his ball found the water on the right side of the green. Unable to shelve his fears about his fiancée, Chase's scorecard posted its first double bogey.

Tank's neck muscles burned. Despite his combat experience, he felt the unusual sensation of panic. It was Saturday and they were back to even par after Chase's first nine holes. If Tank didn't get him turned around soon, then nothing could save Trubird.

A crack of thunder sounded and the wind picked up as Tank and Chase left the ninth green.

"Tank, I know this probably isn't the right time, but I really need the money you guys promised me."

Tank flinched. "We already gave you the five grand sign-on fee," he said.

"Yeah, and I spent it. But you also said I'd get twenty-five thousand for making the cut. Jana and I have plans right after the tournament, and, well, I need it."

Stalling, Tank struggled to find a response when a marshal approached.

"Gentlemen, they've called a delay due to lightning storms. You may take cover in the tent," he said.

"I'm going to run ahead and call my mom. I'll meet you up there." Chase bolted for the telephones.

Tank watched him go, guessing that the young golfer wanted to make Jana a permanent part of his life. He was planning on that nest egg.

*How am I going to tell him we're broke?*

# CHAPTER 18

OneSport's offices were unusually quiet on this Saturday afternoon. Sitting low in the leather desk chair, the drapes pulled tightly, Mort rapped his thumbs on the papers in front of him. With each tap his fury multiplied, and the scowl on his lips grew as he thought through the unpleasant predicament in which he found himself.

First there was the problem of Jake, OneSport's best client handler. His partner may have started out as a two-bit hustler, but nowadays he was magic with both men and women alike. His ability to get them to sign on the dotted line had only improved over the years, and it sickened Mort to see his protégé utterly collapse in his duties.

This thing with Chase McLeary had gotten out of control. Thus far, Jake had failed miserably in his responsibility to control the situation. Not only was he unsuccessful in preventing the initial burst of publicity surrounding Trubird, he was putting them all at risk by enlisting an idiot like Buzz as his point man to destroy McLeary. All the while, Jake was ignoring his other responsibilities, and OneSport could not afford unhappy clients.

Mort batted his thumb on the column of figures in front of him. The financial cost of Jake's efforts was growing every day, and yet McLeary and Trubird were still very much alive. Jake's sizable ego had blinded his ability to get the job done, and he had not yet grasped the seriousness of the situation.

Using his smallest finger like a corkscrew, Mort jabbed it into his ear canal, twisting this way and that, trying to dislodge a loose hair or chunk of wax. Retracting it, he flicked the morsel into the trash and picked up Joe's report. He read it for the third time, careful not to miss anything.

Acquiring Trubird's patents was an excellent move, and Mort was cautiously excited about its future revenue projections. But Joe had unwittingly backed OneSport into a corner by agreeing to the auditors' demands. For the company to continue dominating the worldwide sports industry, it needed to post strong profits every quarter. Any crack in OneSport's armor presented a dire threat that some puny outfit like Trubird could sneak in and infect its body politic.

Rumors of slipping profitability, if spread on the financial news networks, had brought down many a company, even healthy ones, without severe off-balance sheet debts like OneSport.

The thought of anyone losing respect for him was intolerable. Mort was accustomed to being the envy of Wall Street, and public embarrassment was not something he could live with. Never again would he return to the days spent shunned by the beautiful people of the world who now desperately pursued him.

Mort's computer chimed, beckoning him. He swiveled around and opened an email from Dr. Vinny Cochera.

*To: Mort*
*From: Vinny*
*Must meet to discuss Miles' prognosis and protocol parameters. Call my private line ASAP.*

Mort deleted the message, already aware that Miles Callabrio, due to an excess of beta-blockers, was in a coma and was not expected to recover. If he died, an autopsy was unavoidable, and that resulting scandal could ruin them, never mind the related medical costs and Miles' lost earnings for the company.

His eyes narrowed. As usual, it was up to him to protect OneSport and keep the company thriving. Everything was at stake.

He knew exactly what he had to do.

\* \* \* \* \*

Sitting behind the wheel of his silver luxury sedan, Trip looked out over the Atlantic Ocean from the public beach parking lot in Fort Lauderdale, Florida. Anonymous among the Saturday beach revelers, who ignored him while ferrying coolers and inner tubes from minivans and sport utility vehicles to the packed shore, Trip watched fathers and mothers, toddlers and teenagers as they did the normal things families do on weekends. Trip loathed every bit of it; yet, being in this environment, but not of it, oddly comforted him.

Only a few miles from the reserved calm of his private adults-only condominium resort, Trip craved the casual community picnic spot. He watched a blonde-haired boy chase his little sister with a squirt gun while their mother unloaded sand toys from an ancient green station wagon.

Trip had always wanted a son, someone to carry on his name; but his marriages were, at best, passing fads and, at worst, bitter shams. He had no real friends, and aside from an estranged sister and brother-in-law, no relatives to rely on for emotional support.

He put his head down on the steering wheel, covered it with both arms and sobbed. He was ashamed of so many things in his life. Trip had made poor choices before, but none weighed on his mind as heavily as losing Trubird and his decision to take advantage of his partners.

It wasn't that he'd sold out their chances for financial success at the eleventh hour. He also took away their dreams. On the airplane home, when a passenger told Trip about Chase's eagle to make the weekend cut, Trip nearly screamed. The irony was incalculable insofar as Trip's decision to prematurely declare Trubird's death.

He blamed OneSport for everything. Were it not for them and especially Jake Nathan, perfect Jake Nathan, everything would be different. Trip would be a hero, respected amongst the golf industry—instead of a joke. OneSport had an iron grip on the golf world and, try as he might, Trip was unable to break in.

Trip traded in his integrity and reputation for a fee, and after he received Excelsior's final payment, due into his bank account on Monday morning, he would be left completely and utterly alone.

Trip's stomach burned. An overweight woman with a toddler on her bulging hip peered over at him with interest. He turned his head away, and she resumed unloading her van, leaving Trip alone to grieve for all that he was not and all that he had become.

\* \* \* \* \*

At the telephone bank in Montreux's lobby, Chase gripped the receiver like a lifeline as Maddie relayed Jana's condition. The emergency room doctor had confirmed that Jana had ingested a near-fatal dose of Valium. They pumped her stomach, fed her intravenous fluids, and were now waiting for her to regain consciousness.

"You're sure she'll be okay?" Chase asked. He kept one eye on River who was taking turns on a hand-held video game with another scorecard carrier.

"You know how doctors are," Maddie said. "They leave plenty of wiggle room; but, yes, they said she'll be fine."

Chase's shoulders relaxed but his eyes narrowed. Although relieved that she was expected to recover, Chase was seething that someone had done such a terrible thing to Jana, and all because of him. "I swear, no matter how long it takes, I'll make them pay for this," Chase said.

"Who?" Maddie asked.

"OneSport," Chase answered.

"You don't know for sure it was them. Jana was slurring her words while in and out of consciousness, but I did hear her say that someone named Buzz gave her the drinks."

"Buzz, the caddie?" Chase repeated.

Tank took the telephone. He instructed Maddie to have Jana file a police report as soon as she was fully alert. "And, doll," Tank added, "be extra careful. From here on out, it's gonna get ugly."

Ten minutes later, Tank and Chase, sipping coffee in paper cups, sat down in a quiet corner of the lobby.

"I saw Jana talking with Buzz earlier today," Tank said to Chase. "Now he's lapping at Jake Nathan's heels. What do you know about Buzz?"

Chase shook his head. "He's one of the worst caddies on Tour. His yardages never take into account things like wind and rain, he can't keep his mouth shut about his players' personal lives, and he's got a huge chip on his shoulder. He thinks he's owed fame and fortune, a huge ego freak. There's no way Jake Nathan would hire him as a caddie, but he'd probably sign Buzz on to do his dirty work."

Tank studied Chase's countenance. "I've never seen you like this before."

"Like what?" Chase yanked off his cap, flexed the brim and pulled it back on tightly.

"Like a hit man with two bodies in his trunk . . . who doesn't break a sweat when a cop pulls him over for speeding. You think you can handle a little more bad news?"

"What are you talking about?"

"Kid, we're broke. Trubird is completely tapped out, and it looks like Trip walked out on us and maybe even set us up. The only way any of us will see a nickel out of Trubird is if you shoot the lights out over the next twenty-seven holes. You need to finish top ten. It's the only way."

Chase's mouth hung open. "Broke? How can you be broke? What about the money you promised? I had plans. Jana and I—"

It was Tank's turn to be angry. "Can you stop thinking about yourself for one minute? You started out with nothing, so winding up in the same place ain't much of a stretch. But look at what happened to Satch, or look at Dick and me, broke at our age, or what about your own mother who might wind up losing her house. She'd do anything for you, and you're so freaking selfish that you'd let her. When are you going to handle your own problems? Maddie's been bailing you out your whole life. Now it's time to carry your own weight."

Chase leaned in, his eyes inches from Tank's. "Who are you to lecture me about my own mother?"

Tank tipped his head even closer. "I ain't your father, and I ain't your priest, but I know enough not to keep my mouth shut about something this important. I care about your mother, more than you know, and I care about you, too—you snot-nosed brat. So are you going to lay down and be beaten, or are you ready to fight OneSport?"

Chase screwed up his face—ready to fire back, but then changed his mind. He folded his arms across his chest and leaned back in his seat. "Okay, now I get it. Save your breath, because I don't need any encouragement to battle them. I don't care about the money anymore. After what they did to Jana, and nearly to me, I'll make it my life's work to take those guys down."

"Good, because I've got a plan," Tank said.

"I'm guessing it's a long shot."

"Kid, it's our only shot."

\* \* \* \* \*

In a private corner of the scorekeepers' tent, Jake Nathan and Paul Kilroy faced off.

"No, for the last time, I won't do it," Paul Kilroy said, shaking his head.

"Paul, I need this one. It's important to OneSport," Jake said.

"No way. You know as well as I do that Buzz is a terrible caddie. What has he got over your head that you would even consider letting him carry my bag, especially right in the middle of the tournament?"

Jake squeezed Paul's arm. "Keep it down. Come on, Paul, the way you play, the Queen of England could be your caddie and you'd still win the tournament. Don't play hard to get. What if I sweeten the pot? I'll match whatever size check you take home from here for hiring Buzz. How about it?"

Paul sucked in his breath. For the first time, he considered the proposal. "You're seriously willing to put up that kind of money for this guy?"

"You heard me, and I know you need the money. It's no secret that you're screwing around again. Lena won't put up with it, and she won't walk away empty handed. Do yourself a favor and do this. Deal?"

Paul bit his cheek. The lightning storms had subsided and play would soon resume. "I'm not making any promises. I'll try him out on spec, but only for the rest of my round today. If it works, he can continue tomorrow for the finals. But if I don't like him, he's gone after today. I don't need your money that bad."

"Fine, but you only get the bonus if he caddies tomorrow," Jake countered.

Paul swore. "One more thing, you're the one who has to tell Manny that he's off my bag. He's not going to be happy."

"He was happy enough to grab the cash I already offered for accommodating our request. Right now he's showing Buzz the ropes, taking him through all the stuff you like, don't like, need, and might need. Like I said, I've taken care of everything. You just do your job."

\* \* \* \* \*

Manny Fortunato was more than a little perturbed to be knocked off of Paul Kilroy's bag, especially considering how well they were doing in the tournament. But money was money, and he was well compensated for the inconvenience. Plus, it was never a good idea to turn down a man like Jake Nathan. According to Jake, making this accommodation would be "favorably remembered," and being owed a favor from OneSport was like money in the bank.

"Hey, am I wasting my breath here or what?" Manny said to Buzz, who was overly enamored with the twelve-hundred-dollar custom golf bag.

"Man, is this ostrich leather?" Buzz rubbed the textured bag.

*What an idiot.* "I don't know, and I don't care. Did you hear that last thing I said about the grips?"

Buzz took a turn hoisting the bag on his shoulder. "Yeah, yeah. You said Kilroy always thinks he needs new grips, but I should humor him," he mumbled.

Five teenage boys raced up to the men. "Excuse me, are you Paul Kilroy's caddie?" one of the boys asked Buzz.

Manny turned away, disgusted. "I'm out of here. Good luck," he said, hurrying off.

"I sure am Paul's caddie," Buzz said, touching the nametag on his pinafore.

"Wow. He's doing great," said one of the boys. "I bet he wins the tournament. Hey, will you sign an autograph for me?" He thrust a pen and a tour program at Buzz.

"Sure, I'll sign an autograph," Buzz said loudly enough for any interested passersby to hear. He set the bag down.

"Mine, too!" said the two other boys, jumping in front of the first.

"Boys, boys, slow down. Everybody can have one," Buzz said, fending off the young fans that surrounded him.

"What's Paul Kilroy like?" asked one of the boys. "Is he nice?"

"He's a great guy, but without me, who knows?" Buzz said, abandoning any hint of modesty. This is exactly where he belonged—in the limelight.

"Will you sign this one for my dad?"

"Sure, kid."

"And one for my brother?"

"You got it. Hey, back up a little, you're practically in my lap," Buzz said.

After peppering Buzz with questions for another minute or two, the sneaker-clad boys took off as fast as they had arrived.

An announcement sounded. Play would resume in fifteen minutes. All players and caddies were to return to the course.

Buzz turned, picked up Kilroy's bag, and headed for his new boss, who, he had no doubt, would be exceptionally impressed with his new caddie.

\* \* \* \* \*

On the tenth tee, Chase pulled his cap low on his brow and zipped up his windbreaker. "Good, I like wind. Bring it on."

Tank nodded. "Well, the benefits of Trubird clubs are definitely highlighted in this kind of weather. Good thing it didn't rain, or the course would be slow enough for everyone to score well."

A slight dogleg right, Chase stared at the bunker straight ahead. In its back corner there was a steep lip that jutted out like a ledge above the trap. A poor shot would prove disastrous.

"It's supposed to be four hundred and eleven to the pin. But with these gusts, I need to club-up, maybe times two. I'm guessing most players will go for the safe shots. Not me. I'm going for the pin."

They were all depending on Chase now: Jana, Maddie, River, Tank and Dick. He was not going to let them down.

"You know there's trouble on the left, and a big old bunker in front of the green, right?" Tank asked.

Chase readjusted the zipper poking at his neck. He swallowed hard, choking back the need for a double vodka.

"Believe me, I know."

\* \* \* \* \*

Resuming play on the second hole after the thunderstorm delay, Paul Kilroy was cautiously optimistic about his new caddie. After all, he might as well give him the benefit of the doubt. Buzz had handled himself well on the tee and during the walk up the number two fairway.

## McLeary's Mulligan

Aside from spending too much time cleaning his wraparound sunglasses and trying to look overly important, Buzz was behaving appropriately, thus far anyway.

Paul marked his ball on the green and motioned for Buzz to hand over his putter. Running his hands through the golf bag, Buzz finally pushed his trendy sunglasses onto his head so that he could see into the bag.

Now Paul was getting angry. "If you want to be back tomorrow, you better speed it up," he hissed.

Buzz looked irritated. "Take it easy. Here."

"What's that? That's not my putter."

\* \* \* \* \*

After nailing a three hundred yard tee shot from the tenth tee, a nine iron sent Chase's ball to the backside of the sloping green, within eight feet of the cup. Triumphant, Tank handed Chase his Trubird putter as they waited for his playing partner.

Overcompensating for the strong breeze, the other golfer hit his ball too hard and it rolled fifteen feet past the hole. The first to putt, he left it eighteen inches short of the cup, and marked his ball.

"I'd have given anything to see Buzz's face when Kilroy asked for his putter," Tank whispered as Chase lined up his putt.

There was no hesitation as Chase gently squeezed the grip; the ball was destined for the hole as soon as he stroked it. He looked up and a smile creased his left cheek.

Tank winked. "Nice."

Chase's partner holed his second putt and Tank replaced the flag.

"How much money did you pay River's friends for distracting Buzz?" Chase asked.

"Ten bucks each," Tank said. "With an extra twenty for the one who got him to turn his back on Kilroy's bag."

"You don't think they'll get in any trouble do you?"

"Nah." Tank pawed the air. "All they did was ask for autographs. I'm the one who snuck up behind Buzz and switched putters. You should have heard him bragging about his golf prowess. I almost puked."

Chase wore his poker face, already focused on the next hole. "Okay, one birdie down. Let's go get another. This next one's a two hundred and twenty-five yard par three. My five wood will carry the Jones Creek Ravine, and I'll aim for the left side, away from that bunker."

Tank nodded. "In this weather that ain't exactly the safe play, but you know what you're doing."

"As you once told me, watch and learn," Chase said, stone-faced.

Tank allowed himself a smile. In times of war he had seen brave men turn into cowards and ordinary men act extraordinarily brave. He was banking that Chase was one of the latter.

\* \* \* \* \*

"How are you feeling?" The doctor gingerly perched at the end of Jana's bed.

She rubbed her head. "Like someone ran over me with a dump truck." She sat up, nearly vomited, and inched her hand over toward the plastic pitcher of water.

"Here," Maddie said, handing her a cup with a straw. Next to the tanned doctor and the bright peach walls, Jana's complexion was ghostlike.

After checking her vital signs, the doctor flipped through her chart and scratched a few notes. "You're a lucky lady," he said, pulling a stethoscope from around his neck to listen to her breathing. "The nausea will be gone by tomorrow, but I want you to take it easy for another day or two." He stood and brushed lint the front of his blue lab coat. "The police are outside. They're ready to take your statement."

"Wait a minute," Jana said. "My fi—my boyfriend . . . I'm caddying for him. He's playing in the Reno-Tahoe Open and—"

"Not anymore. You're not strong enough. I'm sure he can find someone else for tomorrow. Besides, if the wind doesn't die down," the doctor said, "it might take another day or two for him to finish."

"What are you talking about?" Jana asked.

The doctor reached for the remote control connected to the headboard and flicked on the television. "I don't know who your boyfriend is, but he's probably in the same boat with everyone else, except for the one guy who's been getting lucky. Check out the scores. Since they resumed play after the weather delay, it's been one bogey after another. The winds are fierce."

Jana squinted at the screen. Maddie walked over for a closer look. They gasped. The leaders going into Saturday's round were stumbling, whereas Chase had virtually scorched the course on the back nine, shooting a thirty thus far. Coming off the eighteenth green at six under, he sat amid a pack of five players tied for second place.

The doctor flashed a patronizing smile. "No offense intended, but it's a good thing the World Golf Championships are getting most of the airtime." He turned to leave. "That's where all of the best golfers are playing."

Jana beamed at Maddie. "Not all of them."

Maddie rushed to gently hug Jana, whose pride in Chase rivaled her own.

\* \* \* \* \*

*We're doomed*, Tank thought.

Half an hour earlier, after celebrating Chase's record-breaking score on Montreux's back nine with a few beers and a juicy steak, Tank returned to his hotel room elated. Trubird's luck might be holding on by a thread, but it was still intact. Tank was optimistic that Chase would finish top ten, and thereby cement the support of Hal Vos.

A scalding shower loosened up the sore muscles in his back and neck from carrying the heavy golf bag. By the time he sat down in the plump armchair with his reading glasses and the documents Dick faxed over, Tank felt every bit his age. But, as his eyes shifted back and forth across one of the pages, he became stiff and alert as his optimism turned to panic.

Tank again read the piece of paper. It was a log of Trip's email transmissions. Items between Trip and someone at a company called Excelsior Investments were circled. Dick had scrawled a note across the top: *Look at this printout I got from our Internet service provider. Is this legal? Can he really do this without our consent? Call me ASAP!!!*

There it was in black and white. Trip sold Trubird's patents to his own outfit, Boswyck Partners, which in turn sold them to something called Excelsior Investments.

Tank rifled through a copy of the loan document between Trip and Satch. He laid it, side by side, next to the loan paperwork between Trip and Dick. They were identical demand notes, callable and due within forty-eight hours of notice. Tank kept flipping pages until he came to the smoking gun. Both notes listed its debtor's twenty-five Trubird shares as collateral. Tank knew that with seventy-five of a hundred shares, Trip could do whatever he wanted with Trubird.

Tank ran his fingers through his hair and considered the implications. Without the patents, Trubird was worthless. He pounded the table with both fists. After all the obstacles they had gotten over, after Chase's impressive day on the course, was this it? Had Trubird finally been defeated, not by OneSport, but by one of its own partners? And if Trubird fell apart, would Tank ever see Maddie again? The thought of losing her was even more devastating to Tank than being penniless.

Tank swallowed hard. He double-checked the execution date of Dick's loan paperwork and the payment delivery details. They only had time for one Hail Mary pass. What he had in mind might work, but he wouldn't know for sure until tomorrow afternoon, and even then, only if Chase finished top ten.

He scratched his afternoon shadow. There was no sense in putting any more pressure on Chase by telling him of their desperate situation. If the kid managed to pull off a great finish, only to discover it was all for nothing, Tank couldn't begin to predict Chase's reaction. At least he wouldn't be lying to the kid, technically.

Tank shook off a chill and put on his game face. Right now he needed to make two vital telephone calls. Then, he'd try to get some sleep.

Tomorrow, Sunday, would be Trubird's final test of survival. Last call.

# CHAPTER 19

As he waited in Montreux's lobby for Jake to arrive, Mort Epstein removed his blue pinstriped suit jacket and Brooks Brothers tie. The fashion antithesis of the other early morning spectators who sported pastel polo shirts, khaki shorts and sneakers, he hid behind his black Prada sunglasses and eavesdropped on the golf gossip.

Last night a private jet picked him up at Teterboro Airport in New Jersey and flew him to Nevada during the wee hours. Never one for excess sleep, he snoozed for about three hours, and had the airport car service take him directly to the golf course upon landing. His only luggage was a laptop bag that doubled as a briefcase.

Unaware his senior partner was waiting for him, Jake stepped through the doorway with Buzz nipping at his heels. Mort frowned as he caught wind of their conversation.

"You blew it, and you're fired! There's no amount of money I can throw at Paul Kilroy now to let you carry his bag. Your reputation is totally ruined," Jake snapped. "Excuse me. I've got work to do."

Buzz stepped out in front of Jake and turned to face him. The two men stood eye to eye.

"You can't fire me." Buzz bobbed up and down on tiptoes. "You owe me, and you promised me a top player to work for. I'm not going to disappear. I know things. The police already questioned me about Chase's caddie and where I got the drinks. Maybe I'll tell them the real story."

Mort slipped his jacket and tie over his arm, gripped his briefcase and, like a stalker, appeared behind Buzz's shoulder. Jake froze at the sight of his partner.

Buzz turned, surprised to see the man standing behind him.

Ignoring Buzz's presence, Mort spoke to Jake. "Come with me." He turned on his heel.

Jake wordlessly obeyed.

"Hey. Where are you going? We're not done talking yet," Buzz called out, scurrying behind the two figures. "Mr. Nathan? Mr. Nathan?"

With no more interest than he would regard an ant upon which he was about to stomp, Mort turned to Buzz. "Don't," was all he said, in the softest tone. He waggled a finger back and forth as if warning a naughty child to behave.

Buzz stopped in his tracks, and the men disappeared through the right side foyer.

Once alone, Mort shook his head. "For the first time in your life, Jake, you look like hell."

"People in glass houses—"

"Enough. I want you out of here on the next flight to New York."

Jake steeled himself. "You know I can't do that right now."

"You can, and you will. Do you realize how many of your other clients are suffering because of all the time you're wasting on this McLeary thing? It's costing us a fortune."

"You're the one who said to finish him off, to make sure no one will ever again think twice about him and Trubird. Now you want me to walk away?"

"Yes. We've got the patents, or we will in a matter of hours, and that means we hold all the cards. Trubird is mine, and if we can just control the spin throughout the rest of the day, we've won," Mort said.

"You don't know what—"

"As usual, I know more than you think. I know all about what happened in 1992 with you and Trip Boswyck and why this is so personal to you."

Jake blanched. "Look, I didn't ask for your help, and I don't want it."

"That's too bad. OneSport is in deep right now. Between what happened to Miles Callabrio, what's going on with our auditors, and the numerous illegal things we've already done regarding Trubird, our next mistake could be our last. One scandal is all it would take for us to implode, and you've got your pants around your ankles."

"Enough with the melodrama," Jake scoffed. "I'm sure Joe cooks the books pretty well, but you're not seriously telling me that we could go under. I don't believe it."

"Oh, you'd better believe it if you want to continue in your luxurious lifestyle. Even with the money we're anticipating from our born-again Trubird clubs, it won't be enough to ward off rumors that our profits are slipping, and you know what that'll do to our stock price and, by extension, your personal net worth."

Eyes locked, Mort waited for Jake to blink.

Mort could see Jake mentally taking inventory, considering the stock options that funded his extreme hobbies. Could he stand life without them? And what of his apartment in Soho, and his many opportunities to "see and be seen"?

Inside of a minute, Jake nodded his ascent, thereby ending the power struggle.

"I miss New York anyway." Jake shrugged. "I assume you got my message about Kilroy losing the putter."

"Yes. That idiot I just met has got to be Buzz."

Jake nodded. "He's going to be a problem."

"I'll take care of him. You've got other things to worry about. I gave Tonya a long list of clients and possible recruits that you're scheduled to see on Monday. Get going and impress me, will you?"

"Bite me," Jake replied.

Mort jammed a knuckle into his left nostril. "Call me when you get to New York."

"Don't wait up," Jake said.

Mort watched his partner strut down the hallway, noting how many heads turned Jake's way. He shrugged. Vanity, greed, power. Jake, Joe and Mort were not so different; they simply had different points of reference. And, as OneSport's leader, it was up to Mort to protect all three.

\* \* \* \* \*

Tank, Chase, and every other golfer not playing on the course jockeyed for space on Montreux's putting green. The skies were overcast, and for the second day in a row, the wind whipped through the trees, gusting at thirty to fifty miles per hour.

"You're sure?" Chase asked, pulling his turtleneck higher up around his neck.

"Positive," Tank answered, zipping up his windbreaker. "I double-checked the board three times. You are definitely in the final pairing today with Kilroy. Out of the four guys tied with you for second place, you were the first one into the clubhouse to post his score. Funny, though, I can't help thinking that OneSport had something to do with this."

"If they did, it's going to backfire because now I've got a lot more time to practice with my favorite putter. I'd almost forgotten how sweet this thing feels," Chase said.

"Man, you must have woken up on the right side of the bed. You actually sound competitive," Tank said, triple-checking the power on his cellular telephone. Although he was not allowed to talk on the phone during the tournament, Tank would be able to receive text messages.

"I almost feel sorry for poor Kilroy. He hates the wind. That guy is so cocky. I loved watching him give back strokes yesterday, and I'm gonna love it even more today."

Tank peered into the crowd. "Your mom should be here any minute with Jana. You're gonna have your hands full with that filly. She's stubborn as a mule. The doctor told her to stay in bed another day, but she told him she was coming here whether he liked it or not."

"I can't wait to see her. Just having her on the course will bring me luck."

Tank rubbed his hands together. "I don't know about all that. I wish we'd get started. Hmm. What have we got here?"

Paul Kilroy, the tournament leader, headed their way with Manny, his reinstated caddie, in tow.

Chase kept his chin down, pretending not to notice.

"Let's see if we can get in his head," Tank whispered with a wink. "You stay here out of trouble and let me do the dirty work." He backed up slowly, retrieving Chase's practice balls, one by one.

"Kid, your putting is unbelievable," Tank called out loudly as his backside drew nearer to Paul Kilroy's knee. "With this wind," he continued, "nobody's gonna catch you today." He bumped into Kilroy, sending the tournament leader forward to stumble over his putter. He wound up on one knee.

"Watch where you're going." Red-faced, Kilroy puffed out his cheeks and glared at Tank.

"Sorry," Tank answered, hands innocently raised shoulder height.

A reporter snapped a picture of the humbled Kilroy.

"Stay out of my way," Kilroy softly hissed at Tank as he wiped his pant leg clean.

"No offense intended." Tank removed his cap and slicked down his hair. "I'd be scared of Chase McLeary, too, if I were you," he called out before bending down to tie his shoe.

"I'm not." Kilroy snapped his jaw shut and turned his head to Tank. "I'm not scared of a has-been hack with one lucky round under his belt. Especially one whose alcoholic girlfriend couldn't even stay sober through the weekend."

Tank nonchalantly scratched his neck and looked up.

"Yup," Tank said. "Even your agent is running from you. I just saw Jake Nathan fly out of here. Guess he was anxious to draw up Chase's contract like he promised."

"You're full of it," Kilroy said. He strolled to the opposite side of the putting green.

Tank joined Chase.

"What happened? What did you say to him?" Chase asked.

"Nothing."

"Then how come you've got that cat-who-ate-the-canary look in your eye?"

"No reason," Tank said, smirking. *This is gonna be fun*.

\* \* \* \* \*

While the rest of his family sat in a church pew, singing and worshipping, Joe slouched in front of his plasma television set. His cell phone rang and he knew, without answering, who was calling.

The day before, Joe had placed a large wager on Paul Kilroy to win the Reno-Tahoe Open. Thanks to the stolen Trubird putter, and Paul's natural talent accented by beta-blockers, it was a sure thing. Almost.

"Looks like lady luck ain't with you," Mike, his bookie, said.

"The tournament won't be over for another nine hours. Get off my back," Joe said.

"You know very well your bet has already been lost. Even if Kilroy wins, he won't cover the spread. That tip you had about his newfangled putter was bunk."

Joe squeezed his eyes shut. This was all Jake's fault for not taking care of McLeary. "We'll see."

"I'll meet you at Murray's Bar at six, and you can give me my money."

Joe rubbed his stomach. "I've got plans with my family. We've got a big wedding tonight in Scarsdale, and you know how it—"

"Don't jerk me around, Joey. You know the rules. You begged me to take this stupid golf bet, so suck it up. If you had any sense you'd be betting on baseball like a real man."

Joe rooted through his pockets for antacids.

"Take it easy, take it easy. If Kilroy doesn't cover the spread, I'll get you your money. But today's Sunday. I need a day to exercise some stock options and get the cash. I need some time—"

"You listen to me. I want my money, and I want it today. You've ripped me off before, crying about your little stock-option routine. You should have taken care of that before making your bet. I'd better see your face—and your money—at Murray's at six o'clock."

Like a death-knell, the low-pitched dial tone throbbed against Joe's ear.

\* \* \* \* \*

This was it, Sunday, the final day of the tournament. For Chase, despite his proximity to the top of the pack, he knew enough not to take his score for granted. Many a player had gone into his final eighteen holes of a tournament near the lead, only to take home the tiniest of checks, or no check at all. He could not afford to merely protect his score, he had to attack the course and go for the win. As far as Chase knew, a solid finish was the only thing between Trubird's success and demise.

For Tank, however, Trubird's viability was much more complicated. Because of Trip's deceit, Trubird was the property of Excelsior Investments unless Tank could invalidate the sale. And he had the added stress of knowing that, by itself, Chase's success on the course today would be for naught, unless Tank's Hail Mary pass made it to the end zone.

Tank checked his watch and said a prayer. *Come on, Gina, don't let me down.*

It was twelve fifty-two, tee time.

Hitting into significant wind, most players opted to tee off with a club that would keep the ball safe and low, or else adjust their swings, utilizing a stinger technique.

Paul Kilroy's air of superiority, upon noting Chase's club selection, registered about a twenty on a scale of one to ten. Kilroy's caddie handed him a three iron, and they shared a private laugh as Chase loosened up with his driver.

Chase ignored them, and proceeded to rip the ball two hundred and seventy-five yards, straight down the middle of the par four first hole.

Tank gave the brim of his cap a squeeze. "Yeah," he said, waiting until Kilroy was as close as possible on his way to the tee, "this ain't no place for scaredy-cats today, boss."

Kilroy didn't acknowledge the remark; but Tank knew, from the way his jaw muscle tightened up, that the dig hit its mark.

Kilroy's ball also found the middle of the fairway, but didn't have the same length, landing only two hundred and twenty yards from the tee.

For his second shot, Kilroy chose a four iron, which left his ball a full club short of the green. Chase's second shot, a seven iron, caught a huge break when it bounced in front of the green, and landed in the first cut of rough. It exploded onto the green and rolled within four feet of the pin.

Tank, again, looked around for Maddie to share the moment, but settled for the look on Kilroy's caddie's face. Manny had that look of fear, and Tank loved it.

Kilroy's wedge sent his ball to the back of the green, where it rolled down to the very edge. Chase nailed his birdie putt, but Kilroy missed his long uphill par putt and carded a bogey.

"Not bad," Tank said. "You picked up two strokes on the guy, and we've only played one hole."

Chase grinned at his caddie. "Forget about top ten. Today I'm going all the way."

\* \* \* \* \*

Trip, still in his pajama bottoms at two o'clock, sat on the balcony of his Florida condo and watched the waves meet the shore. Stretched out on a white lounge chair, he stirred his fourth Bloody Mary, and studied the small particles of pepper and horseradish that floated to the top of the glass as he struggled to relax.

In addition to guilt, he was trying to drown out the anxiety that gripped him. He would not be able to relax until tomorrow when Excelsior deposited the final payment into his bank account. Screwing over your partners for money was one thing, but getting screwed out of the money was something else, entirely.

Trip reached for his cell phone. Unable to stem the angst, he dialed the only telephone number listed on Excelsior's letterhead. After risking so much, he was simply looking for reassurance that everything was on schedule.

Because it was Sunday, he expected to reach only a voicemail message, but he listened to all of the recorded options in the hopes of getting an alternate telephone number. Bingo. An "in case of emergency" number was recited. Trip snapped the telephone closed and re-dialed the new number.

After a brief welcome, sequential options were listed. *Press one to page Roger Lemur; press two to page an on-call legal representative; press three to reach a representative from OneSport; press four . . .*

OneSport?!

Trip's glass shattered across the tile floor. Excelsior is a part of OneSport? But that meant that OneSport now owned Trubird's patents.

Trip cried out in anguish as visions of Jake Nathan assaulted him; Jake, deeply tanned the first night they met; Jake, satisfying him like none of the others could; and Jake, laughing at his tears when he no longer needed or wanted Trip.

Jake had used Trip, like he had so many others, to achieve a purpose. In his case, it was to gain access to the tight, privileged inner circle of top golfers, back when OneSport first entered the golf market. He'd immediately picked up on Trip's hidden preferences. Jake knew just what to say, just what to do, all the while using every shred of information and contact Trip provided to advance OneSport's agenda.

Trip's sobs came out in gasps until he retched. The shame and humiliation of what Jake had done—not once, but twice—ravaged his mind. With Trubird's technology, Jake and OneSport would be unstoppable.

# CHAPTER 20

Mort expected a larger gallery than the fifty or so people following along as Paul Kilroy and Chase McLeary duked it out on the golf course. It was due, partly, to the unseasonably cold and windy weather. But Mort suspected many of the missing spectators could be found watching today's broadcast of the World Golf Championships with its all-star cast.

A man approached and Mort groaned.

"You're that guy, aren't you? Mr. Nathan's boss?" Buzz asked.

Mort removed his sunglasses. "Epstein. The name's Epstein."

"I'm Buzz. Look, Mr. Epstein, sir, I helped Mr. Nathan, and he promised to set me up with a big player. We had a little problem, but you owe me."

"Do you have a signed contract?"

"Contract?" Buzz scratched behind his earlobe. "No, the stuff I was doing was—"

"How about a letter of understanding?"

"No, it wasn't like that." Buzz yanked off his cap and slapped it against his thigh.

"Buzz, I'm an attorney, and I'll tell you right now that you have nothing by way of an enforceable agreement," he said, bringing his nose close to Buzz's. "Whatever arrangement you had with my associate was, at best, informal and, at worst, imaginary. Consider yourself outgunned. This is OneSport you're dealing with, and we've got dozens of attorneys on retainer. If you make any trouble for us, first, we'll bury you in paperwork—

you'll be paying off lawyers into the next century. Then we'll bankrupt you. When you think things can't get any worse, you'll get a visit from some men who will make you sorry you were ever born. Are we done?"

Buzz took a step back and collided with an approaching man.

"Excuse me," the man said, a pocket notebook in his hand.

Mort slid his eyes over. "Can I help you?"

"I'm a sports journalist. Are you the guy from OneSport? I was told you want to give an interview about your new golf line."

"Absolutely," Mort answered.

Buzz took off running.

The reporter arched his eyebrows at the abrupt departure, but Mort ignored the implied question and got to work spin doctoring. Mort regaled the reporter with tales of OneSport's forthcoming miracle clubs. Most importantly, he revealed that Chase McLeary had begged OneSport to take him back as a client; and OneSport, ever mindful of its obligation to help a fallen athlete, had offered to let poor Chase McLeary debut its prototype golf clubs in order to help turn around his luck.

\* \* \* \* \*

Both Chase and Paul Kilroy managed to make pars on the second and third holes, leaving Kilroy in the lead by three strokes. So far, the other players on the course were generally shooting par and above, making Chase's match the one to watch.

Tank stood on the fourth fairway, waiting for the group ahead to clear the green. The sudden vibration in his pants pocket startled him. He checked his watch. It was too soon for his daughter to be calling. He flipped open the telephone, read the display, and nearly passed out. The brief text message was from Trip. It read: *Tank, I screwed up. Sold patents to Excelsior for cash. Found out Excelsior is part of OneSport. Stop it if you can. Tell everyone I'm sorry. Trip.*

"Tank? Hey, I said back up a little. You're crowding my swing," Chase said.

Tank pulled back, still reeling from the news. OneSport. It was OneSport all along. He should've known.

\* \* \* \* \*

"Look at the board. He's doing great," Jana said to Maddie as the two women hurried across the course to catch up with Chase.

"Keep your fingers crossed. It'll all be over soon. Are you sure you're up to this?" Maddie asked.

Jana trudged on, untied sneaker laces flapping. She willed away the burning ache in her stomach from vomiting all morning. "You bet I am. There's no way I'm going to miss any more of Chase's final round. Is that . . . Buzz!"

Jana blocked the approaching figure. He looked into her angry eyes.

"I can't talk to you," Buzz said, quickly looking over his shoulder.

"Oh, yes, you can. One minute you're giving me a cold drink and the next minute I'm passed out cold. Why did you do it?"

"Jana, we should go," Maddie said, pulling her elbow.

"Not until I get an answer."

"Look," Buzz explained, "those guys from OneSport will do anything. They're crazy, but they make the rules, and they can break the rules. Their own players take beta-blockers, and half of their caddies do, too. I'm sorry you got hurt, but I gotta go before they see me talking to you," he said, looking back around again as he fled.

"That man was either scared stiff or totally paranoid. Did you see the way he kept looking over his shoulder like someone was about to attack him?" Jana asked.

A huge roar erupted from the gallery.

"Come on," Maddie said, hurrying along. "We've got bigger fish to fry."

They pushed their way into the crowd in time to see Paul Kilroy make an exaggerated bow and toss his putter fifteen feet in the air to his caddie.

"Unbelievable," an applauding fan said. He turned to Maddie. "You missed it. It looked like Kilroy was about to drop another stroke when his approach shot nicked a sprinkler head and took a bad bounce. But he kept his cool and sunk an unbelievable forty-footer to save par."

"I wonder if he would have saved par without taking those drugs?" Jana whispered into Maddie's ear.

"This is turning into quite a horse race," the same fan said to his friend as they headed for the next tee. "With that birdie, McLeary's only two shots behind Kilroy."

"Yeah," the friend replied. "Considering that none of the top twenty-five golfers are here, the level of play is awesome. At least, so far as Kilroy and that McLeary guy are concerned."

"That's because they're both with OneSport," the man said.

Maddie, walking alongside, let out a huff. "I can assure you that OneSport does not represent Chase McLeary."

"Sure they do," the man said over his shoulder. "A reporter just said so. Chase is even using OneSport's prototype golf clubs."

Maddie halted and turned to Jana, causing a backlog of pedestrians to circumvent the twosome.

"What is he talking about?" Jana asked.

"I don't know," Maddie said. "But, if Chase can keep it together, it won't matter anyway."

"There they are," Jana said.

Chase looked up and drank her in, the dark circles beneath her eyes, the perky tenaciousness, and the blouse sticking half way out of her shorts. The wordless exchange left both of them comforted and energized. He tipped his cap, she blew him a kiss, and he continued to grind his way through the tournament. Now it was personal. He wanted to win for her, for him, and for them.

On the fifth and sixth holes, both Chase and Kilroy made workingman's pars, leaving Chase's deficit at two strokes. But, on the par three seventh hole, Kilroy's near perfect tee shot put him on the green only feet from the pin; a certain birdie that would put him three up on Chase. Chase fired back, also hitting the green, although farther from the hole; and he also made birdie to contain Kilroy's lead to two shots.

The competitors matched pars on the eighth hole and birdies on the ninth, which brought Kilroy to twelve under and Chase to ten under at the turn. Both scores were much better than anyone predicted, given the intense gusting winds, and five strokes better than the next best score. The gallery's applause escalated along with the neck-and-neck competition.

Chase opened up the back nine with a birdie against Kilroy's par, bringing him within one shot of the lead. Both players made par on the eleventh, but, on the twelfth hole, Kilroy holed a bunker shot to make birdie while Chase's birdie bid took a last minute turn away from the cup.

Kilroy kept his lead at two strokes until the fifteenth, where Chase's powerful drive gave him an easy birdie. But Kilroy fired back with a birdie on the sixteenth, capitalizing on the shortest hole on the course to restore his lead at two strokes.

The seventeenth hole was a par five six hundred and thirty six yard monster; but, with the wind at his back, Chase made an eagle to Kilroy's par. Jana and Maddie shrieked with joy when Chase's putt dropped into its home, and River tossed the score sign in the air.

Chase and Kilroy were all square going into the eighteenth hole and the crowd was frenzied.

Tank squeezed his watch. It was five-thirty.

"You look a little nervous," Chase said.

"Yeah, you could say that."

"Don't worry, I've got him right where I want him. Besides, we're way ahead of top ten now, so quit your fidgeting. Hal Vos and his bankroll are in the bag. Long live Trubird."

"I think I'm gonna have a freakin' heart attack. I can feel the blood pumping through my neck like a fire hose," Tank said, squeezing the top of his shoulder blade. *Come on, Gina, baby, don't let me down.*

Chase patted Tank on the shoulder. "Try to relax."

"Will you shut up and finish this thing?"

Chase made a mock salute. Having made eagle on the previous hole, he enjoyed the honor of teeing off first.

Under normal conditions, Montreux's finishing hole requires careful consideration of the tee shot. Using a driver requires you to carry the bunker on the right, and also risks the possibility of running off the fairway into the right-hand rough. But a three wood must be left of the tiny bunker on the hill to avoid the big fairway bunker on the right. Given today's wind, club selection was crucial.

Perched as close as she could get to the twosome, Jana willed Chase to look at her. He turned his head.

*I love you.* She mouthed.

*I love you, too.* He mouthed back.

Chase pulled back his driver, and let the centrifugal force take charge. His ball flew three hundred yards, and looked perfect, until a gust of wind sent it into the second cut of rough on the right hand side of the fairway.

Kilroy made a clucking sound and Tank nearly clubbed him over the head.

Mort tipped his sunglasses and nodded at Kilroy. Kilroy emerged from his huddle with a three wood.

"Wimp," Tank whispered to Chase, resisting the urge to audibly meow.

Kilroy waited for a break in the wind to strike a beautiful shot. All smiles and ego, he sauntered past Chase. Behind the ropes, Mort pumped his fist in a show of support.

For his second shot, Chase grabbed his eight iron and fired a knockdown to twenty-five feet from the flag.

Kilroy's second shot, a safe five iron, flew the green. But his third shot was a beautiful recovery, and his ball rolled to five feet, a certain par.

Chase squatted in front his ball. A slippery downhill birdie putt would win the tournament.

"Let her rip," Tank commanded.

As soon as the ball came off his club, a slow growl came from the crowd until it collectively exploded into pandemonium, as Chase's ball caught the left corner and dropped into the hole.

Tank caught Chase up in a bear hug and lifted him off the ground. "You made it! You won! You did it!"

Stomping to his ball, Kilroy finished out his round with a par, gave the briefest of handshakes and hustled toward the scorers' tent.

Chase broke from Tank and took off running to meet Jana. He picked her up and smothered her mouth. River jumped on top of the couple, whooping and hollering.

With fans encircling them, it took Chase a minute to recognize the couple next to him. Tank had his mother wrapped in his arms and she was enthusiastically kissing his neck.

"Come on," Tank said, tearing himself away. "We've got to hurry." He grabbed Maddie's hand.

"Why?" Maddie said. "We won."

"This ain't over yet," Tank said. "Chase, meet me in the scorers' tent with your card. Don't let Kilroy pull any last minute tricks. Take your time reading his card. I'll explain later. Get going!"

Recognizing the severity of Tank's tone, everyone obeyed. Tank took off across the grass, dragging the heavy golf bag with him. He flipped open his phone and dialed. The number rang and rang. No answer. *Damn!* It was five-fifty. Where was she?

The crowd was bubbling with news of Chase's spectacular victory. A fresh round of applause began when Chase arrived at the scorekeepers' tent.

Tank, Maddie, Jana and River stood like sentries as he signed his card and attested to Kilroy's. Reporters lined up to talk to the new champion.

Mort entered the tent and made straight for Chase's side. He licked his lips. "Chase McLeary, you just made me a fortune."

"Who are you, and what are you talking about?" Chase asked.

Tank's telephone rang. He turned his back to answer it.

"I'm Morton Epstein," he said, smugness plastered all over his face, "co-owner of OneSport Corporation. We own all of Trubird's golf club design patents." Mort reached into his pants pocket and extracted a photocopied document. "This is a copy of our sales contract with Trip Boswyck. It's all legal. Once again, you've come up on the wrong side of OneSport."

"You're out of your mind. Tank?" Chase grabbed his arm. "Tank, are you listening to this?"

Tank slipped the telephone back into his pocket. His face was set in stone. "He ain't lying."

Chase's stomach churned with adrenaline and fear. "Go on," he said, rubbing his navel.

Arms folded across his chest, Mort's nods were punctuated with smirks as Tank explained to his partners how Trubird was now worthless.

"There's only one thing Mr. Epstein here doesn't know," Tank continued. "The loan documents between Trip and Dick didn't have a prohibition against assigning the debt. Dick Fischer assigned his loan to me, and I paid it off."

Mort's arms dropped to his sides.

Tank checked his watch. "Yup, just minutes ago Dick's loan was fully repaid to Trip, within the forty-eight hour time limit, which means that Dick keeps his twenty-five shares. And, since Trip only had fifty percent of Trubird's shares when he sold Trubird's patents, he did not have enough authority to make the transfer. You're an attorney, Mort. You know you can't sell a company's main asset without sixty-six and two-thirds percent of stockholders' approval."

Mort's cheeks purpled as Tank continued. "Oh, Trip probably told you he had enough shares, but you didn't do your homework. Trip assumed that Dick couldn't pay him back. He assumed that Dick would forfeit his twenty-five shares, just like

Satch. But, that's not the case. Sorry, Mort old buddy, but the sale is null and void. You don't own squat."

Mort reached for his telephone. "Nice try, Mazzola. You don't have that kind of money to pay off his loan. None of you do. And besides, you could never raise it in such a short amount of time, especially on a weekend. You can't bluff me, you idiot."

Tank pushed his shirtsleeves farther up his arms, and balled up his fists. "Listen up, you piece of crap." He snorted up a deep breath before continuing. "Doctor Gina Mazzola, my daughter, is on the Board of Directors of the National Bank & Trust of Raleigh. Early this morning she called her buddy, the bank's Chief Financial Officer, and asked for a loan. She used her certificates of deposit, cash, and her business accounts as collateral for the note. The CFO had the authority, and the code to the vault, and he gave her the cash this afternoon."

Spit flew from the corners of Mort's mouth. "You say your daughter is in Raleigh? Well, Trip Boswyck is in Florida. There's no way she could have delivered the money to him."

Tank smiled. "All she needed to do was deliver it to his address, just like the loan document stated. Trip's address was the place of delivery stipulated, and she had three witnesses watch her drop off the cash before six o'clock tonight, the deadline for repayment."

"Will somebody please explain what's going on here?" Jana asked.

Tank held up a finger, motioning for them to be silent while he savored hearing Mort's wrath spew out into his telephone. He was not accustomed to getting outsmarted.

Jana, Maddie and River held their breath as Mort confirmed what Tank had told him. He swirled around, glowering at Tank, while shouting into the mouthpiece.

Tank waived his fingers at Mort. *Bye Bye, OneSport*, he mouthed.

Hal Vos ran up and slapped Tank on the back. "Partner, you sure know how to rise to the challenge. Congratulations, Chase. We're going to make a fortune together."

"Jana, where are you going?" Chase asked.

She returned with a man in tow. "I can't wait any longer. I want you to meet one of your fans. This is Pastor Olive," Jana said.

Chase looked at Tank. "We're okay?"

"Ship shape, kiddo. Go tie the knot."

The wedding party assembled around the eighteenth green. The bride held a bouquet of flowers borrowed from the caterers' table, and the groom had a white golf tee as a boutonnière. The crowd cheered as Chase and Jana said their vows. The tournament official was all smiles as he offered them their pseudo-dowry in the form of an oversized check for half a million dollars, Chase's winnings.

Even Tank couldn't stop the tears from flowing. "Hey, Jana," he said, trying to compose himself.

"Yes?"

"How do you want to split up the caddie fee?"

"Tank, it's all yours. You earned it," Jana said.

"How much do I get for carrying the score-keeper sign?" River asked.

"Nothin', you're a volunteer," Tank said.

"Volunteer? I should get at least half. Come on, please? Then I can buy that new scooter and an X-Box," River begged.

Tank handed him a driver and a ball. "Tell you what. Go over there and hit this ball a hundred and fifty yards straight down the middle, and I'll give you a grand. That's a thousand bucks, kid."

"A thousand bucks? You got it!"

River practically knocked down everyone in his path on his way to a safe spot on the fairway. He closed his eyes, focused on his father's advice, and sent the little white ball one hundred and eighty yards straight down the middle.

# Epilogue

On Monday morning, the New York newspaper obituary section had one prominent article. Trip Boswyck was found dead, in his Florida condominium, of a self-inflicted gunshot wound.

Mort Epstein was too busy to notice.

As soon as the stock market opened, OneSport's stock price plummeted on rumors that its new miracle golf clubs would not be released as promised. An article also reported that Nevada police were questioning top OneSport officials in connection with both an alleged poisoning incident and an alleged kidnapping at the Reno-Tahoe Open. North Carolina law enforcement also wanted to interview OneSport personnel regarding a suspicious fire that resulted in one fatality.

"Mort?"

"No calls."

Tonya swallowed. "It's a sports reporter asking about Miles. He's doing an investigative expose on beta-blockers and wants a quote. He claims to have a copy of Miles' medical records."

"No calls!"

As the morning wore on, one financial news commentator predicted that OneSport might not survive its auditors' mandated financial statement revision, and there was talk of an investigation into its overall accounting practices.

"Get Jake in here," Mort barked.

Tonya's voice echoed through Mort's office. "I can't. He's on the Concorde to Paris with Madame de L'Enfant."

*Sucking up to that billionaire's seventy-year-old widow*, Mort thought, correctly guessing that Jake had every intention of hedging his financial future.

"Then get Joe."

"Sorry, he's still at lunch. An old friend named Mike, a big creepy looking guy, stopped by a little while ago. Funny, it didn't look like Joe was too happy to see him."

Mort jabbed his intercom button too hard; the telephone crashed to the marble floor and shattered.

\* \* \* \* \*

Sitting on the patio of her house, in her bathing suit and cover-up, Maddie accepted the champagne flute that Tank handed her. He wore navy blue swim trunks and an unfastened white terry cloth robe. As he bent toward her, she pulled him in for a deep kiss. She let her finger run up his muscled chest and touched the thick gold cross dangling from around his neck.

"Doll, keep that up and you'll never get rid of me," he said.

"Maybe I don't want to."

Tank grinned and scanned the surf for River who was boogie boarding with three other boys. "I'm glad you get to keep your house. I like it here."

"Me, too," she said. "And I like you here."

"How long until Chase and Jana get back from their honeymoon?"

"Another five days. River will be glad to see them."

Tank took her hand. "Let's talk about us."

# About the Author

Bridget Bell Webber, a high-handicapper with an avid slice, resides in Annapolis, Maryland with her husband and two sons. This is her first novel.

Visit her Web site at http://www.bridgetbellwebber.com.

*If you enjoyed this book, please visit the publisher,*
**Grace Abraham Publishing**
*at* http://www.graceabraham.com
*to read about additional mysteries in the Dark-N-Stormies line.*

Printed in the United States
45572LVS00001B